THE GUILD CODEX: SPELLBOUND / FOUR

DEMON MAGIC
AND A MARTINI

ANNETTE MARIE

dark owl
fantasy

Demon Magic and a Martini
The Guild Codex: Spellbound / Book Four

Dark Owl Fantasy Inc.
PO Box 88106, Rabbit Hill Post Office
Edmonton, AB, Canada T6R 0M5
www.darkowlfantasy.com

Cover Copyright © 2019 by Annette Ahner
Cover and Book Interior by Midnight Whimsy Designs
www.midnightwhimsydesigns.com

Editing by Elizabeth Darkley
arrowheadediting.wordpress.com

ISBN 978-1-988153-30-8

MORE BOOKS BY ANNETTE MARIE

STEEL & STONE UNIVERSE

Steel & Stone Series

Chase the Dark

Bind the Soul

Yield the Night

Reap the Shadows

Unleash the Storm

Steel & Stone

Spell Weaver Trilogy

The Night Realm

The Shadow Weave

The Blood Curse

OTHER WORKS

Red Winter Trilogy

Red Winter

Dark Tempest

Immortal Fire

THE GUILD CODEX

CLASSES OF MAGIC

Spiritalis

Psychica

Arcana

Demonica

Elementaria

MYTHIC

A person with magical ability

MPD / MAGIPOL

The organization that regulates mythics and their activities

ROGUE

A mythic living in violation of MPD laws

DEMON MAGIC
AND A MARTINI

"NO," I SAID.

"*No?*"

"No."

Darren slammed his hands down on the bar top. "You're the bartender. It's your job to give me a drink."

I thoughtfully tapped my chin as I appraised all six-foot-whatever of furious combat sorcerer trying to lean across my bar and tower over me at the same time. Darren wasn't my favorite person when he was sober, and drunk he was as pleasant as a skunk and porcupine combined into one stinky, stabby animal.

"You're cut off." I buffed my fingernails on my apron. "Which I told you an hour ago. And half an hour ago. And ten minutes ago."

"You can't cut me off!"

"Yes, I can. I'm the bartender, as you pointed out."

"I'm not drunk," he snarled, leaning even farther across the bar and wafting my face with reeking alcohol breath. "Serve me or you'll regret ever having—"

He broke off when I also planted my hands on the bar top and got in *his* face. Bullies never expected their intimidation tactics to be used against them.

"I'll regret *what?*" I demanded as he backed up. "Go on, finish the sentence. Speak up nice and loud so everyone can hear how tough you are."

Since I was already talking nice and loud, several people turned, their expressions brightening with anticipation. Tori was about to humiliate someone again and they had front-row seats. I swear that's why the tables nearest my station were always full.

Ah, I love my job.

Darren sluggishly considered his options, then muttered, "Come on, Tori. Just one more drink."

I laughed. "You can't play nice *after* threatening me. Get lost, Darren."

His hands clenched into fists, thick muscles bunching in his upper arms. He glowered like a two-year-old denied his sippy cup, but he was drunk enough to really lose his temper— assuming he could slur his way through an incantation. Better not chance it. Combat sorcerers were never pushovers, and Darren was meaner than most. He wasn't a person I should antagonize.

Keeping that firmly in mind, I stuck my tongue out at him.

His eyes bulged, then he stormed back to his table. I smirked. See? I wasn't scared. With careful nonchalance, I slipped my hand out of my back pocket where I'd been holding my Queen of Spades card, ready to whip the artifact out to defend myself.

Totally not scared at all.

But seriously, I wasn't a dunce with no concept of self-preservation. I knew Darren could mess me up if he wanted to, but sometimes, showing no fear was the best defense.

My bad attitude—"bad" according to every former employer—was the reason I'd landed this job. A human bartender … working for a magic guild.

I glanced fondly across the pub. Busy for a Tuesday night, but the twenty or so mythics scattered around had quieted down since the dinner rush. It was almost eleven, and I planned to clean up soon. Tomorrow would be a crazy night—and I had no one to blame but myself.

It all started with pumpkins.

I'd spotted them at the grocery store in early October and got the brilliant idea to decorate my bar for the spookiest month of the year. But I couldn't carry an armload of pumpkins home alone, so I called my favorite pyromage to pick me and my over-large squashes up from the store. Aaron, who can't hear an idea without going enthusiastically overboard, added another ten to my order and drove it all back to his place.

The look on Ezra's face when we walked in with the first load of pumpkins was only slightly less memorable than the look on Kai's face when Aaron informed him we'd *all* be carving pumpkins before Halloween.

I smiled at the dozen jack-o'-lanterns arranged in clusters around the pub, their glowing orange faces grinning or scowling—or in the case of Kai's single pumpkin, staring disapprovingly. How a pumpkin could convey ultimate displeasure, I didn't know, but Kai had achieved it to great effect. I might have laid the guilt trip on too thick when I begged him to carve "just one little pumpkin or else Halloween will be *ruined*."

Somehow, the jack-o'-lanterns had led to orange and black paper streamers, which had mysteriously appeared on my bar top one afternoon. What else was I supposed to do except decorate the pub with them? Then Aaron had shown up with a box full of fuzzy, posable bats, which now hung from the ceiling. No one was taking credit for the red and orange lights strung across the liquor shelves behind me, but I suspected they were Clara's doing.

And *then*, even more mysteriously, everyone started talking about "the Halloween party" and asking me what the plan was.

I wasn't planning a party. I'd never *intended* to plan a party.

Footsteps thudded down the stairs that led to the building's two upper levels. With her brown hair spilling out of its messy bun, Clara wheeled around the corner, clutching a bulging folder. She careened toward me, her face a mask of urgency.

"Hi Clara," I said. "You're working late tonight."

"Candy corn!" she blurted. "We need candy corn for the party. It's not Halloween without candy corn."

"I'll add it to the shopping list." I pulled a paper out of my apron pocket and added candy corn to the "everything I forgot during my last shopping trip" list, then frowned at her. "You're worrying about the party, aren't you? You have enough to deal with. I'll handle it."

"I can't help myself." With that crisis averted—everything with the assistant guild master was a crisis—she set her folder down and slid onto a stool. "I can't remember the last time we celebrated Halloween as a guild. It'll be a full house. A lot of guildeds are bringing family members or dates."

Yes, I'd firmly and clearly told everyone I wasn't planning an event of any kind, but had they listened? Did they care? No. I was now hosting the guild's biggest party of the year, all because I'd wanted to carve a damn pumpkin.

"We'll help with bartending," Clara added, straightening her folder, "so you can enjoy the party too. Have you chosen a costume yet?"

Parties I could do. Candy was awesome. Decorations were fun. But I *hated* dressing up. Before I could stop it, a scowl overtook my face. "Aaron wants to go as Jane and George Jetson because they're both redheads, but Kai wants us to go as two characters from *Mad Men*. I've only seen, like, three episodes."

"Kai just wants to wear a suit and call it a costume," Clara observed wisely. "What about Ezra? You two can dress up as Jon Snow and Ygritte."

"*Game of Thrones?*" I mused. "At least I'd be a badass wildling."

Clara's eyes lit up. "Ezra even looks like Jon Snow. You two in costume would be so cute. You only have a day to get it ready, though. I bet you could hit up the specialty shop on—"

I quickly waved a hand. "I'm good. Costumes are optional, and I'll be wearing an apron anyway."

Her face fell. "But it's your party. You have to wear a costume."

Holding my smile in place, I just nodded. *My* party. Ugh.

She picked up her folder and half the contents made a bid for freedom. I grabbed at the papers as they slid across the bar top, and together, we stuffed all the paperwork back into its cardboard prison.

"Thanks." She heaved a sigh. "I have so much to do, and Darius wants me to—oh!"

"Oh?" I asked warily, disconcerted by her sudden horror.

"I forgot! Darius asked me two weeks ago to—but I got distracted by—and I didn't tell you—"

"Tell me what?"

She winced guiltily. "Darius wants to update the pub menu. It hasn't changed in years and we're well overdue to spice things up. He suggested you might like to do it."

"Me?"

"You and Ramsey work the most hours in the pub, but Ramsey is busy with his apprenticeship and doesn't want the extra responsibility. I've mentioned to Darius several times that you might enjoy having a voice in the pub's management."

A voice in management? It was a paltry bone—not even close to a promotion—but giddy delight bubbled in my chest. Never at a single job in my life had anyone offered me a larger role or more responsibility than whatever grunt position they'd hired me into. I'd been demoted before, but that was it.

"I'd love to!" I grabbed my grocery list and flipped it over to take notes. "What do you need me to do?"

Clara blinked at my immediate excitement, then smiled. "Darius wants a written proposal that covers what menu items to remove and what to add. You'll need to include information about pricing, ingredients, suppliers, prep time, etcetera."

I scribbled that down. "Okay, sure. When does he want it by?"

"Ah." She winced again. "He suggested it two weeks ago, so I think he's expecting your proposal … next week."

That might be a bit tight. "When next week?"

"Um, probably Monday. He likes to get the week's paperwork done on Mondays."

Five days, and one of them would be consumed by a giant party. I clamped down on my apprehension and smiled confidently. "Got it."

"I can tell him I forgot and you'll need more time to—"

"Nope!" I stuffed my notes in my apron. "It's fine. No problem at all." This was my chance to prove I was worthy of more responsibility and I wasn't blowing it by asking for a deadline extension. If Darius wanted the new menu on Monday, then he'd get it on Monday.

I glanced at the back counter where my laptop was waiting, a half-finished college assignment on the screen. *That* might not make it to the instructor by next week, though. Hmm. I'd figure it out. I had two days off between now and Monday. I could do it.

Clara headed back upstairs to continue her late-night work session with Darius—odd but not entirely unusual. Darius, the guild master, traveled a lot and whenever he returned from a long trip, he and Clara would disappear for a day to catch up on all the work that required the GM's input or approval.

That, or they were having a secret affair, and after his trips, they barricaded themselves in his office to … nah. Too weird with the guild officers' desks right outside his door.

A few minutes later, I was sitting on the bar top and staring with mild panic at the chalkboard menu above the back counter. The stool behind me scraped across the floor as someone pulled it out.

"Do I want to know what you're doing?"

I didn't turn at the sound of Aaron's voice. "What's your favorite item on the menu?"

"The burger."

"What about you, Kai? Ezra?" I didn't need to look to know they were there too.

"The burger," Kai answered without hesitation.

"The burger," Ezra said in his meltingly smooth voice. "But it's not a fair question."

"Why not?"

"Because there's only one menu item."

I twisted around to give him a puzzled look. "What do you mean? There are ten entrees."

His dark eyebrows rose above his mismatched eyes. One was chocolate brown while the other was pale as ice with a dark pupil and outer ring, the iris damaged by the scar that ran from his temple down to his cheek. With his curly hair and the scruffy shadow along his jaw, he did kind of look like an olive-skinned Jon Snow.

He leaned on the bar and whispered conspiratorially, "*Everyone* orders the burger. I don't think they stock ingredients for anything else."

Huh. Now that he mentioned it, I always ordered the burger too. You'd think I would be sick of it after five months, but who could get sick of a delicious burger? "What's your least favorite meal?"

They shrugged, leaving me to wonder if they'd ever tried anything else.

Kai sat on a stool. "Why the sudden interest in the menu?"

"Darius wants me to revamp it." I hid my desperation. "He wants a new menu proposal on Monday."

"Monday? That's short notice." Aaron propped his elbow on the counter. "How about Poison Ivy?"

"What? You want to add poison ivy to the menu?"

"No, for your costume. You can be Poison Ivy and I'll be Batman."

I snorted. "Kai is way more of a Batman than you."

Ezra laughed, while Aaron sulked. Feeling guilty, I hopped off the bar and faced the three mages. Aaron was perched on his favorite stool, his copper hair tousled and the sleeves of his casual sweater pushed up his hard forearms. Kai sat beside him, his dark hair a stark contrast to his fair complexion, the first few buttons of his shirt undone. Ezra had one hip propped against the bar, his black t-shirt declaring, "Winter Is Coming."

Hmm, right, he was a *Game of Thrones* fan. Maybe I *could* convince him to do a couple's costume with—wait, what was I thinking? I didn't *want* to dress up.

"I'm not wearing a costume," I announced fervidly.

"But it's your p—" Aaron began.

"It's not my party! These are my *pumpkins*. I never proposed a party, let alone volunteered to organize one! And I *never* said I would dress up like a—" As a grin took over his face, I cut myself off. He'd heard this rant two or three times a day since the party became a thing. "This is all your fault."

"*My* fault?"

"You wanted extra pumpkins. If you hadn't—"

A bell rang, announcing the opening of the guild door. The bell was a new addition, installed a few weeks ago. I didn't know the whole story, but something about a drunk human wandering in while Clara was upstairs. The ward on the door repelled humans by triggering a sudden wave of fear, but it didn't work so well on the inebriated—or on the stubborn, like me.

So now we had a bell.

I glanced over, expecting to see patrons on their way home for the night—half the pub had emptied in the last half hour—but instead, two people stepped inside.

The man was average in height but above average in muscle, with dark hair buzzed close to his head and a beard only slightly longer. His tawny skin and leather jacket glistened with raindrops, and a fat, ugly silver pendant rested against his chest.

The tall, willowy woman walked like she was floating, her long black hair fluttering behind her and her russet complexion flushed pink from the cold rain. Her fitted leather coat was stylish, dark blue jeans fashionably tight, and black-leather boots knee high. Hanging from her belt were two narrow-bladed daggers with odd S-shaped hilts.

Neither was a member of the Crow and Hammer.

2

THE NEWCOMERS HESITATED inside the doors, unsure of their welcome. When they started toward the bar, their every movement screamed guardedness. Yeah, they definitely lacked confidence in their entry—an impression backed up by the sudden silence in the room.

"Who's that?" Aaron muttered. "Gotta be from Odin's Eye."

I snapped to attention. In the five and a half months I'd worked here, I'd never seen a member of another guild enter our headquarters. On top of that, Odin's Eye had a rough reputation. They were bounty specialists—hunters of rogues, criminals, and beastly bad things.

Suffice it to say, Odin's Eye and the Crow and Hammer did not get along.

Kai pushed off his stool and strode toward the approaching pair. The woman's gaze slashed across him—then a broad smile erased the cool appraisal from her face.

She took two quick steps ahead of her companion and threw her arms around Kai. My mouth fell open.

Then Kai wrapped *his* arms around *her* and my jaw hit the bar top.

I dragged my stare off them to see what Kai's best friends thought of this unexpected turn. Aaron was smirking, and Ezra was … uh … where was Ezra?

His spot was empty. Where had he disappeared to?

Kai pulled back from the mystery woman and murmured something, then drew her toward the bar with a hand on the small of her back. I eyed the placement. Gentlemanly politeness or a bit *too* familiar to be good manners?

He nudged his stool out for her. "Tori, a martini for Izzah, please—dry with two olives. Put it on my tab."

"You don't have to-*lah*, Kai," she exclaimed in a throaty voice tinged with an accent I didn't recognize.

"It's my pleasure." He sat on the stool beside her. "Izzah, you remember Aaron Sinclair?"

"Hey Izzah." Aaron offered his hand. "Long time no see."

Izzah's smile returned, dimples appearing in her cheeks. "Good to see you again, Aaron."

Kai tilted his head toward me. "Izzah, this is Tori. Tori, Izzah Ramesh."

As Izzah and I said hello, conversation resumed around the room. Completely forgotten, Izzah's companion slunk up to the bar and perched on the stool on her other side. She introduced him as Mario and another round of polite greetings ensued.

Aaron's curious gaze jumped from Izzah to Kai and back again. "What brings you here from Odin's Eye, Izzah?"

Oh, of course, Aaron was straight to business. I should've gotten out a question first—something like, "Kai, how do you know this lovely lady?" or even better, "What is the exact nature of your relationship?"

Okay, maybe Aaron had the right idea about noninvasive questions.

Izzah pushed her thick hair, damp from the rain, off her shoulders and cast the pyromage a playful look. "*Wah*, not even going to try small talk first?"

"We don't do small talk very well," Kai said, a subtle teasing note in his voice. Kai … teasing?

"That you don't, *leng chai*," she replied with a laugh.

Musing about the very specific drink order—how did he know exactly how she liked her martini?—I dropped two olives in the cocktail glass and slid it to her, then asked Mario, "Can I get you anything?"

"I'm fine," he muttered. I felt a spark of sympathy. He'd become an instant third wheel.

"To be fair, though," Kai continued, his gaze locked on Izzah, "you only show up when there's trouble."

Oh, so this girl had a habit of recurring visits? I made another mental note. Was I snoopy? Oh, hell yes. Kai's reputation as a playboy was surpassed only by the complete mystery surrounding the women he dated. I'd never met a single one. Could this raven-haired beauty be one of them? Was she the current short-term lady in his life? Did she *know* she was a short-term lady?

"Trouble *konon?*" she repeated, amusement in her smoldering brown eyes. "What a thing to say."

"It is trouble, isn't it?"

"Of course. But nothing as bad as … you know-*lah.*"

Aaron and Kai exchanged looks like they were remembering their last visit to the local torturer.

"Better not be," Aaron groaned. "How many hearings did we have to sit through?"

"I lost count." Izzah sighed as though the thought alone exhausted her. "How many hearings can you fit in six months?"

Kai rolled his eyes up in thought. "Is that how long it took?"

"Well, it was kind of a big deal," Izzah pointed out. "MagiPol interrogated us for breaking and entering, fraud, theft, damage to international treasures—"

"I didn't *mean* to destroy those artifacts—" Kai interrupted.

"—millions in insurance claims, people panicking in the streets—"

"That wasn't my fault," he muttered. "It was just a power outage."

"—and it made international news, so there was a major cover-up—"

"*All right*," he burst out. "Stop reminding me. That whole thing was a nightmare."

As he glowered, Izzah's face lit up in a triumphant grin. Oh man. She was needling him on purpose. She knew how to push cool, collected, unflappable Kai's buttons.

I liked her already.

"So, what kind of trouble are we looking at this time?" Aaron asked.

I silently cursed him for derailing the cute moment.

Izzah's good humor faded. "Have you heard anything about the Keys of Solomon?"

The what now?

"Nothing recently," Kai replied.

She nervously tapped her fingernail on the stem of her martini glass. "They're in town."

"That's never good news," he murmured, his expression darkening. "How many are we talking?

"Most of the guild is what I heard. Four or five teams."

Kai swore under his breath. "Any idea why?"

"Why else?" She lifted her martini and took a long sip. "Demons."

Oh goody. Demons, i.e. Demonica, i.e. the magic class only ever mentioned in tones of grudging respect, repulsion, and fear.

Not knowing what to ask first, I muttered to Aaron, "What are the Keys of Solomon?"

His lip curled in disgust. "They're a nomadic guild that specializes in demon hunting. It's all they do. They travel around, following rumors of demons and contractors they can kill."

My mouth made a gulping motion like a fish out of water. "I'm sorry, did you say *kill*? They go looking for people *to kill*?"

"*Har*, what else?" Izzah asked, confused by my reaction.

"Tori is new," Kai told her. "Very recently discovered."

She offered me an apologetic smile. "Sorry-*lah*. Welcome to the fold."

Though I'd been "discovered" as a witch two months ago, it was all a big fat lie. But despite being entirely human, I was now registered in the MPD database as a bona-fide witch. My phone number was in the mythic phonebook and there was no hiding it.

"Are they a rogue guild?" I asked as I pulled out two rocks glasses, unable to believe the Keys of Solomon guild was allowed to run around killing people.

"In everything but name." Izzah took another sip of her martini. "Officially, they're a legal guild, though they trample the line whenever it suits them. They only choose targets with DOD bounties."

"Dead or Deceased," Aaron explained. "As opposed to Dead or Alive."

I pulled a face. Mythics. They had the weirdest sense of humor.

"An untethered demon is automatically 'kill on sight,'" Izzah explained. "And contractors who screw up badly enough to get tagged with a bounty … well, those are always DOD bounties, because how else do you stop their demon?"

"It's a game to them," Mario rumbled unexpectedly.

Surprised, I turned to the second Odin's Eye mythic, a bottle of rum in my hand. I'd forgotten he was there. For such a beefy guy, he did an excellent impression of a stone statue.

"They collect kill points as much as bounty payouts," he continued. "It's all about ego and battle lust. There are stories about the Keys provoking a contractor into a fight, killing them, then claiming the contractor attacked first."

"Mario is a contractor," Izzah informed us. "Contractors keep close tabs on the Keys. They have to, when the Keys are so dangerous."

I stared at the dude, my ears buzzing. He was a contractor. A Demonica mythic. I'd never met one before, and I squinted suspiciously as though he might morph into a demon at any moment. Not that I had any idea how Demonica magic worked.

"Why would the Keys come here?" Kai asked. "Aside from the Grand Grimoire, the city has few contractors and none of them have bounties."

Izzah leaned closer to him and lowered her voice. "There are rumors of an underground summoning operation, right here in the downtown area."

"Why haven't we heard about this?" Aaron asked tersely.

She shrugged. "Your guild has no Demonica mythics, so the rumors pass you by. Now you know-*lah*."

"Thank you for sharing the information," Kai murmured. "I appreciate it."

Her dimples reappeared. I passed him a rum and coke, then slid the second one several spots down the counter. "Hey, Aaron, I want your opinion on a costume."

"Huh? Oh, okay." He joined me down the bar. "Change your mind about dressing up?"

I passed him his drink and whispered, "Of course not. I want to give Kai and Izzah some space to see what they do."

They sat side by side, deep in murmured conversation and completely ignoring Mario a seat away. Were Kai and Izzah sitting closer than platonic acquaintants would?

"Look how focused he is on her," I added in amazement. "Who *is* she?"

Aaron snickered at my reaction. "She's an Odin's Eye hydromage. I don't know her well, but she's smart and tough."

"Is she his ex? She seems to like him too much for him to have dumped her."

Aaron shrugged.

"Where did Ezra vanish to?" I asked, changing the subject. Guys sucked at gossiping about their friends.

"He went upstairs. Bathroom, maybe?" Another shrug.

Hmm, well, I'd have to investigate his disappearance later. For now, I braced my arms on the bar top. "Tell me more about this Keys of Solomon guild."

Aaron grimaced. "Them showing up is always bad news. First, it means there's illegal Demonica activity nearby. And second, it means shit is about to get ugly. The Keys don't let ethics or discretion get in the way of a kill."

"They're gladiators," Mario said, walking over to join us, "who only care about winning. Can I get a water?"

"Sure." I scooped ice into a glass and filled it. "Are they morally opposed to demon summoning or something? Is that why they're so bloodthirsty?"

"Half the Keys are contractors." Mario perched on a stool beside Aaron. He probably didn't want to watch Izzah and Kai flirt. "It takes a demon to kill a demon."

"And it takes even more to kill an untethered demon," Aaron added. "Though the Keys claim they're good enough to do it with a three-man team."

I frowned. "*Untethered* demon? What does that mean?"

"A contracted demon is under the contractor's complete control." Mario rubbed his fingers across his knuckles. "An untethered demon is one that escaped its summoning circle without a contract. It's stronger, faster, and has full command of its magic. Demon magic is the stuff of literal hell."

"Unbound demons do only one thing." Aaron tossed half his drink back in one gulp. "They slaughter every living creature that crosses their path. They kill nonstop until they're killed. It's the biggest reason summoning is so heavily regulated."

A shiver of fear ran through me. "Why doesn't MagiPol ban it?"

"Because some people will do it anyway. By making it legal but regulating it, MagiPol ensures most summonings are done under their supervision. Illegal summoning is rare nowadays."

Mario glanced impatiently at Izzah, but she and Kai were still talking. "The laws are strict. A summoner caught performing without permits can face the death penalty. A contractor without proper registration is always put to death."

I swallowed. "That's harsh."

"It has to be. Once a demon is bound in a contract, killing the contractor is the safest way to eliminate the demon. Summoners are punished almost as harshly because illegal summoning is how you end up with untethered demons, and every one of those results in a body count."

Aaron noticed my disquiet. "Don't freak, Tori. Unbound demons are so rare you don't need to worry about it. MagiPol tightened a few laws ten years ago, and I haven't heard of a demon on the loose in about—"

The clamor of twenty phones chiming at the same moment interrupted him.

I froze, my wide eyes flicking between Aaron and Mario. Everyone in the guild had gone still, surprise and unease written on every face. In perfect unison, we all reached for our phones. Screens lit up across the pub.

On my phone's screen, a message glowed brightly.

> **MPD Emergency Alert:** --CODE BLACK-- Suspected unbound demon active in your area. All CM assemble at GHQ ASAP. NCM take shelter. PROCEED WITH UTMOST CAUTION.

The words glared mockingly. This was a joke, right? Because we'd just been talking about how rare and horrific unbound demons were? It was a joke message … sent to every mythic cell phone in the pub.

Aaron looked up from his phone, his face white. "Guess I spoke too soon."

3

I WAS STILL SHARING a look of dread with Aaron when footsteps thudded rapidly down the stairs.

Darius jumped the last step, Clara right behind him, followed by the guild's second and third officers, Tabitha and Felix. The latter carried a white tub with a laptop balanced on the lid.

As the guild master strode into the pub, his voice rang out like a whip crack. "Combat mythics—if you're sober, gear up and report to Tabitha. If you're not sober, down to the basement. Venus, dose them with cleansing drafts, then tally our stock of potions and make more if you're short. Non-combat mythics, report to Felix. He'll divvy out assignments."

The mythics at the tables went from shocked stillness to scrambling action in two seconds flat. Mario was already making a beeline to the door, and Izzah called a hurried farewell to Kai. The two mythics disappeared outside, presumably rushing back to their guild.

All CM assemble at GHQ ASAP. Translation: All combat mythics assemble at guild headquarters as soon as possible.

"Tori." Darius's commanding voice made me flinch. "No more alcohol until the MPD lifts the alert. Everyone needs their wits about them tonight."

"Yes, sir," I said quickly.

Aaron and Kai joined the five mythics heading into the basement, leaving me alone at the bar. Darius stood in the center of a swirl of activity, giving orders.

"Felix, organize the non-combats into teams and have them contact every member who isn't present. Prioritize combats first. All healers and alchemists to the guild immediately. Apprentices can wait on standby. Anyone who isn't combat trained needs to take shelter, no exceptions. Ensure they don't travel alone.

"Clara, choose two assistants and set up the main floor as our command center and emergency intake. Tabitha, while you wait for the combat members to gear up, collect extra laptops from upstairs. Felix, do you have enough communication gear to equip five or six team leads?"

He pulled a tablet out of his tub. "I'll check my spreadsheet."

Clara waved me over. "Tori, help me. Ramsey, you too."

Ramsey, who came out of the kitchen following the alert, turned to the guild master. "Darius, I request to join the combat teams. I'm only a few months from completing my apprenticeship."

"Granted."

Nodding, he jogged toward the basement stairs.

Clara looked around, but the remaining mythics were getting assignments from Felix. "You and me, Tori. Let's go."

I raced around the bar to join her. "Just tell me what to do."

Together, we cleared an open space in the middle of the pub, then set up three separate areas: a group of tables for Felix's helpers, a healers' corner with two tables and a line of chairs to keep people out, and a "command center" of four tables pushed into a row, on which Tabitha had set three laptops.

"Once Darius submits our team numbers," Clara explained breathlessly as we stacked spare chairs in a corner, "MPD will assign our grid. We'll use the computers to track the teams' movements and progress."

I nodded as though I understood. The corner for Felix's helpers was already filled with bustling noise—six mythics on their phones, papers spread in front of them as they methodically contacted every guild member. About twenty people were in the building, leaving another thirty to call. Presumably, they'd all received the text alert, but Darius wasn't relying on that.

By the time Clara and I finished arranging the command center, another half a dozen members had arrived. They swept in and were immediately sent to either gear up or set up. Sanjana, our apprentice healer, arrived alongside a huge man with rich teak skin and a shaved head. Miles had enough muscle to be a combat mythic, but he was one of our two experienced healers—as well as a renowned surgeon. Arcana magic required intensive study to master, but healing Arcana was by far the most demanding; many healers completed med school alongside their apprenticeships.

Sanjana and Miles joined Venus, an alchemist, in preparing the healers' corner—and their work had anxious butterflies tickling my stomach. They laid out two gurneys, lined the table with various potions, and produced a surgery cart. Yeah, an actual surgery cart full of surgical tools straight from an emergency room.

Just what were they expecting to happen?

The geared combat mythics started gathering in the middle of the room—Aaron and Kai, decked out in leather, armored vests, and weapons; petite Zora with a huge sword on her back and other weaponized artifacts strapped to her thin limbs; Lyndon with his belt lined with artifacts, even though he didn't normally go on combat missions; Darren, sobered up by a potion and adjusting his leather duster; and Laetitia, our hydromage, sporting a pair of steel batons.

I scoured the group again. Where was Ezra?

As though summoned by my thought, the aeromage descended from the upper level, one hand trailing on the banister as he glanced across his comrades. His expression was calm, but tension lined his shoulders.

"Rowe," Tabitha barked at him, "why aren't you geared? Get moving."

Darius looked up from the laptop Felix was working on. "Ezra is off on injury. He stays." The guild master straightened as he looked across the non-combat mythics. "I know it's difficult to stay behind, whether injured or inexperienced or the wrong class to fight. We all want to protect our homes, loved ones, and the innocent strangers at risk tonight. Protect them, and our fighters, by staying safe and helping here."

Nods circled the group. Ezra slunk to my side, his hands jammed in his pockets and misery in his eyes. Before I could ask when he'd been injured and why no one had told me,

Aaron and Kai broke away from the combat mythics and hastened over to us.

Aaron clapped Ezra on the shoulder. "It'll be a boring march around downtown anyway."

As Ezra muttered a reply, Kai took my elbow and drew me away. "Tori," he said in a low voice, "keep an eye on him, okay? He'll worry about us and he might be tempted to sneak out, but he needs to stay inside the guild."

"I'll watch him, but I don't understand why—"

"The grid is posted," Darius announced. "Teams! Tabitha, you're leading Weldon, Zhi, and Ming. Andrew, you're leading Zora, Ramsey, and Darren. Aaron, you're leading Kai, Gwen, and Drew. Sylvia, you're leading Laetitia, Lyndon, and Philip."

Whoa, wait. *Philip?* Wasn't he a witch? I didn't know combat witches were a thing.

"If your team isn't assembled yet, wait for them," Darius continued. "If you're ready, get your grid point from Felix—and don't forget your stickers."

Kai gave my arm a squeeze. "Time to go."

I grabbed his wrist as he stepped away. "Kai—" My voice cracked. I scarcely understood what was happening, but only a dumbass would fail to recognize the level of danger. "Be careful."

"We will." Aaron pulled me against his side in a quick hug. "This will be over before you know it. Just hang in there."

Heart in my throat, I watched the two mages, Gwen the sorceress, and Drew the telekinetic march over to Felix. The officer pointed at something on the laptop screen and handed Aaron an earpiece with a coiled cord, which he plugged into his cell. He tapped on the screen, then stuck his phone in the chest pocket of his vest. Felix stuck a reflective diamond sticker on each mythic's shoulder.

"Remember," Darius told them, "stay in the open. Be vigilant. Expect an ambush. At the first sign of the demon, call it in and *follow procedure*."

Aaron nodded. Then they were out the door and into the rainy streets where a monster lurked.

The last combat mythics arrived in a rush, and all I could do was stay out of the way as they geared up, formed a team, and received their instructions and stickers. Ezra stood beside me, unhappiness rolling off him in waves.

The fourth and final team sped out into the rain, and the noise level dropped significantly. I rubbed a hand over my face, taking in the healers and alchemists waiting quietly in their corner and the non-combat mythics sitting at their tables, a few calling the last members they hadn't gotten through to yet.

"What's with the stickers?" I muttered. Not the most pressing question I wanted to ask, but what the hell was the point of stickers?

"They identify mythics," Felix answered. I'd been asking Ezra, but I hadn't realized the guild officer was walking up on my other side. "A Code Black means the MPD has brought in human law enforcement to help. They're closing roads and clearing all humans from the area where the demon is suspected to be, and the stickers keep the police from stopping our teams."

"And what's all that about grids?" I asked.

"We're doing a grid search of the area. The MPD has assigned every guild to a section of the grid, based on how many teams we can provide." He turned to Ezra. "Can you bring two TVs from the second floor? I need larger screens."

Ezra nodded and headed upstairs.

Watching him go, sympathy flickered across Felix's features. "There's nothing more difficult than being left behind."

Footsteps thumped, but it wasn't Ezra returning with a TV. Darius trotted down the stairs—and the GM had transformed. He now wore leather gear, his belt weighed down by two sets of long knives, their silver hilts gleaming. Girard followed, decked out in sorcery artifacts, and last was Alistair, carrying a heavy *bo* staff carved with runes, his tattooed arms bared by his leather vest. As a volcanomage, the rain and cold probably didn't bother him.

"All right, we're off," Darius declared. "Felix, you're in charge. Keep me informed of any developments."

"Yes, sir. Good luck."

Alistair chuckled with dark humor. "Luck is for beginners."

Slapping stickers on their shoulders, the three men marched outside. The door banged shut behind them.

"That's the most terrifying team I've ever seen," Felix muttered almost too quietly for me to hear. "I pity the demon that tries to go through *them*."

Over the next few minutes, Ezra brought down two TVs and Felix hooked them up to the laptops. An image filled each screen. On one was a map showing a square of city blocks twenty across, the Crow and Hammer on its northeastern edge. A big red X glowed in the center, and all around it were blinking dots. Red squares highlighted different sections, and two squares had turned to a solid green.

"The dots are teams from all the guilds. The GPS updates every few seconds." Felix sat at the table and pulled on an over-the-ear headset with a mic. He pointed to the other screen. "The green areas have been checked by a team. See the update?"

On the second TV, messages scrolled upward like stuttering movie credits. The last two read, "OE T2: Grid 6 clear. GG T1: Grid 2 clear."

"OE," I murmured. "Odin's Eye?"

"GG is Grand Grimoire. They'll be out in force since the entire guild is contractors and champions."

"Champions?"

"Those are—hold on." He pressed a button on his headset. "Copy that, proceed east to Grid 11. Over."

His fingers flew across the keyboard, and a second later, "CH T3: Grid 8 clear" popped into the update feed. Twenty seconds after that, another square on the map went green.

Clara rushed down the stairs, sweeping her escaping hair into a bun and twisting a rubber band around it. "All right. We don't know how long this will take, so Tori, can you put on coffee and boil water for tea? After that, please make as many sandwiches as we have ingredients for. Ezra, why don't you help her?"

Without waiting for a response, she moved on to the other loitering mythics, giving more instructions—clean up this, set up that. Felix sat at the command station, manning the headset and laptops.

I grabbed Ezra's arm and pulled him into the kitchen. The saloon doors swung shut behind us, offering a semblance of privacy.

"You're injured?" I asked sharply as I turned on the giant coffee maker and pulled out packets of dark roast.

"Not precisely." He scrubbed a hand over his face and into his hair, tangling his brown curls. His shoulders slumped forward, his gaze skittering away from mine. "This sort of thing ... I don't do well with it. Darius knows that, so he ..."

"So he made an excuse for you." Dumping the coffee grounds into the filter, I wondered if this was related to Ezra's temper or the terrifying crimson magic he could command in emergencies. What did Darius know? All this time, I'd assumed only Aaron and Kai were in on Ezra's secrets.

"Demons," I said hoarsely. "I know nothing about demons." I'd had lots of opportunities to ask over the past months, but honestly, I hadn't wanted to know how scary they were.

Apparently, Ezra had a similar distaste for the topic, because he let out a long, weary breath like he'd prefer to discuss literally anything else. "Demons are kind of like fae, but they come from a world that's completely separate from ours. We don't know anything about it or even what demons are … aside from powerful and vicious."

I pulled out loaves of bread and counted the deli meat packs in the fridge. The pub's "super club sandwich" wasn't a popular item. Note to self: propose cutting it off the menu.

"Why do people summon them, then?" I asked as I piled tomatoes on a cutting board.

He leaned against the counter, staying out of my way. "Because it's a power that anyone, human or mythic, can acquire. The only requirement is their willingness to pay the price for it."

"Which is?"

"A lifetime contract binding you to an evil creature that wants to kill you. And your soul."

I looked up, expecting one of his deadpan jokes, but his eyes were dark with an emotion I couldn't read. "Your *soul*?"

"It's called the banishment clause, and it's part of every demon contract. Once a demon is summoned, it's stuck here. It needs a contractor—or rather, the contractor's soul—to leave this world. When the human dies, the demon takes their soul and returns home."

I stood with my knife poised above a tomato, trying to remember how to rehinge my jaw. "That's … insane. Why would anyone ever enter into a demon contract if they have to give up their *soul*?"

Ezra shrugged and shifted over to the sink to wash his hands. "What can I do to help?"

"Lay out the bread for me, please." I finished slicing tomatoes. "How does a demon get loose like this?"

He placed a dozen slices of bread across a large cutting board. "The summoner made a mistake. They let it loose without a contract."

"And now it's going to kill people," I finished in a whisper, feeling ill.

"They say unbound demons kill because they're trying to go home. They want a soul, but it doesn't work without a contract." He went quiet as he slathered mayo on the bread. "Every guild has sent combat teams to the area. They'll find the demon."

"And then what? What did Darius mean about following procedures?"

"Our teams will call in the demon's location, then wait for the nearest contractors to arrive. It takes a demon to kill a demon."

Mario had said that too. "Why?"

"Because it's so dangerous. No one wants to fight a demon, especially not an unbound one, which is in full command of its magic, strength, speed, and wit. Plus, a demon can survive a lot of damage. They're difficult to kill. Defeating one …" He trailed off, his hands unmoving, mayo dripping off the knife.

A nauseating chill washed over me and I shivered. "Aaron and Kai … and everyone else … Ezra, how much danger are they in?"

Ezra stared at the half-made sandwiches, then lifted his haunted stare to mine. "I don't want them to find the demon. I don't want them anywhere near it."

The cold in my veins deepened. Ezra wasn't a coward and he knew what Aaron and Kai could do, but if he was afraid … Even if it was selfish, even if it meant it took longer to stop the demon, I hoped Aaron and Kai never laid eyes on it.

4

HOW LONG DID IT TAKE to find a demon on a killing spree?

A long-ass time, that's how long.

I slumped at the bar, an empty plate in front of me. I'd eaten half a sandwich just so Clara would stop nagging me, but I was too anxious to be hungry. The last four hours had crawled by, and a portion of my attention was always tuned to Felix's voice. Waiting for Aaron's next check in. Waiting to see an update from the other Crow and Hammer teams—all people I knew and cared about.

Well, *mostly* people I cared about. I wouldn't cry if Sylvia got tossed around a bit, but I still wanted everyone, including the insufferable sorceress, to come back safely.

Swiveling on my stool, I scoured Felix's screens again. The ever-changing map now featured three X's: the original one, plus two more. Suspected sightings of the demon. As squares turned green, red ones appeared elsewhere. The search kept shifting, but despite every combat mythic in the city out there looking, they couldn't find the demon.

It was starting to feel unreal, like maybe it was all a disgusting Halloween prank. I might have believed that, except the MPD had no sense of humor.

Felix sat at the table, his attention moving from screen to screen. "Copy that. Proceed northeast to Grid 31. Wait—repeat that." A pause. "North of you? Team Three is north of your position." Another longer pause. "Okay, I'll relay the message."

He typed on the keyboard, then spoke again. "Aaron, do you copy? I have a message from Tabitha. Two KS teams just passed her location, heading north toward your position. If they interfere in your search, cede your grid and move to the next."

Tapping his headset again, he huffed angrily.

"KS teams?" I prompted cautiously. "The Keys of Solomon?"

Pushing his dark-rimmed glasses up his nose, he nodded. "They aren't following the grid or communicating with other guilds. They want the demon kill for themselves." His hand flew to his headset. "Copy that, Team Two. Proceed ... northeast to Grid 33."

I rubbed my hands over my face, my eyes burning. It was way past my bedtime, but there was no way I could sleep. Aaron and Kai weren't the only ones I was worried about. The MPD had the regular police force helping with this operation, which meant my brother was out there too. Unlike the mythics, Justin had no idea the danger he was in.

After my dramatic induction into the mythic community at the beginning of September, things with my brother became ... strained. I'd told him almost everything, from my first shift at the Crow and Hammer to my recent brush with the law. His knowledge of mythics was limited to what he'd learned after joining the force—meaning he knew very little—and he was highly prejudiced since the police only ever encountered mythics who were causing havoc.

Needless to say, he wasn't happy about me joining a "magical street gang"—his words, not mine. He was convinced it was dangerous and excessively illegal, but most of all, he was hurt that I'd lied to him for months. Rogue witches had attacked me right in front of him, but instead of coming clean, I'd doubled down on the deceit.

Twisting my lips, I held my phone for a long minute, then sent a brief message warning him to be extra careful. Maybe it would help.

I glanced at the big clock on the wall: 4:23 a.m. In another hour or two, the morning rush hour would begin—a mass migration of humans the MPD couldn't hope to stop. Thousands upon thousands of people would flood downtown, putting themselves in the demon's path and making the search all the more difficult.

I was still staring at the screens, my stomach churning as I watched the blinking dots, when a male torso in a black "Winter Is Coming" shirt appeared in front of me.

"Tori." With my name alone, Ezra's silk-smooth voice lowered my anxiety levels by several degrees. "Here."

I blinked at my laptop. "Huh?"

He set it on the counter and slid onto the stool beside me. "Let's work on the new pub menu."

"Now? I'd have more success concentrating on calculus equations. By the way, I failed calculus."

"I need a distraction, and you do too. You've been fixated on those screens for hours. Give yourself a break."

Like a moth drawn to a light, my head turned back to the TVs. "But …"

He tugged gently on my ponytail until I straightened, then nudged the laptop in front of me. I booted it up and opened a new document, then stared blankly at the white page. "I don't even know where to start."

"Let's look up other pub menus for ideas."

A quick Google search produced a list of the best bars and pubs in the city. I pulled up the number one restaurant's menu.

Ezra leaned close to skim it. "Avocado mash. Avocado toast. And avocado … chili? Why didn't Clara think of this strategy before? So much effort wasted in buying multiple ingredients."

I snorted, half my attention on Felix's voice as he directed Team One to a new grid. I scrolled through more dishes. "What's *with* this menu? Salads? Perogies? Cheese boards? This isn't real bar food. Where's the greasy, deep-fried stuff?" I exited the window and tried the next restaurant on the list.

"Mediterranean stuffed chicken breast," Ezra read off the new menu. "I tried to make stuffed chicken breasts once."

My eyebrows shot up. "I thought you didn't cook."

"I don't. I *tried* for a few months, then I got banned."

"Banned?"

"Hmm." His eyes brightened with rueful humor. "I never learned to cook when I was younger, so I'm awful at it. Kai and Aaron tried to teach me, but …" He propped his chin on his hand. "When I'm alone in the kitchen, I don't knock things over because I remember where I put them. But with someone else, they move things around and I don't know where everything is anymore, and …"

"And you knock things over," I guessed, an easy conclusion to reach.

"Mm-hmm. After a tragic incident involving a plate of barbequed steaks, Aaron jokingly banned me from the kitchen, but I decided I wasn't meant to be a great chef and took the ban literally. It was for the best," he finished somberly.

"You just don't like cooking, do you?"

"No, not really." He grinned. "You're a great cook. Who taught you?"

"I'm mostly self-taught, but I learned the basics from Justin, who learned from my mom. She made the best lasagna I've ever tasted." I scrunched my face. "Though I haven't had it since I was a kid, so maybe it's just really good in my memory."

"Sometimes it's better," he murmured, "not tarnishing those really good memories with adult sensibilities."

"Yeah, I think so. What about you? What's your favorite childhood meal?"

"Me?" His eyes went distant with thought, and I held my breath, expecting him to evade the question or answer with a joke. "I would say my mother's *moqueca*."

"Moqueca? What's that?"

"It's a kind of fish stew eaten with rice and *farofa*. When she took the lid off the pot and all the steam escaped—the aroma." He sighed wistfully. "Definitely my favorite."

I couldn't help grinning at his half-longing, half-starving expression. "I've never heard of it before, but it sounds delicious."

"It's a Brazilian dish. I don't know anyone who makes it."

I surreptitiously reexamined his beautiful bronze skin. "Is your mother Brazilian?"

He nodded. "She and my father moved to the US when they were eighteen. They cooked a lot of traditional dishes before …"

As he trailed off, his expression shuttering, I quickly asked, "Do you know how to make moqueca?"

"I sometimes watched my mother make it, but I don't have a recipe."

"We could look one up," I said excitedly. "Not your mom's version, but something similar, and we could try making it. It'd be fun!"

He blinked, and I froze, kicking myself for being insensitive. Then his face relaxed into a smile. "I think I'd enjoy that. We should try it sometime."

Relieved that I hadn't upset him, I returned to the laptop. We went through several pub menus and found little in the way of ideas, but we entertained ourselves by making fun of the weirdest dishes. Time slipped by faster and I stopped listening to Felix's every word.

That is until a distinct change in his tone brought my head around. Ezra looked over as well, his tension returning in an instant—and a distracted part of me wondered how much effort he was putting into hiding *his* concern to alleviate mine.

"Yes, sir," Felix said brusquely. "Yes. Right away."

He tapped on his keyboard. "Attention all teams. MPD agents and the GMs have conferred on the search strategy. We're switching to a rotation so teams can rest. Teams One and Three, return to the guild. Teams Two, Four, and Five, stand by while the MPD recalculates the grids."

Felix muted his headset. "Okay, everyone," he announced to the room. "We pushed our teams hard to track this demon down before sunrise, but it's proving evasive. The good news is that the demon hasn't attacked anyone yet. The bad news is that it's making it difficult to find, and once dawn arrives, keeping humans safe will become a job in itself."

"Are we sure there *is* a demon?" Sanjana, the apprentice healer, asked. "After six hours of searching, no one has confirmed a sighting or even a dead body."

"That doesn't make it any less dangerous, just more elusive." He rose to his feet. "We're one of the two closest guilds to the search area, so we'll be taking half the teams who are going on rest, while the other half will go to the Seadevil's headquarters. We're about to have a lot of company. Clara, did you get the second level prepared for people to sleep? Good. Healers and alchemists, get ready with vitality potions and strength boosters. Tori, prepare hot drinks. How much food do we have?"

"The fridge is full of sandwiches," I told him. "We'll be good for a while. I can always make burgers if we need them."

He nodded. "Get to it, guys."

As he took his seat, I left Ezra at the bar and headed into the kitchen to put on more coffee. Relief mixed with my anxiety. Aaron and Kai were on their way back. They'd be safe for a while.

I'd just emptied the coffee machine and restarted it when a surprised shout burst from the pub. Dropping the coffee packet, I flew through the saloon doors as half the room rushed toward Felix's monitors.

"What?" I demanded, racing up to Ezra. "What happened?"

"The demon is five blocks from here," he said tersely, stretching onto his toes to see over people's heads. "Odin's Eye just reported it—in an area that was already cleared."

Five blocks? My heart slammed into my ribs. Five blocks was way too close.

"The demon jumped our lines and is fleeing northeast of Grid 22," Felix barked into his headset. "All teams, check in with your position. Team One?" He paused. "Confirmed. Team Two? Confirmed. Team Three?" Another pause. "Team Three? Team Three, do you copy?"

My entire body went cold. No one moved, every person as still as a statue, half of them watching the screen, the other half watching the guild door like the demon might burst through at any moment.

"Team Three? Team Three, I'm not receiving." Felix focused on another screen. "Where's their signal? It's—"

He leaped to his feet and spun toward the door—and that's when I saw the blinking GPS dot marking a team's location. The indicator was speeding toward our guild, almost on top of us, about to—

The front door flew open.

Several people screamed and backpedaled, but it wasn't the demon. Dark-haired and russet-skinned Izzah burst into the pub in a splatter of rain.

"Healer!" she yelled. "*Where's the healer?*"

"Here!" Miles boomed as a mash of eight people squeezed through the doorway. Aaron pushed through, a limp man slung over his shoulder in a fireman carry, and Drew carried Gwen piggyback-style. Last in line, Kai backed through the door with his sword out, then slammed it shut and flipped the heavy, rarely used bolt down.

Aaron lowered the injured man onto a gurney and the healers surrounded him. Miles and Elisabetta—a tall blond woman—shot rapid observations back and forth as they cut their patient's clothes off.

As Kai helped Gwen off Drew's back and supported her over to a chair, Aaron stormed up to Felix, his black vest shining with rain and blood. "Get Darius for me."

Felix sat again and tapped on his laptop. "Darius, do you copy? I have Aaron here."

Aaron took the headset and shoved it on his dripping head. "Darius, *the demon has wings.* The bastard was probably watching our search from the rooftops. How the f—" He cut off the curse. "Yeah, we're okay. Gwen sprained an ankle, that's it. An Odin's Eye man took the hit and he's with our healers."

A pause while he listened.

"We ran into their team on our way back. We stopped to trade notes, and the beast dropped on our heads. It knew our guards were down." He swore again.

Aaron listened for a minute more, then yanked the headset off and passed it back to Felix. He strode away from the table, cursing in a low, continuous growl. The three healers were huddled around the injured mythic, and as I watched, the shifting bodies parted, offering me a glimpse of the gurney.

The man was lying face down, his bare back streaked with blood. Three deep gashes ran from shoulder to shoulder.

The horrific wounds were enough to make me lightheaded, but they weren't the reason the floor was shifting under my feet. The way the three parallel cuts swept across his flesh like monstrous claws had torn him open … I'd seen wounds just like that before.

I'd seen them in the form of white scars that raked across Ezra's torso from hip to sternum.

AARON SLUMPED on a stool. "Tori, I need a drink."

I shook my head. "Darius said no liquor until the alert is over."

He looked up with pleading, exhausted blue eyes. "Just one. My next rotation doesn't start for two hours."

Shifting my weight, I considered. "Only if you promise to eat a sandwich. What do you want to drink?"

"Something that'll burn."

I pulled out a shot glass and filled it to the brim with whiskey. He downed the shot with a grimace.

Kai dropped into the next seat, his sword sheathed. My stomach twitched unhappily at the sight of him and I ducked into the kitchen to grab sandwiches and a wet paper towel.

Returning to the bar, I put a sandwich in front of each guy, then told Kai, "Hold still."

He squinted tiredly, then recoiled when I started scrubbing his cheek with the paper towel.

"Tori," he complained.

"You're splattered with blood. Just hold still." I scrubbed his temple, checked he was clean, then pitched the paper towel into the garbage. "Okay. Now eat."

As they robotically bit into their sandwiches, I surveyed the pub. The healers were working on the injured man, his team members hovering nearby—Izzah, Mario, and another mythic. It was reasonably quiet again.

No sooner did I think that than the door banged. The bolt rattled, then someone knocked loudly. Clara hastened to unlock it, and three wet strangers stumbled in. Outside, rain poured, the rippling puddles reflecting the building's lights.

"Guild?" Clara asked.

"Pandora Knights."

She made a quick note on a clipboard. "We have hot drinks, sandwiches, and cots upstairs. What would you like first?"

They conferred, then chose beds. She led the weary trio to the stairs, where the second level had been converted into a bunk room. As they passed the bar, Aaron and Kai nodded to the men, and they nodded back.

"Mages," Aaron said once they'd vanished upstairs. "The Pandora Knights are exclusively Elementaria. They invited me to join but I passed. They're snobs."

I glanced worriedly at the stairs. With the arrival of the Odin's Eye team, Ezra had vanished, just like when Izzah and Mario had shown up last night. There were only so many places he could've gone. "Is Ezra up there?"

"I checked on him a few minutes ago," Kai said. "He's camped out on the third floor where it's quiet."

That was good. Ezra was unpredictable when it came to chaos. Sometimes, he was the calmest person in the room, and other times ... he didn't cope well. I now suspected that demon-related chaos always pushed his buttons.

I pulled my spare stool over and sat across from them. "What happened out there?"

Aaron rubbed his forehead. "It was ugly, Tori. The demon dropped on us from off a building and ripped Roberto open before we even knew what was happening. Mario called his demon out, and the unbound demon jumped right over it and tried to take Mario's head off. Izzah was fast—she's his champion—and landed a direct hit with a water blade, but the demon barely flinched. The thing is a tank."

"What do you mean she's Mario's champion?"

"It's a tongue-in-cheek term for a contractor's protector," Kai explained, picking at the crust of his half-eaten sandwich. "Since no one wants to fight a demon, they try to kill the demon's contractor instead. As soon as the contractor dies, the demon is gone."

"It takes most of a contractor's concentration to command and maneuver his demon, so the champion protects him." Aaron stared at his sandwich like it was made of playdough. "Mario's demon was way too slow for the unbound one. I thought we were all dead."

"Not that I enjoy admitting it," Kai muttered, "but the Keys of Solomon saved our asses. Their team charged in with two demons of their own, and the unbound one took off. The Keys chased it while we rushed Roberto back here."

Huffing painfully with each step, Izzah stumbled over to the bar and sat beside Kai. "*Aduh.* Tori, anything to eat? For Mario too, please."

"Coming right up." I grabbed two more sandwiches, and when I returned, Mario had taken the stool beside Izzah, his shoulders drooping. "Here you go."

Izzah started unwrapping her food. "It's bad, this demon. With its ability to fly, we'll have a hell of a time catching it, let alone killing it."

"We can wear it down," Kai said. "It's one demon against thirty combat teams. Sooner or later, it'll make a mistake."

"But how many mistakes will we make first? How many will die?" She took an unenthusiastic bite. Why did no one like my super club sandwiches? They were only a little soggy.

"Mario," Aaron began, "do you know anything about winged demons?"

"They aren't common." He picked the tomato out of his sandwich. "Summoners keep mum about demon lore, so I don't know much about types. I've heard about winged demons but I've never seen one until now."

I sank onto my stool. "Are all demons equal, or does their power vary like fae?"

"They're all powerful, but some more than others. I can only base it on my own experience, but some are larger with more physical strength."

"Our issue is magic," Izzah said. "Bound demons can't use their magic, only the small amount the contractor can command through them. Unbound demons can do who knows what with theirs."

"Who knows what ..." Aaron muttered. He shoved back from the bar. "I need to sleep if I want to be of any use in a couple of hours. Tori, can you ask Felix about a replacement phone for me? Mine got smashed during the ambush."

"Okay. Have a good rest." Chewing on my lower lip, I watched him, Kai, Izzah, and Mario limp tiredly upstairs to catch a few hours of sleep. None of them had finished their sandwiches, and I threw out the remains. I needed better food for them. Something more appetizing than slimy deli meat. Something they could scarf down fast.

I hung around the bar for another hour, dispensing unappealing sandwiches to the mythic teams that arrived in trios and quartets, wet, dirty, and exhausted. They'd eat, have a drink, then traipse upstairs to sleep.

When all the expected teams had settled in, I headed up the stairs. Passing the open doorway to the second level, I glimpsed the dark room filled with cots and mats, still bodies stretched out under thin blankets and gear piled around them.

I continued to the third level and headed down a short hall. In the room at the end, the three officer desks were buried in folders and papers, all work abandoned when the alert had gone out.

Ezra sat on Girard's desk, feet resting on the seat of his chair, and stared out the rain-streaked window. As I walked in, he glanced over, his face dimly lit by the single lamp glowing on Tabitha's desk. His expression was a mystery.

I stopped beside him, at a complete loss for what to say. How did I broach the topic of his scars? How did I ask if a demon had inflicted them? Should I suggest he hadn't joined the search because he couldn't handle confrontation with demons? Should I point out that he fled whenever Mario showed up because the man was a demon contractor?

I didn't want to ask any of those things, so I said nothing. Sitting on the desk beside him, I too stared out the window at the street beyond, illuminated by the first gleam of dawn. In silence, we watched the wet pavement brighten with shades of orange and gold.

It had been a long night, but the dawning day promised to be even longer.

5

SLEEPLESS TORI is a grumpy Tori.

I squinted blearily at the clock. 6:35 p.m. Over eighteen hours since the alert had gone out, and everyone's energy was flagging. I'd napped for the afternoon, curled up in Clara's chair in the office at the back of the kitchen, but it hadn't helped much.

Aaron and Kai were due back from their third rotation at seven. A couple dozen mythics were sleeping on the second level, and another ten were hanging around the pub, too wired to sleep.

At one table, a pair of older men and a woman were poring over a map. According to Felix, they were the GM of Odin's Eye, the GM of Smoke & Mirrors, and the first officer of the Pandora Knights. Their teams were sleeping, but they couldn't rest.

I filled three mugs with steaming black coffee and carried them over.

"Thank you," the woman murmured as I set them down. "The movement patterns don't make sense, Lee. The demon could only have reached this point by flying directly there and attacking immediately."

She jabbed at the map. All the locations where the demon had been spotted were highlighted. The creature was jumping all over the Eastside, an expansive and disreputable neighborhood with a mix of low-income housing, small businesses, and industry. Since ambushing Aaron's team, the demon had struck three more times ... and its victims hadn't been as lucky as the Odin's Eye survivor.

Three mythics had died in the streets. Another hadn't made it to the healers in time. Two more were with the Seadevil guild's healers, hanging on to life.

Lee folded his hands together and tapped them against his narrow lips. "These four locations are confirmed engagements with the demon." He indicated the highlighter marks. "The rest are signs or sightings. They could be wrong."

"Grand Grimoire is confident about the damage they found—only a demon could have inflicted it, and it was recent," the woman said. "Either this demon is moving exceptionally fast, or there are multiple demons."

"Um," I interjected hesitantly. "There *are* multiple demons, though, aren't there? Any of the contractors' demons could have caused some damage, right?"

The two men looked at me like I was a moron, but the woman frowned thoughtfully. "Grand Grimoire wouldn't report damage caused by their own demons, but ... do we have any record about the Keys' movements?"

They resumed their debate, and I headed back to the bar, wishing I'd kept my mouth shut. Slipping into the kitchen, I checked on our food supply. An MPD agent had stopped by a few hours ago to see what we needed and promised a grocery delivery would arrive later this evening, but we were down to two sandwiches that had surpassed soggy and devolved into beige gelatin. I'd served most of our burgers—a bit charred compared to Ramsey's cooking, but edible.

Sighing, I wandered out again, helplessness weighing on me. What use was I? I had two artifacts and a familiar with just enough magic to make puffs of wind. Hoshi was sleeping in my purse, where she spent most of her time when I was out of the house. She liked being close to me, and since I always kept my purse nearby, the arrangement worked well.

My phone buzzed against my butt cheek. I yanked it out, terrified it might be Aaron—or worse, the police department calling Justin's emergency contact, which was me. I didn't recognize the number.

"Hello?" My voice wavered with nerves.

"Hello, Tori Dawson? This is Puffs & Pastries Bakery."

I wilted in relief. "Oh. Yeah."

"I'm just calling to see if you're coming for your order? Your invoice says you planned to pick it up at three."

"Uh, right." Baked goods for the Halloween party—which, safe to say, wasn't happening anymore. I glanced around the pub but couldn't see any of my jack-o'-lanterns. I wondered where they'd ended up. "About that. I've had a, uh, family emergency so I'm not sure when …"

I trailed off, considering our barren kitchen. I'd thrown out a lot of food today, but fresh-baked cupcakes might tempt the tired mythics to eat.

"I'm not sure when I can come," I said quickly, "but I'll try to get over there. How late are you open?"

"Until eight."

"Okay. Thanks." Ending the call, I strode over to Felix, who was manning the command center with bloodshot eyes and a mug of black coffee.

"Felix." I pulled out the chair beside him. "You know how I ordered eight dozen cupcakes for the Halloween party tonight?"

"No." He smiled tiredly. "But okay. What about it?"

"Can I go get them? We're almost out of food, and something sweet and easy to snack on might wake up some appetites."

"Where's the bakery?"

"It's in Gastown—a ten-minute walk west of here." I pointed at the map screen, which showed that all the demonic activity was to the east. "That should be okay, right? Gastown isn't closed down or anything."

"The area is in the clear, but we're keeping all members under cover." He rubbed his goatee. "We do need something to snack on, and it isn't far. Take Ezra with you. It'd do him well to get out for a few minutes."

"Great. We'll go right now."

He nodded. "If they have muffins or buns, buy those too."

"Got it."

I hurried up to the third level to wake Ezra from his nap on the floor by the officers' desks, his head pillowed on his folded jacket. I grabbed my coat and purse, and checked that Hoshi was snoozing in orb form at its bottom. Two minutes later, we were stepping out into the crisp evening air.

The streetlamps were already lit, their orange lights gleaming on the wet pavement. The rain had let up, but the air was so damp it was like breathing underwater. Ezra and I walked fast, looking over our shoulders every few steps, but all was quiet. I clamped my arms around myself, shivering from nerves and cold.

Within a few minutes, we'd entered the better-lit neighborhood of Gastown, and suddenly, the streets were full of people. As laughing groups and costumed partiers filled the sidewalks, I remembered that Halloween festivities hadn't come to a screeching halt for the rest of the populace. A handful of tense police officers were scattered around, presumably to prevent people from wandering off, and I scanned them for any sign of Justin.

As the sidewalk grew crowded, Ezra shifted behind me, and I led the way through droves of revelers. The cafés were bursting with lines out the door, their patios filled despite the chilly air. Dodging teenagers in anime costumes, I tugged my thin jacket tighter around me. How could those girls stand wearing such short skirts in this weather?

Catching my arm, Ezra pulled me out of the flow of foot traffic and into a shop, so fast I didn't see what store we'd entered. Warm air washed over me, and I blinked at the shelves of toys.

"This isn't the bakery," I pointed out dryly.

"I know." He raised his eyebrows. "But I saw these."

Stepping over to the window display, piled high with *Harry Potter* collectibles, he plucked a red- and gold-striped scarf off a rack and looped it around my neck. I picked up the end to examine the embroidered coat of arms. "Gryffindor?"

"It's perfect for you."

With a goofy smile I couldn't quite squash, I lifted a second one off the hook. "You too, then."

He took it away before I could put it over his head. Hanging it back up, he chose a yellow and black one and slung it around his neck.

"Hufflepuff? You're not a Hufflepuff."

"Definitely am."

"How would you know?" I teased. "You don't even like *Harry Potter*—which I don't understand at all, by the way. What don't you like?"

His amusement faltered. "It ... it's stupid."

Curiosity lit through me. "Come on, tell me."

He picked up a Harry figurine, stared at it, then sighed. "It's the scar thing."

I glanced from the figurine to the jagged white line that cut down Ezra's face, an injury that had stolen half his vision. In the near six months I'd known him, how many times had complete strangers stared at him, pointed, or rudely asked what had happened? He had a collection of ridiculous explanations for the obnoxiously curious; last time, he'd warned the person to be extra careful with knitting needles.

I plucked the figurine from his hand and set it on the shelf, then unwound the Gryffindor scarf from around my neck, replaced it on a hook, and put on a Hufflepuff one instead. "Hufflepuffs are loyal and hardworking. That's where I want to be."

Smiling crookedly, Ezra adjusted my new scarf, snugging the soft knit up under my chin. The backs of his fingers brushed my cheek. "There. You're ready."

My skin tingled, but I pretended to be unaffected. "Ready for what?"

"To run for it. The cashier will never catch us. On the count of three. One—"

"Whoa, *what?* We are *not* shoplifting—" I belatedly noticed the sparkle in his eyes and growled. "Oh my god! *You!*"

Huffing, I playfully—mostly—swatted his shoulder, and his laughing grin broke free. With a roll of my eyes, I stalked up to the counter and dug into my purse, but he appeared beside me, bills already in hand. The cashier rang up the scarves, passed Ezra a handful of change, then cut the tags off our new winter wear.

"I can't believe I fell for that," I muttered as I swept ahead of him and pushed the door open. "Just wait until—*AAHHH!*"

The high-pitched shriek erupted from my throat as a blood-splattered face loomed six inches from my nose, mouth gaping in a loud moan. I fell backward into Ezra.

"*Gaaahhhg*," the zombie burbled.

Dragging one leg, it lurched past me—and behind it followed two dozen bodies in torn clothes, their pale faces artfully smeared with glistening gore. As the horde shambled down the sidewalk, pedestrians stepped aside, laughing or pretending to cower in fear.

I clutched Ezra's coat, wheezing as my brain caught up to reality. Halloween. It was Halloween, and those were costumes. A zombie walk. Fun downtown event, with professional makeup and all that. Pretend dead people. Ha ha, fun.

Sliding an arm around my waist, Ezra nudged me away from the shop's doorway. I sucked in air and told myself I'd only freaked because my nerves were shot from the real-life horror show going on right now, unbeknownst to the public.

"I didn't scream, did I?" I muttered.

"No, not at all," Ezra lied solemnly.

I puffed out a breath, amused and embarrassed, then drew away from the safe circle of his arm. Straightening my jacket, I took one step—and a girl's purse smacked me in the face as she flung her arm up to wave at someone.

"Oh, sorry," she said brightly and hurried away.

Holding my throbbing nose, I took another step. Ezra grabbed my hand and hauled me back as a trio of knee-high kidlets in dinosaur costumes ran past, a frazzled dad chasing after them.

Ezra led me into the chaos, weaving through the jostle with better coordination than I'd displayed; he could use his air magic to sense movement around him. After half a block, we broke free of the worst of the crowd and I fell into step beside him. My fingers were curled around his, his warm palm engulfing mine. I didn't need a guide anymore, and it was silly to pretend I did. I should nonchalantly free my hand. I really should.

Only when the bakery's glowing windows were one shop away did I finally withdraw my hand from his. As I shoved the door open and stepped into the humid interior, my mouth immediately watered.

"Oh," Ezra murmured. "It smells really good in here."

It smelled like heaven, if heaven were made entirely of chocolate, vanilla, caramel, and cream cheese icing. The place was packed with salivating customers, and I got in line, Ezra right behind me. We slowly made our way to the front counter, and surrounded by warm light, chattering people, and delicious aromas, I could almost forget why I was bone tired and jittery with apprehension.

I finally stepped up to the counter. "Pick up for Tori Dawson."

"Oh, you made it! Excellent." The pretty eighteen-ish-year-old tucked a lock of blond-streaked hair behind her ear. "Can I get you anything else?"

I asked about buns and muffins, and she piled a dozen on the counter, then disappeared into the back. She returned with four big bags stuffed with cupcake trays, and we wrestled the new items into the bags. As we finished, she peeked at Ezra, who was drooling over the cake bombs in the glass display.

"Would you like to sample a pumpkin-spice cupcake?" she asked him, smiling shyly as she held up the bite-sized goody with pale orange icing. "They have orange buttercream icing and they're to die for. I have one left."

"Thanks." He took the cupcake and offered it to me. Unable to resist anything sweet, I unwrapped it and bit off half. The moist cake exploded with flavor, its smooth, light icing melting on my tongue. "Oh hell, that's delicious. You have to try this."

As I held the second half out to Ezra, I started to ask the cashier if this flavor had been included in my order, but her gaze was darting from me to Ezra and her expression had dimmed with disappointment.

Sometime in the last eighteen hours of hell, I'd lost all coordination. Instead of holding the cupcake out for Ezra to take, I'd stuck it up toward his face—as though to *feed* it to him, like the cutsiest newly-in-love-and-revolting-everyone-around-them couple.

Ezra hesitated, caught off guard. Embarrassment ricocheted through me and I yanked my arm down to navel height—now weirdly low like I was trying to pass it to him in secret. Failing to maintain any dignity, I stuffed it into his hand and turned back to the counter.

"Are we good to go, then?" I asked gruffly.

"Yes, that's everything," she replied in a glum tone. "Have a nice evening."

As Ezra took two bags, I heaved the other two off the counter and sped onto the sidewalk—almost crashing into a group dressed up as plastic green soldiers, faces painted and everything. I squeezed past them, my bulky bags bouncing off their legs. Behind me, Ezra apologized to someone he'd knocked into a bus stop bench.

We inched through the throng, trying to protect the cupcakes, but it was impossible. Spotting a group of thirty people, probably in the middle of a Halloween pub crawl, I ducked into the opening of a nearby alley. Ezra slipped in with me, just missing the oncoming swarm.

I watched them pass—but another group came in right behind them. If I tried to go through that horde, I was likely to punch someone out of my way. And then I'd get arrested for assault, and the police would confiscate all the delicious cupcakes before I got to eat any.

"Let's cut through here," I said, turning away from the sidewalk. "Skip some of the crowds."

Ezra hesitated, then nodded. He didn't like crowds either.

With the space to walk together, we fell into step side by side. He glanced warily around the alley, the darkness broken by lonely bulbs hovering above the back doors of shops. I watched him out of the corner of my eye, seeing what the bakery cashier had been admiring. Soft, loose curls in a perpetual tousle tumbled across his forehead and teased his eyes. Dark, sexy scruff edged his strong jaw, and his full lips formed a serious but somehow sultry line when he wasn't smiling—but he usually had a quiet tilt at the corners of his mouth, subtle but warm.

His head swiveled, shoulders tight.

My steps slowed as I broke out of my reverie. "What's wrong?"

Stopping in the center of the narrow alley, he turned in a circle, his smile nowhere in sight. As his brow scrunched with focus, he faced the way we'd come—then his head snapped back, gaze jumping to the rooftops three stories up.

He dropped his bags and the cupcake containers hit the ground with a crunch. Grasping my arm, he yanked me so hard I almost fell.

"Ezra?" I gasped.

"Run!"

I let go of my bags. The plastic containers broke open, spilling orange cupcakes onto the wet pavement. He hauled me into a stumbling run and we sprinted to an intersection of alleys. Fifty feet away on our right waited the brightly lit and bustling street. The other three directions were dark, narrow alleys full of dumpsters and graffiti-marked overhead doors.

Ezra glanced at the bright street, then pulled me in the opposite direction.

"Ezra!" I yelped, his grip on my arm painful. "What's wrong?"

His gaze shot upward. This time I turned fast enough to follow his line of sight, my neck craning back. The rooftops loomed over the narrow alley, the silhouettes marred by power lines and rickety fire escapes.

Fear hit me like a bolt of arctic lightning, seizing every muscle in my body.

Two buildings down, perched on a rooftop, was a shape that belonged only in nightmares and horror movies. Something blacker than ebony, horns rising off its head, curved wings like a bat, and eyes that glowed like twin drops of magma.

6

EZRA AND I FLED down the alley.

Panic squeezed my lungs but my legs pumped anyway, driven by animalistic terror. Death stalked us, and my lizard brain knew it. Survival instincts screamed in my skull, and I clutched Ezra's hand as we dashed through the maze.

My blind fear said to run, to flee, to escape, but human logic was screaming something else. *How do you outrun a demon that can fly?*

I didn't look back to see if it was following us. I just ran, half a step behind Ezra, struggling to keep pace. He kept pulling away until our arms were stretched between our bodies, then he'd slow again to let me catch up.

We reached another intersection and he wheeled into an even narrower alley. Heading east. Fleeing toward the Crow and Hammer.

Yes. Yes, yes, yes. The guild was full of combat mythics resting between shifts. We didn't have to outrun the demon. We just had to reach the guild before the demon attacked us.

We sprinted between buildings, and I prayed I wouldn't trip. Couldn't fall. Had to run.

Ezra slammed to a halt. I flew past him before he yanked me off my feet and into his chest. He scrambled backward, holding me tight against him, the soles of my shoes brushing the wet pavement.

Metal creaked overhead, then groaned under a heavy weight. Two stories up, dark wings unfurled from atop a fire escape.

Ezra dragged me backward, keeping the demon in sight. Hysterical babble filled my head. Demon. The demon was here. It was stalking us. Why was it here? *How* was it here? It was supposed to be terrorizing combat mythics twenty blocks east of Gastown.

Reaching what he must've considered an acceptable distance, Ezra spun around and broke into a run, pulling me with him. We raced back to the intersection, and he turned north. Yes. Go north, cut east again, bolt for the guild. We weren't that far. Only a few more blocks.

We got six steps before Ezra pulled up short again. He backpedaled and I almost fell from the sudden change of direction.

Black wings flared as the demon landed on a wooden beam above a set of power lines, halfway along the northern alley. Waiting for us. Taunting us with our inability to outrun it.

Ezra backed up step by step, his breathing fast and harsh. I clutched his hand, my limbs shaking. We retreated into the intersection of alleys. The demon had cut us off when we went east. It'd moved to stop us from going north. Just south of us was the crowded street the alley paralleled.

With nowhere else to go, we ran west—away from the Crow and Hammer. Where else could we go? I raced beside him, too frightened to think beyond the next moment. Just run. No time for strategy. Just—

We skidded to a stop again, but not because the demon had cut us off.

A four-story wall rose in our path. A dead end. I scoured the rows of tall overhead doors, all shut and locked. A single lightbulb glowed above a recessed metal door with a heavy padlock hanging from it. We were trapped.

Ezra and I spun around.

The demon prowled into the alley, its magma-red eyes radiating malevolent power. A low, growling laugh throbbed from its throat.

Terror buckled my legs. Ezra grabbed my waist and pulled me against his side.

The demon was huge—seven feet tall with a heavy head and monstrous wings. Four thick horns rose off its hairless skull, covered in dark skin with a reddish undertone. Bands of muscle crossed its broad chest and its thick arms were weaponized by the spines protruding from its elbows and the curved talons tipping its strong fingers. Black cloth, covered by interlocking metal armor and a wide belt, wrapped its hips and upper thighs. A heavy tail dragged behind it, ending in a bony plate that could crush a human skull with one hit.

Petrifying fear like I'd never felt before closed my throat. No mythic had frightened me this much. No black-magic rogue. No darkfae. This was something else, something *worse*.

It was pure evil. It was death given form, the embodiment of murder and bloodlust.

As though it could hear my thoughts, the creature's lips pulled back to reveal huge, flesh-tearing fangs. Its quiet, gravelly laugh echoed down the alley, and it took another step. The beast was toying with us, drinking in our terror as it stalked closer. Even fifty feet away, its suffocating presence filled the alley. I couldn't breathe through the icy chill.

Ezra's arm tightened around me—and I realized the cold was coming from him.

He grabbed my upper arms and pushed me on stumbling legs until my back hit the locked metal door. Then he forced me into a crouch in the alcove, where I trembled against the frigid steel.

"Tori." He took hold of my wrists, his skin like ice. "*Tori.*"

I forced my gaze up to his, hyperventilating in rapid wheezes.

"Listen to me. I'll keep you safe—I swear I will—but I need you to promise me." His fingers tightened painfully around my wrists, then he lifted my hands to my face and pressed my palms over my eyes. "Keep your eyes covered. Don't look."

Confusion fizzled through my panic and I tried to lower my hands. "Ezra—"

He held my palms against my eyes. "Promise me, Tori. Cover your eyes and stay here and don't move until I come back, or—" He stuttered. "Until I come back."

"But—"

"Tori, *promise me.*"

With my eyes covered, I couldn't see the expression that accompanied his hoarse, desperate command. I swallowed hard. "I promise."

He released my wrists. Squeezing my face with my hands, tears wetting my palms, I trembled at his quiet footsteps walking away from me. Alone, cornered in a doorway, my eyes covered, a demon stalking closer.

Ezra's steps retreated until I couldn't hear them, then came the quiet sound of the demon's deep breathing—close. Much closer than before. Panic swept through me, so potent my muscles convulsed.

"*Tūiranā thē, hrātir. Eshanā paissum adh'sūv thē.*"

The harsh, gravelly rumble vibrated in my bones, a language I'd never heard before. The demon continued in its guttural tongue, then broke off with a deep growl. The temperature plunged and the orange glow leaking around my hands disappeared as darkness overtook the lightbulb.

Red light flared, shining through my palms.

The air, searing with painful cold, turned electric and power scraped across my bones like thousands of tiny knives. The demon barked something in its harsh language, then came the grind of claws dragging across pavement.

With a sickening thud, flesh struck flesh.

The demon roared. Thumps, grunts. Crimson light flared again and frigid wind blasted me. I pressed into the alcove, knees pulled up to my chest. Arctic cold clawed at my exposed skin, stealing my body heat. My tears froze to my cheeks.

Red light blinded me through my hands, then a clanging boom as something hit an overhead door. My instincts screamed at me to look, but I didn't want to. I didn't dare. Huddling into a tighter ball, I crushed my eye sockets with the heels of my hands.

Crack. The sound of breaking bone. A deafening howl echoed off the alley walls, and air boomed with the labored beating of wings. The sound grew distant, then silence settled around me.

Shaking in my alcove, I waited. And waited. And waited.

Silence. Nothing but silence.

Trembling so violently I could barely control my limbs, I lowered my hands. The lightbulb overhead buzzed and flickered, casting a weak glow across the alley.

Glittering white fractals covered the ground, the damp sheen of recent rain turned to pale ice. Frost coated every surface, and thick crimson blood had frozen to macabre pink. A huge dent, smeared with icy blood, had caved in a steel door.

Exhaling in a wintry-white cloud, I pushed out of the alcove and onto unsteady legs.

Ice crunched under a heavy footfall. I spun toward the shadow-swathed dead end. Ezra limped out of the darkness, heavily favoring one leg. His face was splattered with blood and he held a hand over his left eye, covering his scar and pale iris. Blood dripped steadily off his elbow.

"*Ezra.*" My mouth formed his name, but only a croak escaped my dry throat. I stumbled across the frozen pavement, reaching for him.

"I was coming to get you." His normally smooth voice was a rough, painful rasp, no louder than a whisper.

I grabbed his arm to steady him—and my fingers slid through slick, warm wetness. Jerking back, I looked in horror at my hands, coated in bright red human blood.

"You're hurt." With those two words, I threw off my helpless terror and pulled myself together. Ezra was injured and it was my turn to be the strong one.

My purse was gone—lost while we'd been running. I ran my hand over Ezra's front pockets, feeling for the shape of his phone. With no time for bashfulness, I reached around and grabbed his ass with both hands. He jumped.

"Tori …" he muttered hazily. Was he going into shock?

My fingers pressed into the hard shape of a cell. I yanked it out of his pocket and pressed the power button. The screen lit up but a spiderweb of cracks had turned the display into a hideous pattern of black and neon streaks. Useless.

We needed help. Ezra was limping too much to walk far, and I didn't know how much blood he'd lost.

"Hoshi?" I called.

A breeze washed over me, then a bluish-silver shape appeared. The sylph's pink eyes glowed faintly, her gecko-like head adorned with two pairs of antennae that ended in little blue crystals. Her body was mostly tail, and her long, sinuous form undulated weightlessly, as though the air were thicker than water.

"Sorry I dropped you," I said hastily, relieved she'd followed me even after getting accidentally dumped somewhere. "Hoshi, Aaron is at the guild. I need you to bring him to me." I squinted, forming an image of the guild and Aaron in my mind, then imagining Hoshi leading him through the alleys to me and Ezra.

Hoshi touched her cool nose to my forehead and the image replayed in my head. The sylph spiraled around me, then sped down the alley like a fluttering blue banner.

Throwing Ezra's broken phone aside, I pulled off my scarf—his he'd lost during the battle. I wound it around his bleeding arm, then tied the limb against his chest in a sling. He was swaying, so I pulled him over to the wall and sat him against it. He finally lowered his hand from his face. His eye looked normal—as normal as the pale iris ever looked—and I wondered why he'd covered it.

"Hold on, Ezra," I whispered. "You'll be okay."

He smiled faintly and my heart twisted. I tried to check him for injuries, but he was covered in blood—some his, some the thick, crimson-black demon blood.

Forcing myself to breathe deep, I scanned the alley for signs of movement—praying Aaron and Kai were at the guild and would come as fast as they could. And praying the demon didn't return.

My gaze landed on a dark shape lying on the pavement amidst the splattered blood. For a long moment, I didn't understand what it was, then I realized it was the demon's horns—two of the four horns that had risen off its head, shattered at the base. I remembered the bone-like crack before the demon fled.

How the hell had Ezra done *that*?

Swallowing my questions, I pushed myself up and approached the broken appendages. It took a swift but stern lecture to convince myself to touch them. Gingerly picking them up, I speed-walked down the alley, away from the signs of battle, and shoved the two horns deep into a garbage bin. After replacing the lid, I strode back to Ezra.

He watched me return. Said nothing.

I crouched beside him, took his hand in both of mine, and waited for help to arrive. He closed his eyes, breathing harshly and sagging forward with the passing minutes. Panic swirled through my gut—then I saw the flash of pale blue at the end of the alley. A sinuous shape, accompanied by two human silhouettes.

"Tori?" a familiar voice called, sharp with alarm.

"Aaron!" I screamed. "Over here!"

He and Kai sprinted up the alley, fully geared with their weapons drawn. Hoshi trailed after them. When they reached the frosted ground and saw the battle damage—the dented steel door, cement walls gouged with claw marks—Aaron slid to a horrified stop.

Kai ran straight to Ezra, sheathed his sword in one quick motion, and flicked on the light attached to his vest. As brightness bloomed, Kai pulled the bloody scarf away. My stomach turned over.

A triple line of claw marks raked down Ezra's arm from bicep to wrist, and even deeper gouges in his leg were leaking blood. Ezra cracked his eyes open, pupils dilated and unfocused.

"Aaron!" Kai barked as he unbuckled his belt. "The others are right behind us."

Aaron nodded. As Kai slid his belt around Ezra's thigh and pulled it tight to stanch the bleeding, Aaron raised both hands. Fire burst from his palms. Swirling steam rose from the pavement and the air warmed to a normal temperature.

Four people appeared at the alley intersection.

"Here!" Aaron shouted.

Drew, Lyndon, Venus, and Sylvia ran to join us. Venus dropped to her knees beside Kai, her brown eyes darting over Ezra as she opened her alchemy kit. He'd closed his eyes again, and I was no longer sure he was conscious.

"Good lord," Lyndon said hoarsely, staring at the damage. "What happened?"

Everyone except Venus, who was pouring a sizzling potion over Ezra's arm, looked at me. Aaron's blue eyes were electric in their intensity, and Kai's dark stare cut with warning.

I understood: No single mythic should've been able to fight a demon and survive. Aaron had melted the frost, the same way I had hidden the broken horns. Ezra's secrets balanced on a blade's edge and a single wrong word could expose them.

"We were walking back from the bakery," I said shakily. "The demon showed itself … and chased us." I gulped down the very real panic rising in me, triggered by the memories. "I sent Hoshi for help, and the demon chased us into a dead end. Ezra tried to protect me but … I think the demon was toying with him."

I looked at Ezra, slumped against Kai, and lied with all the skill I possessed. "The demon was about to kill him, then it took off. I think it heard you guys coming."

Drew whirled around in a panicky circle. "Is it that close? Aaron, did you report it?"

As Aaron spoke into the mic on his earpiece, Venus closed her bag. "I've stopped most of the bleeding, but if the demon threw him around, he might have internal injuries. Let's get him back to the guild."

Drew and Kai loaded Ezra onto Aaron, piggyback-style, and they walked away in a tight cluster. Sylvia pulled me to my feet.

"You did good, hun," she murmured, patting my arm. "You did good."

I blinked. Sylvia never said nice things, like … ever.

She kept an arm around my shoulders as we hurried after the others. I glanced back at the caved-in steel door. I'd lied and now I had to hold to that story—but what had really happened? How had Ezra survived the demon's attack?

And how dangerous were the secrets that he, Aaron, and Kai were so desperate to protect?

7

"AND THEN," I said wearily, "the demon flew away. Aaron, Kai, and the others arrived a minute later."

Cearra, Alyssa, Liam, and Riley listened with expressions ranging from rapt fear to scarcely suppressed disbelief.

"Just like that?" Cearra asked skeptically. "It flew away?"

I ignored her since I'd literally just said that.

Liam adjusted the round sunglasses he always wore. "Why do you think it fled, Tori?"

I'd repeated my story so many times now—to Felix, to Darius, to an MPD agent on the phone, to four GMs from other guilds—that the details came easily. Considering the authoritative positions of the people I was lying to, I couldn't afford any inconsistencies.

"The demon either decided that killing us wasn't fun anymore," I answered, "or it didn't want a big fight right then.

Either way, if Aaron and Kai had arrived a minute later, Ezra would be dead. Me too, probably."

All five of us glanced across the pub to the healers' corner. Ezra was stretched out on the second gurney in a weird half-clothed state—one sleeve and one leg of his pants cut off—while the healers worked on his injuries. He'd lost a lot of blood, but the wounds weren't as bad as they'd looked. Elisabetta had assured me, Aaron, and Kai that he'd be back on his feet in no time.

"You got lucky for sure," Cearra said, worry softening her normally acerbic tone. "I can't believe the demon stalked you guys like that."

"Do you think it followed you into Gastown?" Riley asked, nervously adjusting her hair—a mop of wild brown curls that made mine look tame in comparison. "Why would it do that?"

"If it followed them," Alyssa cut in shrilly, "does that mean it's watching our guild?"

The four mythics shifted uneasily. I didn't comment, but I suspected the same. How else would the demon have picked me and Ezra out of the crowd like that? It must have followed us, but Ezra didn't sense its movements until after we'd left the chaotic Halloween crowds behind.

Riley's question was the big one on my mind: *Why?* Why had the demon targeted us?

"I heard Felix say the police are clearing out Gastown," Liam said, "but no one's found any sign of the demon. Do you think it's watching us again?"

They all shuddered, and I wondered if they wanted to leave. Like me, they'd been stuck in the guild for almost twenty hours now. It wasn't safe to go out alone, and the combat mythics were too busy hunting the demon to escort them anywhere.

The guild door banged open. Aaron and Kai swept in, an assortment of other mythics following them. Kai tossed me my lost purse, and I gratefully stuffed it on the back counter.

Felix looked up from his computers expectantly.

"No sign of the damn thing," Aaron told him. "Who knows where it is, and the Keys are making themselves real obnoxious. They're all over Gastown."

Felix muttered something foul. "I'll report to Darius. He and his team are heading back this way."

The two mages moved toward Ezra and the healers, and I hastened to join them. I slipped between Aaron and Kai as they watched Miles draw a rune on Ezra's inner forearm. He didn't have much unmarked skin left—the healers had drawn all kinds of shapes and symbols around his injuries. The gouges from the demon's claws had healed to thin pink lines, smears of dried blood the only sign he'd been seriously injured.

"Okay," Miles said. "Time to wake him up. *Ori expergefacio.*"

The rune shimmered, and Ezra inhaled sharply. His eyes flickered open, bleary and disoriented. Miles and Sanjana helped him sit up, then they fed him three back-to-back potions. He gagged on the last one, spilling the green liquid down his chin.

"Drink up!" Miles commanded. "I don't care what you think it tastes like."

Ezra swallowed the last of it with effort, then wiped his mouth with the back of his hand. "What if it tastes like Brussels sprouts and burnt engine oil?"

Miles asked Ezra a few questions about pain or stiffness, then patted him on the shoulder. "You'll feel better once you've washed up and changed. Aaron and Kai, help him downstairs to clean up and make sure he stays on his feet."

Kai pulled Ezra's arm over his shoulders and drew him up. Ezra leaned on his friend, limping as they walked toward the basement stairs. Aaron started to follow, then reached back and grabbed my hand. Uh, okay. I'd figured "cleaning up" would involve showers and things, but I guess I was still invited.

The basement staircase was situated underneath the one to the upper level, the door tucked out of sight of the main pub floor. I'd only been in the basement a few times. The main room consisted of exercise equipment and a sparring arena, with shelves of gear lining the far wall. Behind one door was a large alchemy lab, and behind another was a heavily reinforced room for spell testing.

Eighties action movie posters covered every spare inch of wall space, and Sylvester Stallone's crazy Rambo stare followed me as we passed a row of treadmills. Kai pulled Ezra into the men's showers, the door marked with an alien face instead of a men's room stick figure, and I sat down on the nearest workout bench to wait. Aaron hung back with me.

I scrubbed my face. "I'm so tired."

"Yeah," Aaron agreed, sitting heavily on the mats beside me. "What a day."

My throat constricted and I whispered, "How bad is it?"

"I think we'll be okay," he answered, understanding what I was asking. "Your story is believable, and they're attributing the damage in the alley to the demon showing off its strength to frighten you two. It's already proven that it enjoys ambushing and terrifying its victims."

I swallowed back the sick feeling in my stomach. "What about the horns?"

In the few minutes I'd gotten alone with Aaron and Kai before they had to go back out, I'd whispered a high-speed rendition of the real fight and warned them I'd hidden demonic body parts in a garbage bin—evidence that would shatter my fragile explanation of my and Ezra's survival.

Aaron shook his head. "We tried to search when no one was looking, but the place was crawling with mythics from multiple guilds. It was safer not to draw attention to it. No one has any reason to search the trash."

"This is all my fault." I pressed my hands together. "Kai told me to keep Ezra inside the guild, but I thought he meant I had to keep Ezra from following you two. I thought it was safe to go to Gastown. Even Felix said it was safe."

"It's not your fault. No one could have predicted the demon would be there and attack you."

Though he said it sincerely, I wondered if he was being honest. I almost felt like he and Kai had been fearing something like this would happen …

A few minutes later, Kai and Ezra walked out of the showers, the aeromage limping but steady. His hair shone wetly and he wore a clean t-shirt and black sweats. Every guild member kept spare clothes and a full set of gear at the guild; after becoming a member, I'd been assigned a locker in the women's shower room. Come to think of it, I should probably make use of those resources.

They sat on the mats with Aaron, Ezra leaning wearily against the weight bench I was perched on, and I slid off it to sit cross-legged between him and Aaron.

"So," Kai said, "we need a plan."

I squinted one eye dubiously. "A plan for what?"

"Oh, nothing important," Aaron replied breezily. "Just luring out and killing a demon without involving anyone else."

"Uh … what?"

Ezra pushed his damp hair out of his eyes. "I'll try not to bleed as much next time."

"Whoa, whoa, *whoa*." I pointed accusingly at Aaron. "What the hell are you talking about?"

Kai propped himself up on one arm. "Your story is good, Tori, but the whole thing will fall apart if anyone sees the demon with half its horns ripped off. It was sighted multiple times with its horns intact, and if anyone discovers its newly injured state, they'll start asking questions."

"They're already asking questions," Aaron added. "We don't want any more."

"So we have to find the demon and kill it first," Kai concluded.

I looked between them, waiting for someone to yell, "Gotcha!"

"You want to find the demon," I clarified, "which *thirty teams* of mythics haven't found yet, and then you want to kill it, when it's already butchered *four combat mythics*."

"Yeah," Aaron agreed darkly. "But the demon's already gone for Ezra once. If he goes outside again, the demon should come after him a second time."

My gaze swung to Ezra. He looked away, avoiding my eyes.

"But it could be *anywhere*," I protested, unable to believe we were having this discussion. "It can fly."

"Not very well … not anymore," Ezra muttered reluctantly, as though worried he was causing us even more trouble. "I broke one of its wings."

"See?" Aaron said. "It's gotta be nearby."

I squeezed my temples. "Okay, fine, maybe that would work. But what about the second part? You know, the part where the demon tore up Ezra once already and how it almost ripped the both of you apart too. The three of you going up against this thing by yourselves is suicide."

The three mages exchanged glances as though wordlessly debating something. The silence stretched for a full minute, and I considered closing my eyes and humming loudly so they could speed things up with an actual discussion.

Finally, Aaron shrugged. "We should bring her."

"No," Ezra snapped.

"The area is crawling with teams and we can't risk any witnesses. She can help by delaying or distracting anyone who approaches. She'll run interference while we handle the demon."

Ezra pressed his lips together. "No."

I glanced at him, his jaw flexing and arms folded, then back to Aaron. Secrets hung between us like ghosts and half-formed suspicions filled my head, but the handful of puzzle pieces I held didn't form a complete picture. The broken glimpses they offered, however …

My questions died on my tongue. I didn't want to know. I didn't want to know how Ezra had survived the demon, why it had gone after him, or why they thought it would attack him again.

"So, we're going to hunt the demon," I said slowly.

Ezra's jaw tightened until it threatened to crack his teeth. He wouldn't look at me.

"We're going to *kill* a demon," Kai clarified. "And we're going to do it before anyone else gets the chance."

"But first," Aaron added, stifling a yawn with one hand, "we're going to sleep. I'm so tired I'd lose a fight against a poodle."

My stomach sank. Was this really happening? Were we going after the demon ourselves? No guild support. No backup. Aaron, Kai, and Ezra would face that deadly beast, all on their own.

"Guys." I stared at the three of them. "This is insane."

Kai shook his head. "No, Tori. This is survival."

8

THERE ARE TWO KINDS OF GIRLS: those who've fantasized about a threesome with a pair of hot guys, and liars.

I'll be honest here. I was a hot-blooded woman without a boyfriend, and my three best friends were excessively attractive. All else aside, they had the hard-muscled bodies of professional athletes, and I'd seen enough of their skin to fuel my fantasies until my ovaries turned to dust.

That didn't mean I intended to *act* on my fantasies, but come on. How could I resist a few steamy daydreams? In retrospect, I really should've resisted—because now every one of those inappropriate thoughts was parading through my stupid brain. Every. Single. One.

Heaving a sigh, I stared at the ceiling and focused on the uncomfortable mat beneath me. If I thought extra hard about the way the waistband of my sweatpants was pressing unpleasantly against my lower spine, I might forget about Ezra's warmth on my left, and Aaron's warmth on my right.

Kai was asleep on Ezra's opposite side, and I was still trying to figure out exactly how this had happened. Yes, we needed rest, and yes, the only available place to sleep was on the second level, which was crowded with a mixture of tables, cots, and sleeping mats, plus a lot of mythics—four of whom were snoring.

But how had I ended up having a slumber-party foursome with the guys?

Another sigh slid from my lungs. Of course I knew. They weren't about to leave me all by my lonesome in a corner.

The guys were my best friends. Aaron and I hadn't made a compatible couple for some stupid reason, and I was damn lucky our friendship had emerged unscathed. Aside from some awkward moments in the first few weeks after the breakup, nothing had really changed between us. He was still the same fun, teasing, supportive troublemaker as before, which only confirmed we weren't meant to be more than friends.

As for the other two, Kai had so much romantic baggage he could open his own suitcase depot. And Ezra eschewed any form of relationship—no dating, no flings, no one-night stands.

They were undateable, and that was perfectly fine with me.

Five minutes later, I gave up on sleep. Flipping my blanket off, I carefully extracted myself from the pile. The guys didn't stir; they were out like three sexy rocks. With a longing glance over my shoulder, I tiptoed across the room and down the stairs. A drink of cold water—and maybe a splash in the face—then I would try to sleep again.

The pub was quiet. The clock read 2:32 a.m. and only a dozen people were awake. Elisabetta sat at the empty healers' station, her head lolling forward. Felix had finally succumbed to exhaustion, so Tabitha sat at the computers in his place, watching updates scroll past. Six or seven strangers were resting at the tables. A few looked familiar but I didn't know their names.

Only one small group was accomplishing anything besides keeping upright in their chairs. Four people were clustered at the end of the bar, whispering. As I headed toward them, I spotted Izzah—her makeup long gone, her leather pants scuffed, and her black shirt crusted with dried blood on one side.

Facing three older men, she spoke in a low voice edged with suppressed anger. "There's only one explanation for—"

"You have no proof."

"Do we need proof to act?" she shot back. "Or will you let more people die while you wait to be absolutely positive? What about *your* people, Lee? Our guild has already—"

"That's enough, Izzah," the short, middlemost man interrupted. "We aren't picking a fight with the Keys based on unfounded suspicions."

I recognized him as one of the GMs I'd brought coffee to, and I halted a few feet away, tiredly rubbing one eye. They were blocking my way behind the bar. Though I was tempted to barrel through like I usually did, curiosity got the better of me.

"The Keys are unleashing their demons to create false positives on demonic activity," Izzah insisted. "They are *deliberately* muddying the search so they can get the kill for themselves. How long until having their demons claw up walls doesn't get enough attention? What happens then, *hah?*"

"They wouldn't go that far," Lee said.

"The rumors—and the evidence—say otherwise." She glared at the GM. "The last attack might not have happened if the Keys hadn't faked a demon sighting so far east. Who knows how long we've been searching the wrong areas?"

I tensed. Was *that* how the demon had turned up so far west to attack Ezra and me when we thought it was in another neighborhood?

Lee folded his arms. "What do you expect us to do without evidence?"

"Go to MagiPol." Izzah pointed at the door like there were MPD agents waiting on the front step. "Report the Keys. If you—or even better, if *three* GMs press them to act, they'll eject the Keys from the city."

Three GMs? Wow, Izzah had more grit than I'd realized.

"We have nothing to take to the MPD," Lee said with finality. "Until we do, we can work around the Keys. You should rest, Izzah. Get some sleep."

With that cool dismissal, he walked away. Another GM followed him, while the third headed upstairs. Izzah glared after Lee, then blew out a long, angry breath before giving me a tired smile.

"Hey Tori."

"Hi Izzah. Is that Lee guy your GM?"

"Yeah." She shook her head, her long ponytail swishing side to side. "I was afraid he'd take that stance. No one wants to report the Keys' actions to MagiPol in case it forces a confrontation. So *geram!*"

I glanced at the ceiling as though I could see the guys through it. "Tell Kai about your suspicions. He'll make sure our GM hears about it."

Izzah hesitated, then nodded. "He's sleeping-*mah*? I'll catch him once he's up and let him know. Guild rivalries or not, someone needs to act before the Keys get completely out of control."

At the mention of sleep, a yawn pulled at my jaw. "I came down for some water. Want anything?"

"Water would be great."

With Izzah following, I crossed behind the bar and pushed through the saloon doors. I grabbed two bottles of water from the fridge and tossed her one.

"Thanks." She cracked it open. "How's Ezra?"

"He's doing okay. How's … it was Roberto, right?"

"Yeah. He's already itching to get back out there." She grimaced disbelievingly, then asked, "How's Kai?"

"He's doing fine." As I opened my water, she chewed on a fingernail, a crease between her elegantly arched eyebrows. With the glow from the pub lighting one edge of her face, she radiated mysterious beauty. Exactly the sort of woman I'd expect Kai to go for. "How do you two know each other?"

"Hm." She took a long drink. "We dated for a few months … about three years ago now, I guess. Time flies …"

A few *months*? That was a long-term relationship by Kai's standards. "How did you meet?"

Her expression softened, gaze sliding absently across the counters. "He tried to arrest me for attempted theft."

My eyes popped. "Oh. Sounds romantic."

She laughed. "I was twenty and thought I knew what I was doing, but I was in over my head. He was working a security job, and after deciding I wasn't actually trying to steal anything, he helped me …" She trailed off, musing in reminiscent silence, then added matter-of-factly, "We dated for a few months afterward, then he dumped me."

I winced. Oh, Kai. He was wonderful and considerate and protective, but he treated the woman he dated like Solo cups. "Do you know why?"

"No …" She leaned against the counter, swirling her water in the bottle. "I was naïve-*lah*. We never talked about being exclusive or made plans for the future. I was just … happy and in love, you know? But I guess he wasn't."

Judging by the sad yearning on her face, she was *still* in love with him. I wasn't mean enough to point that out, though. "That's tough. You're friends, though, aren't you?"

"I tried to hate him," Izzah admitted with a sigh, "but I couldn't, especially since we keep running into each other. And sometimes he looks at me like …"

Like he wanted to sweep her off her feet and carry her away. That's what it had looked like to me when she'd strolled into the pub.

Grimacing, she chugged the rest of her water. "I must be tired. Spilling my guts to you. Don't mind me-*lah*. Just oversharing with a stranger."

I laughed. "Hey, any friend of Kai's is someone I want to know."

She grinned, then bid me good night. I watched her go, tapping my water bottle thoughtfully against my chin. I knew part of the reason Kai's love life was so messed up, but I didn't know why he felt the need to date chronically and dump women when he couldn't commit to a relationship.

What were the odds I could wrangle an explanation out of the womanizing electramage on why he'd broken up with

Izzah? I pondered the math. Less than fifty-fifty and definitely not in my favor.

———

DARIUS LEANED AGAINST the front of his desk, facing the three mages. "You're requesting what, specifically?"

Over twenty-four hours after leaving the guild, Darius and his team had finally returned to rest. These old men had more stamina than the young'uns. The guild master's face was pale with fatigue, his clothes were damp from the on-and-off rain, and mud splattered his pants up to his knees. Silver knives were strapped to his hips, and as he spoke, he spun a steel bracelet around his wrist—a sorcery artifact, I was assuming.

"The demon's movements have been unpredictable from the start," Aaron explained. "Since it targeted Ezra once, it's a reasonable bet that it'll target him again."

From my spot behind the three mages, I nodded along. I would've expected Kai to do the talking—he was the eloquent, bossy one—but Aaron had a closer relationship with Darius. Every Crow and Hammer member was assigned a mentor from the guild leadership team: someone to oversee their activities and training, handle personal or professional issues, and administer discipline. My mentor was Felix, while Aaron's mentor was Darius.

"Considering how poorly the tracking efforts have gone," Aaron continued, "it's worth a shot to lure the demon out. I'm requesting permission to form a team with Kai, Ezra, and Tori."

Darius studied Aaron, then his gray eyes turned to Kai, Ezra, and finally me. "With two encounters between the four of you, how would you assess your ability to handle a direct attack from the demon?"

"Ezra will be our early warning system," Aaron answered promptly, "since aeromages can sense movement without seeing it. He'll also act as our defense. Properly prepared, he's well equipped for it. Me and Kai will bring the firepower. We can inflict heavy damage in a short time."

"And Tori's role?"

"Her familiar, Hoshi, will act as backup surveillance, since she can get a bird's-eye view of our surroundings. Tori will be our communications point, since we can't count on having free hands to call in the demon's location. We'll also equip her with tools to help distract the demon in a worst-case scenario."

Considering us with a steely gaze, the guild master folded his arms. I shifted uncomfortably, wondering again how much Darius knew about Ezra's secrets.

"Tori."

I jumped at my name.

"This is an extremely dangerous endeavor, and you're not combat trained. Do you understand the risks of joining their team?"

Gulping back my nerves, I straightened my spine. "Yes, sir."

Darius nodded and told Aaron, "I won't have you wandering the streets unaccounted for. You'll register your new team and join the grid search under the MPD's direction. If you encounter the demon, you will follow procedure. Understood?"

"Yes, sir."

"Be careful and don't put yourselves in harm's way. I expect all four of you back in the same condition as when you left."

"Yes, sir."

With a nod from the GM, we saw ourselves out. I huffed, not sure if I was relieved or apprehensive. Part of me had hoped Darius would forbid us from going out.

"Now what?" I asked as we headed down the stairs.

Aaron cast me a tight smile. "Now we gear up."

I was used to the guys gearing up for jobs—decking themselves out in everything from protective clothing to weapons to communications equipment. I was always a little jealous of how badass they looked with their dark clothes and leather baldrics and big, scary swords.

I hadn't expected to be gearing up too.

Thirty minutes later, I was standing in the pub, dressed for combat for the first time in my life. Sturdy black leather clung to my legs, and a long-sleeved shirt with a texture reminiscent of Kevlar covered my torso. On top of it, I wore a leather jacket with padded elbows, lots of zippered pockets, and several hidden compartments.

Around my waist was the most unusual piece of my outfit. The custom belt, made from wide, polished leather, had several quick-access pouches for my sorcery artifacts, and clipped along my hips were six alchemy "bombs"—glass spheres the size of billiard balls. Three were smoke bombs, and three were alchemic flash-bangs.

Aaron circled me, checking my new outfit. He was already dressed for battle in similar protective clothing and with Sharpie strapped to his back.

"All fits." He tugged my belt, ensuring it wouldn't slip down my hips. "The pants aren't too tight?"

"No, they're perfect." I shifted my weight, feeling more silly than badass. "Where did all this stuff come from?"

Kai joined us, slipping knives into the pockets of his armored vest. "We started putting it together a couple months ago. We planned to surprise you on your first job, whenever that happened."

"We might've mentioned it," Aaron added, "except you've avoided all references to training, and without training, you can't take jobs, so …"

I hid my guilty wince. It wasn't that I was opposed to going on jobs with the guys. It was just that, well, they were already so accomplished—and powerful. In comparison, any attempt I made to train would seem like a kindergartener learning to tie her shoes.

Felix joined us, his expression bleakly disapproving. He handed me my phone, an earpiece clipped into it. "Your phone is all set up. Press this button to activate the mic."

After hooking the earpiece into place, I slipped my phone into a front pocket of my new jacket. I was already sweating under the leather. No wonder some guildeds had been written up over the summer for skipping their leather gear.

Felix gave me a few more instructions on following the grid and reporting our movements, then scowled deeply at Aaron. "You keep her safe."

"We will."

"Are we ready?" Kai asked.

"We just need—"

Ezra walked out from the basement. He was dressed all in black and a thick strap crossed his chest, holding his two-part pole-arm that could be used as a baton, dual short swords, or a double-bladed staff. Long gloves ran up to his biceps, the knuckles and elbows reinforced with steel, and he wore a knitted black hat over his hair. Without the soft brown curls to soften his face, intimidating severity sharpened his features. His pale eye gleamed dangerously.

"—Ezra," Aaron finished. "You ready?"

He nodded.

Felix looked across us. "You're starting on Grid 132. Head southwest."

With no more ceremony than that, the four of us trudged to the door. I could feel eyes on my back—Miles and Sanjana at the healers' station, half a dozen members of other guilds, and scattered Crow and Hammer mythics. They watched us go, and as we filed outside, I couldn't shake the feeling of a funeral march.

9

WALKING THROUGH the empty streets was neither exciting nor mentally engaging, and that was leaving my brain with way too much time to dwell on what was coming.

As the four of us strode along dark sidewalks, I mentally cast about for less terrifying topics. The first one to jump to mind? Why, my chat with Izzah, of course. But there are appropriate times for delicate conversations about sensitive topics, and then there are excessively *inappropriate* times.

I can tell the difference. Really, I can.

Smiling brightly, I fell into step with Kai. He squinted at me with instant suspicion.

"Hello, Kai."

"No."

"'No' what?"

"Whatever you're planning to ask me. No."

Our quiet steps tapped against the damp pavement, but the rain had let up. Empty shops stared with blank windows as we passed. It was four in the morning, and the city wouldn't wake for another couple of hours.

That was how long we had to lure out the demon and kill it.

I squashed my kindling fear and bumped Kai's shoulder with mine. "Oh, come on. You don't even know what I want to ask."

"I know that snoopy look."

A pout pushed my lips out. "I'm not snoopy. Ezra, I'm not a snoop, am I?"

His gaze shifted away from the nearest alley. He smiled at me. "Of course not."

"Ha! See?"

"Snoopy is a mean word," Ezra added. "You're persistently inquisitive."

My victorious grin faltered. "Wait—"

Felix's voice buzzed in my ear, reporting Keys of Solomon activity in our area. I swallowed my retort and passed on the warning. As Kai led us into an alley, the comforting glow of the streetlights dimmed, and my gaze crept toward the rooftops. We didn't *need* to go through alleys, but the whole purpose of this mission was to tempt the demon into attacking Ezra again.

Was the creature really waiting for Ezra to reappear? I tried not to think about the possible explanations for why the demon was so intent on murdering the aeromage. I might be "snoopy" about Kai's love life, but when it came to Ezra's secrets, I had no desire to pry.

Desperate for a distraction, I poked Kai in the arm. "Why did you dump Izzah?"

"I knew it would be something like that."

"You broke her heart."

"I know."

His casual acceptance sparked my anger. "Do you *enjoy* being a complete douche-canoe to women?"

"Tori," Aaron cut in with sudden irritation. "Lay off."

I opened my mouth, then closed it, feeling torn. On one hand, I should respect Kai's privacy and not freak over his romantic decisions, which had nothing to do with me. On the other hand, I had a hard time ignoring his shitty playboy habits.

Kai glanced at me, surprised I'd fallen silent. His mouth twisted. "I broke things off with her because of the death threats."

His flat words took a moment to register. "*Death threats?* Against Izzah?"

He nodded, dark eyes fixed straight ahead. "From my family."

Aaron and Ezra showed no surprise at this revelation, so they must know all about Kai's roots—the runaway son of the mythic world's largest crime syndicate. His two best friends must also know he was engaged to marry a woman his family had chosen.

"But you left," I said quietly. "Don't they realize you'll never go through with the engagement?"

"They still consider me their property. Property has value, and they've promised it to another family. Even if a wedding never happens, anything that threatens the arrangement is unacceptable."

In the eyes of his family, Kai's relationship with Izzah must have threatened the engagement. So they, in turn, had threatened Izzah, and he'd ended things to protect her.

"That's bullshit!" I burst out. "They can't prevent you from dating anyone for the rest of your life!"

Kai snorted. "Actually, they can."

"But—" I bit off my protest. Kai knew what his family was capable of better than me. "That's completely unfair!"

"Life's not fair."

I struggled to control my helpless outrage. "Okay, I get why you ended things with Izzah. But … why do you date a zillion women, then?"

His eyebrows rose. "A zillion?"

"At least I didn't say a *bazillion* women. So? Why?"

"Why not?"

I peered into his face as though I could activate my laser-beam vision and see what he was thinking. His mouth curved in a half smile but he said nothing more.

"His family can't be bothered to keep track of every girl he takes out for dinner," Aaron supplied unexpectedly, "so they mostly leave him alone these days."

"Oh." I supposed that made sense. And he did have an endless line of women waiting to date him. I'd seen firsthand how many phone numbers he received on even the most mundane outings.

As we crossed a street and entered another alleyway, I pondered his dilemma. Did his family intend to thwart him from *ever* having a meaningful relationship with a woman? No, wait. He'd said he was waiting for his fiancée to marry someone else. If *she* broke the engagement, then he'd be off the hook.

Tapping my lower lip, I wondered if there was a way to encourage this fiancée to hurry the hell up and marry some other dude.

"No," Kai said.

"'No' what?"

"Whatever you're thinking. No."

I threw my hands up. "You don't even know what I—"

As we stepped out of the alley and onto a sidewalk, I bit off my protest. So far, the streets had been eerily empty, but half a block away, a dozen people stood in the center of the road. It wasn't a friendly meeting, judging by the angry shouting.

Actually, make that *familiar* angry shouting.

"Is that Izzah?" I asked, squinting at the group.

"Sounds like it." Kai took a step closer. "Who are the others? What are they yelling about?"

Aaron strode past us, taking the lead. "Dunno, but we should find out."

Kai joined him, leaving me standing there. Was I the only one of us with a fully functioning short-term memory? We were expecting the demon to attack us at literally any moment, weren't we? And our plan hinged on having *zero witnesses* to said attack? I glanced questioningly at Ezra beside me.

He shook his head. "Attention span of five-year-olds."

"I suppose we should go supervise."

"The kids might get in trouble if we don't."

We hastened toward the confrontation. Izzah and Mario, plus two other Odin's Eye mythics, stood near a quartet of men and women in a tight cluster. Across from them were three men that couldn't have looked more villainous if they'd tattooed swastikas on their foreheads.

Ezra abruptly stopped a solid thirty feet from the group. "Uh, maybe I'll wait here."

"Why?"

"There are contractors. Mario, plus two more in that group of four; they're Grand Grimoire mythics, I think. And the other three people are—"

"Let me guess. Keys of Solomon."

He nodded. "Two are contractors. See their pendants?"

I squinted. He could see their jewelry from here? Then I spotted the first "pendant" and realized it was hard to miss. Each contractor wore a chain with a palm-sized steel disc hanging from it, displayed on their chests like first-place ribbons.

"What are those things?"

"The demonic artifact—it's called an *infernus*. The demon is bound to the infernus, and that's where its spirit is contained when the contractor isn't commanding it."

It occurred to me, not for the first time, that Ezra knew a surprising amount about Demonica. Was this common knowledge?

Aaron and Kai reached the terse group of mythics, and the latter's voice rolled through the quiet street, low and steady. If anyone could defuse this situation, Kai could.

Izzah said something sharp, pointing at the Keys mythics, and Kai swung toward them.

"They did *what*?" he demanded loudly.

… or not.

"I warned the GMs," Izzah yelled. "Now look!"

"We haven't done anything but try to find a demon in all the pathetic chaos you lot have caused," the oldest Keys member said, his smug undertone begging for someone to smack him. I'd volunteer as tribute, but I wasn't close enough.

"You used your demon to attack the Grand Grimoire team," Izzah accused venomously.

The Keys mythic folded his arms. "Prove it, bitch."

"Watch yourself," Kai growled.

"Watch *yourself*, mage," the man shot back, "or you'll get to meet my demon. Ever seen a demon before, kid? Try not to shit yourself when you do."

Kai's hand closed around the hilt of his katana. "You think you can call it out before I stop your heart?"

Holy shit. Was Kai even *trying* to defuse the situation? Maybe I should step in and bring it down a notch. I did a quick mental run-through of the possible outcomes of my intervention. Visions of screaming and fire and bodies scattered across the pavement flashed through my mind.

On second thought, I'd probably make it worse.

The Keys man snorted derisively. "We're not wasting our time on a runt like you. We're here for a demon."

Ah okay, so Kai did know what he was doing. The Keys man started to back up—

"Then I'll give you a demon!" Mario snarled, grabbing the pendant hanging from his neck.

Deep red light ignited from between his fingers. The streaks of power leaped to the pavement and coalesced into a rippling splash. It expanded upward as though the magic were pouring from the infernus into an invisible mold. The light condensed and solidified, and when it died away, a demon stood in front of the contractor.

I gulped down a surge of terror. The demon had come out of the pendant like a Pokémon out of a poké ball. *Beelzebub, I choose you!*

96 ♠ ANNETTE MARIE

This beast was even taller than the winged one, but thinner and gangly—not that its lack of bulging muscles made it any less terrifying. Its eyes glowed like hot lava and horns lined its head, a narrow mane running from its forehead down its back to a lion-like tail. Giant claws tipped its fingers, and tusks jutted up from its heavy lower jaw.

The red light had barely diffused before more crimson power erupted from the two Keys' pendants. A pair of demons manifested in front of their masters. One was shorter—as in seven feet instead of eight—and built like a tank, its entire back adorned with thick spines. The other was tall and thin like Mario's, but with its limbs covered in plate scale. All three had skin in varying shades of red-tinted toffee, wore minimalistic armor, and possessed the same glowing red eyes.

With my eyes locked on the beasts, I blindly reached for Ezra. My fingers closed tightly around his wrist—and cold radiated through the thick fingerless glove that covered his arm from knuckles to bicep. The air held only a slight chill—he was containing his reaction to the demons as best he could.

But this was still all kinds of bad.

The two demons faced Mario's, but they didn't otherwise move. All three creatures scarcely seemed to breathe, so still and silent they could have been statues. Horrible, nightmare-spawning statues.

Aaron and Kai gripped the hilts of their swords, while Izzah clutched the handles of her narrow-bladed knives and the Grand Grimoire contractors held their pendants, ready to call their demons too.

I whipped my phone out, flipped to the camera, and yelled, "Hey, idiots!"

A dozen pairs of eyes turned toward me.

As I raised my phone, I almost forgot what I'd been planning to say. To the naked eye, the three demons looked as solid as the mythics, but on the screen, they showed up as semi-transparent, featureless shadows. Freaky.

"I'm recording you," I called, "just so you know. Are you sure you want to kill each other? Maybe you could save this for a better time—such as never."

"Who the hell are you?" a Keys man sneered.

I tilted the camera toward my face. "For the record," I told the phone, "Mario called his demon first, but the prickbags from the Keys threatened to kill Kai with their demons before that. I'd call it a defensive move."

What I'd actually call it was an *idiot* move, and if we came out of this alive, I planned to inform Mario of that—with significant volume and a lot of bad language.

I flipped the camera back down to point at them. "Okay, go ahead."

The Keys shifted uncomfortably, then the oldest one barked a laugh. "Fine, girl. We'll play your game."

He touched his pendant. Red magic glowed across the heavyset demon's hands and feet, and streaks of power shot for the infernus. The creature dissolved into crimson magic that whisked back into the pendant. As quickly as it had appeared, the demon was gone again.

The other Keys contractor called his demon back, and only then did Mario summon his into the pendant. Not once had any of the demons so much as twitched.

"All right, cool," I announced. "Aaron, Kai, we should mosey on, hmm?"

Kai glanced at Izzah, and I could imagine the warning look he gave her. "Are you moving along?"

She gave a short nod and turned, grabbing Mario's arm. Hauling him with her, she marched down the street. Her two team members hastily followed. Muttering among themselves, the Grand Grimoire group headed in the same direction, glancing warily over their shoulders at the Keys.

"Aaron, was it?" The older Keys guy looked him up and down. "You'd be the Sinclair kid."

The youngest Keys contractor sneered. "Crow and Hammer fledglings, eh?"

The first time Aaron and I met, Aaron had introduced himself like I should recognize his name, and I'd thought he was an arrogant jerk. It annoyed me that he really was sort of famous among mythics.

Finally showing some sense, Aaron and Kai ignored the taunts and strode back to me and Ezra. Yes. Good. Let's get out of here before things went wrong in a big way. The Keys watched the two mages withdraw—then started after them.

Well, shit.

"Aaron Sinclair," the old guy mused. "So that would make *you* the Yamada boy, wouldn't it?"

Kai grunted eloquently.

"I'm Burke," he introduced himself, sounding almost polite. He gestured at his comrades. "Halil and Fenton." He waited to see if Kai would offer his name. "Anyone from the Yamada family must be a cut above the Crow and Hammer's rejects. We're always looking for new talent."

"A flattering offer. You can shove it up your ass."

The old guy smirked. As he and his pals drew closer, I got a proper look at them. Burke was bald and wrinkled, with a narrow, sinewy frame. He looked tougher than a piece of beef jerky left in the sun, and that was without the demon pendant hanging around his neck.

Halil, the middle-aged one, had cheeks so hollow he must be missing most of his molars, a look his square jaw and sunken eyes didn't help. He was huge—taller than Aaron—with broad shoulders and thick, muscular limbs clad in leather gear. A sword with a two-hander hilt jutted over his shoulder and he wore brass knuckles on his right hand. Either a sorcerer or a mage. I was guessing mage.

The youngest guy, Fenton, was also a contractor. His arms, bared by a wife beater, were heavily tattooed, and his dark hair was greasily combed back from his face. He leered at my boobs—or at the suggestion of boobs beneath my leather jacket.

"Aw," I said, "look at this guy. He's never even *seen* a girl before."

Fenton's gaze jerked from my chest to my face, confusion twisting his eyebrows. "What?"

"Only a basement-dwelling loser would stare like that."

"*What?*"

I looked sadly at Aaron. "And he's deaf too! Poor thing."

Aaron shot the Key's team a scathing look. "Go hunt the demon. We have a grid to search."

Burke's sneer widened as his deep-set eyes ran across me and over to Ezra. "Oh, now, don't rush off. If you're Sinclair and he's Yamada, then this kid would be the aeromage—the one who survived the demon attack last night."

Ezra watched the Keys men with an eerily blank expression—a look I knew as the most obvious tell for his temper.

Nudging Ezra to get him moving, Aaron strode in the opposite direction from the other mythics. I hastened after them, Kai bringing up the rear. The Keys watched us, their stares boring into my back.

They watched—but they didn't follow.

I breathed a long sigh. We cut through three more alleys and down another street, and the Keys of Solomon didn't reappear to harass us. Wherever they'd gone, it wasn't in this direction. Crisis averted.

Now all we had to worry about was the demon.

10

"WHAT'S THEIR PROBLEM?" I grumbled. "Attacking another team? Threatening you guys? How do they get away with this shit?"

"The Keys have been picking fights with people since the search started," Aaron replied as we trudged through another reeking alley. We were only a couple of blocks from the grid we were supposed to search. "They're getting away with it because the demon is a bigger problem."

"My concern is that noisy encounter might have put the demon off approaching us, assuming it's nearby." Kai chuffed impatiently. "I was hoping it'd show up before we reached the search zone."

I glanced apprehensively across the dark rooftops. What were the chances the demon was nearby? Our whole plan hinged on the demon attacking us away from any witnesses. We had to kill it before anyone realized Ezra had injured it.

And by "we," I meant "not me." I was purely a witness protection service. That's what my smoke bombs and mythic-style flash-bangs were for. If anyone tried to approach while the guys were dealing with the demon, my job was to dissuade them.

"Speaking of demons," I began, "what's up with theirs? They didn't move *at all*. They were real, weren't they?"

"Very real." Kai turned down another street. "That's how bound demons behave. The contractor has full control. The demon has no autonomy; it's like a puppet. Without the contractor's command, it can't do anything."

"*Nothing*? Like, it would drown in water if the contractor didn't command it to swim?"

"Precisely. It's part of the contract. The demon gives up its free will to its contractor."

"Some contracts are looser than that," Aaron added, "but they're illegal. Give the demon any leeway, and it'll find ways to kill people. It's dangerous not only for the contractor, but for everyone in the contractor's vicinity."

I shook my head in disbelief. "That sounds—"

Ezra stopped. His gaze darted across the left side of the street. "Something is moving up on the roof."

I squeezed my hands into fists, sternly commanding myself not to look.

Don't look for the murder-happy hellion eager to rip us into pieces? Oh yes, so easy. The spot between my shoulder blades prickled, but I didn't know if it was the demon's eyes I could feel on me. Nightmarish flashes of my last encounter with the winged beast filled my mind, fueling the adrenaline in my blood.

"Which direction?" Kai asked. Without taking his eyes off the buildings, Ezra tilted his head in answer, and Kai swore. "That's the active search area. Is the demon watching us search for it?"

Reaching behind me, I slipped my hand into the large back pouch of my fancy new belt. I pulled out a silver orb, covered in smooth ridges and marked with pink and aquamarine stripes.

"Hoshi," I whispered.

The orb expanded, then unraveled into the sylph's long, sinuous shape. Her pink eyes glowed faintly as she glanced skyward, then ducked behind me, crowding against my back. Couldn't blame her. I wished I could hide behind the guys the same way.

"What's the plan?" My voice was embarrassingly shrill. I felt nowhere near ready for this.

"Where is it, Ezra?" Aaron demanded.

Ezra held perfectly still as though listening. "I lost it. It's either not moving or it's shifted to an incorporeal state."

"Incorporeal?" I yelped. "They can—"

Hoshi's tail whipped around me and cool magic surged through my body. My vision blurred—and a huge dark shape barreled out of the sky at warp speed and passed right through me like I wasn't there. Which I wasn't, because the small fae had shifted me out of reality.

The shadowy beast slammed into Ezra.

My vision steadied as Ezra crashed into the pavement, the monstrous demon on top of him, wings arching off its back— one twisted into a mockery of the other. Hoshi had vanished. She'd drained her small well of magic to protect me.

Ezra had caught the demon by the wrists, and it pressed down, one clawed foot on either side of him, hooked talons at its fingertips straining toward his face. The muscles in Ezra's arms bulged with the effort of holding the demon back, and tendons stood out in his neck.

I grabbed a tiny glass ball from my belt and whipped it at the back of the demon's head from six feet away. It hit the leathery skull and burst.

Blinding light flashed and a deafening bang shattered my eardrums.

My vision went white, and by the time I could see again, the demon had lurched off Ezra, its eyes squinched painfully. It spun with shocking agility and its giant arm shot toward me. Kai drew his sword so fast the steel blurred. A bolt of lightning as thick as a tree branch leaped off the blade and hit the beast in the chest.

The force flung it backward, but it landed on its feet and snarled as it whirled on us again. Now Aaron had his sword out too. He bellowed furiously as he whipped it sideways, and a band of searing blue flame launched at the creature.

The surrounding air turned arctic cold.

The icy chill flowed out of the demon and Aaron's flames shrank. They washed over the demon's hide with barely a sizzle.

Frost spread out from the creature's feet as it loosed a low, throbbing laugh. Its magma eyes gleamed malevolently, no less terrifying for its lopsided appearance—the two foot-long horns on the left side of its head broken off.

Aaron and Kai angled their swords defensively. Behind them, Ezra jumped to his feet, breathing hard with one hand pressed to his face. He stepped into the gap between his friends, eight short yards away from the demon.

The frigid air hurt my lungs to breathe. Not that I was doing a great job of breathing anyway. My panicky gaze jumped over the beast, picking out details like that would somehow help me survive—the spiky crest etched into the center of its belt armor, the shimmering texture of the cloth wound around its waist and thighs, the glint of a thin, dark chain hanging around its neck.

The demon's pink tongue slid out, wetting its lips. Its red stare fixed on Ezra.

"*Hrātir, kah udēisathē nā?*" Growling words in an alien language rumbled from its throat. "*Tenth'ūsanā imailatē vīsh adh'sūv arbh'ētahthēs.*"

One palm still pressed to his blind eye, Ezra bared his teeth. He extended his other arm, fingers spread, and a red glow lit across his fingertips. Crimson power raced over his hand and up his arm in twisting veins.

Magic spiked around his wrist and coiled into the shape of a sorcery circle filled with ugly runes. A second ring sprang around his forearm, and a third formed around his elbow. In a continuous, dizzying flow, the runes shifted, faded, and reformed into new ones, all while crackling power built in the air.

Snarling, the demon lifted its arm, mirroring Ezra. Throbbing red power lit its clawed hand and writhed up its arm. Aaron and Kai braced themselves.

That's when I realized they couldn't take their attention off the enemy to worry about me—and I wasn't supposed to be this close to the battle. Slipping on the wet pavement, I backed rapidly down the alley.

The air shuddered. Ice sheathed the ground around Ezra's feet—then magic erupted from his palm.

Six spiraling spears of glowing red light hurtled toward the demon. Crimson light burst from the demon's hand, and the two forces collided—and exploded.

Arctic wind hit me, followed by a shockwave of red-tinted smoke. I staggered and shielded my face as debris whipped across me. As I lowered my arms, the demon launched itself at the three mages.

Broken wing or not, the thing was *fast*. I didn't even see what happened. Fire, a burst of lightning, then Aaron hit the ground, his sword skittering away. Kai shouted something— and then the demon charged Ezra.

His pole-arm was in his hands and he twisted it apart into two short swords. The demon changed direction, leaping past his blades. As Ezra whirled after it, the demon slammed its good wing into Kai, knocking him into a shop window. The glass shattered and he fell onto the display counter inside.

Aaron was back up and fire raced along his sword as he set his feet. Ezra circled the demon, his back to me. Crimson power snaked over his hands and forearms, and wherever he stepped, the damp pavement turned to frosted ice.

Beneath the demon's feet, ice spread in the same broken fractals.

My headset crackled, and I almost screamed from fright.

"*Tori?*" Felix's voice spoke in my ear. "*Your GPS signal has stopped moving. Is everything okay?*"

I gulped. Right. We were supposed to follow procedure. Kai and Aaron had told me to report the demon once they'd engaged it, because if they hadn't killed it by the time backup arrived, then they probably couldn't kill it at all.

"Demon sighted," I squeaked, holding the mic button. "Demon sighted. My team has engaged."

"*What?*" Felix gasped. The earpiece crackled, then his voice barked over the line as he relayed the message to all Crow and Hammer teams.

Dislodged glass shattered on the pavement as Kai stumbled out of the window. Two short knives were already in his hands, and he threw them with rapid snaps of his wrists.

They struck the demon's back. One bounced off and clattered on the pavement, but the other stuck in place.

Kai whipped his sword up and pointed it at the streetlamp above his head. Electricity crackled over the pole and the casing burst. An electric bolt leaped from the shattered bulb to Kai's sword. White light surged over him, then he cast his sword toward the demon.

Lightning slammed into the beast, hurling it across the street and into a wall. As chunks of brick rained down, Kai pulled more power from the streetlight and channeled a continuous stream into the demon. The other streetlights lining the road exploded in showers of sparks.

Aaron turned his sword sideways and pressed his palm to the spot just below the crossguard. The steel glowed with heat. Face tight with concentration, he slid his hand along the blade in a swift, purposeful motion.

A half circle of fire roared to life around the demon. The blue-white inferno stretched higher, then swept inward, closing the ring. Kai hurled more electric power into the obscuring flames, not letting up on his attack for an instant.

With fire igniting across his arms and shoulders, Aaron charged toward his fire, his blade extended to deliver a killing blow while their attacks had the creature pinned to the wall.

"*Tori, an Odin's Eye team is two blocks out,*" Felix barked in my ear. "*They're on their way.*"

Two blocks? Too close!

As Aaron reached the howling inferno, the flames bulged outward—and crimson magic blasted the fire and lightning away. The concussive force threw Aaron backward. He landed on his feet in a stumble, his sword weaving out of position.

The demon launched out of the hissing smoke. Steam rose off its skin and fury blazed in its glowing eyes as its claws slashed at Aaron's face.

Ezra sprang into the demon's path.

One of his swords hit the ground, cast aside as he grasped the second's hilt with both hands and ran the blade through the demon's outstretched palm. Red light surged down the steel and exploded.

The demon lurched backward, tearing its mangled hand off the blade. A snarl ripping from its throat, it grabbed Ezra's sword and jerked it out of his hands. Without a pause, Ezra slammed his fist into the demon's thick chest. Air boomed and the demon was thrown two yards back.

"*Tori,*" Felix said urgently. "*The other team is around the corner. Do you copy?*"

Panic whirled in my head. Around the corner?

Ezra thrust both hands out. Crimson power spread over his palms, sorcery-like sigils springing out of thin air to surround his wrists. Baring its fangs, the demon called on its magic as well. Aaron scrambled backward to get clear.

Instead of running away too, I ran *toward* the demon.

Yeah, I was crazy.

The combatants faced off perpendicular to me, the mages on the left and the demon on the right. Red magic crawled over Ezra, while the demon prepared its own deadly unleashing.

And approaching from somewhere behind me was a team of mythics I could *not* allow to see any of this.

I snapped an alchemy bomb off my belt, and with my other hand, I reached into a front pouch. As I closed in on the mages and demon, I flung the glass sphere behind me.

It shattered, and as though the sound were a signal, Ezra and the demon unleashed their attacks. The crimson powers collided, and just like last time, they exploded in every direction.

As howling red magic rocketed toward me, I thrust my Queen of Spades card toward the demon and screamed, "*Ori repercutio!*"

The wave of magic about to obliterate my flesh hit the rippling spell and rebounded—directly into the demon.

The redirected force blasted the demon sideways. As its wings flared for balance, magma eyes whipped in my direction. Ezra's arm snapped back, red magic flaring around his arm in jagged spikes, and the temperature plunged below freezing.

That was the last thing I saw before a cloud of impenetrable fog rolled over us.

The spreading smoke screen from my alchemy bomb blanketed the entire street, and an instant later, red power detonated in the spot where I'd last seen Ezra. Icy wind blasted me, the demon howled furiously, then huge wings beat the air.

I gasped in the smoke and tasted something sweet and almost peppery. The thud of the demon's wings faded, replaced by my rapid pulse thrumming in my ears. Adrenaline pounded in my blood and my hands trembled. I stuffed the Queen of Spades back in its pouch before I dropped it.

"Aaron?" Kai called through the impenetrable smoke. "Ezra?"

"Here," Aaron answered close by.

From farther down the street, a hoarse voice I scarcely recognized as Ezra's muttered, "Here."

"Tori?" Kai asked.

"Here." The word came out in a chicken-like squawk. I cleared my throat and tried again. "I'm here. Guys, an Odin's Eye team is almost—"

"Crow and Hammer!" The shout came from behind me. "Crow and Hammer team! Where are you?"

"We're here!" Kai yelled back. "The demon already fled. Stay where you are. It's impossible to see through the screen."

The Odin's Eye mythic agreed, then spoke to his teammates in a quieter tone.

A shadow materialized into Aaron. As he joined me, Kai limped out of the mist. Blood streaked his face, but I couldn't see any glass sticking out of him. Thank goodness.

"Well," Aaron whispered, fury and fatigue competing in his haggard expression, "that was a disaster."

"Did we even injure it?" Kai growled. Sword in one hand, he pressed the other to his side. "I'm either badly bruised or my ribs are cracked."

Aaron sheathed his sword over his shoulder, grunting with the movement as though the weapon weighed half a ton. "I knew the demon was fast and strong, but I didn't expect it to be all but impervious to harm. If that's what it can do—"

"That's not what it can do."

Ezra's hoarse voice floated out of the smoke screen. Following the sound, I picked out his barely discernible shadow in the fog. He stood almost too still to see, making no move to come closer.

"The demon was holding back," he rasped.

My blood chilled. That *hadn't* been a demon fighting at full power?

Aaron and Kai exchanged wary looks.

"Why would it hold back?" Aaron asked, directing the question into the fog. "What does it want?"

A long, empty pause, then Ezra answered in a haunted whisper, the words tinged with cold fear.

"I don't know."

II

WE RETURNED TO THE GUILD, sore, exhausted, and defeated.

After debriefing with the guild officers, we got checkups from the healers. I was fine, but Aaron and Ezra got dosed with several potions to help with the bruising and pain. Kai got a turn on the gurney to have his cracked ribs mended.

That had been two hours ago, and I found myself alone at the bar, perched tiredly on a stool with my laptop open in front of me. My proposal for the pub's menu update was in a pathetic state, but all I could do was stare at the screen, my thoughts in disarray.

Kai and Aaron were on the second level, sleeping. Elementaria was the most physically draining class of magic, and I'd seen before how quickly it fatigued them. After expending so much magic in such a short time, they would need to rest for the better part of the day.

Ezra wasn't sleeping on the second level. He'd disappeared after his checkup, and I had no idea where he'd vanished to.

I should go find him. Make sure he was okay. Make sure he …

Nausea churned in my stomach, competing with gut-clenching fear. Whenever I closed my eyes, I could see it: crimson light veining the demon's arms, sparking over its fingers, surging out of its flesh; an arctic chill rolling off its body, freezing the puddles and frosting every surface.

And I could see crimson light snaking over Ezra. Glowing over his hands. Forming intricate spells around his arms. I could feel the frigid cold radiating from his skin, hear the crunch of ice under his feet, taste the wintry frost in the air.

I couldn't ignore it. I couldn't deny it. I couldn't pretend I hadn't noticed.

Ezra's cold, crimson magic was identical to the demon's.

My throat tightened and I pressed my hands to my face. Ezra's secrets. Ezra's temper. Ezra's power. Power that no one else was allowed to see, that no one could ever know he possessed. Power that was all but indistinguishable from a demon's.

Now I knew why the demon was hunting Ezra. How he'd survived his first fight with the hellish beast. Why Aaron and Kai had been so confident the demon would attack him again. But what did it *mean*?

What was Ezra? Not a mere aeromage, that I knew. He wasn't a contractor either. He hadn't called a demon out of an infernus to fight for him. This was something else. Something … forbidden. I stared blankly at my menu proposal, my gut twisting into knots.

A pink Gucci purse dropped onto the bar beside me. I dragged my eyes off the laptop screen as Sabrina slid onto a stool.

"Hey," I said, attempting to sound normal and not halfway to a panic attack. "Do chili cheese fries sound appetizing to you?"

"Um … not really."

Unsurprised by her answer, I reached for the keyboard to make a note in my proposal, then did a double take at the diviner. "Wait. What are you doing here? Non-combat members are under house arrest until the demon alert is lifted."

"I know." She smiled wanly. "I snuck out."

She'd snuck out of her safe home to trek into the demon's active area? Then she'd entered the guild where an officer could notice her and realize she'd disobeyed orders?

I eyed her disbelievingly, then asked, "Are you okay?"

Sabrina normally looked ready for a photoshoot, with flawless makeup and a salon-styled blond bob, but she wasn't wearing a fleck of makeup and her hair hung limply around her face.

"I needed to see you." She twisted her hands together. "I've been doing a lot of readings … trying to predict something useful to help with the demon search … but none of my readings will work."

"They won't work?" I repeated in confusion.

She rubbed under one eye, the fragile skin marred by tired circles. "The spreads are nonsensical. The cards have nothing to do with one another or outright contradict each other, but … two cards have turned up in every single reading."

Reaching into her purse, she pulled out two black and gold cards. On one, a carefree traveler was about to step off a cliff, and on the other, a black-cloaked grim reaper held a bloody scythe.

"The Fool and Death," she whispered.

I scowled to hide my apprehension. Those two cards had shown up before: the Death card had made itself a nuisance shortly before a near-deadly confrontation with an evil sorceress, and the Fool card had popped up right before my new life at the guild had fallen apart. Neither image inspired happy feelings.

"I think," Sabrina said slowly, "the deck keeps showing me these cards because they're tied to you. It's a message."

"Not another message."

"That's the purpose of the cards—to deliver messages. I need to do a reading for you, Tori."

I opened my mouth to refuse, but her stress and worry were so blatant I couldn't. Whatever was up with her cards, it was urgent enough that she'd risked her life to come and see me.

Puffing out a breath, I turned on my stool to face her. "All right. Let's do it."

She smiled in relief, recovering a fraction of her usual energy, and pulled a fabric bundle from her purse. She unwrapped her deck and spread the silk scarf over the bar like a tablecloth, then set the Death and Fool cards aside.

"I cleansed the deck before I came," she said, shuffling the cards at warp speed. "A clean slate. And I'm leaving those two out"—she tilted her head toward the rejected pair—"so they don't dominate your reading."

Placing the shuffled deck face down on the silk, she spread it into a broad fan. "Choose six cards. Take your time, but don't overthink it."

Rolling my shoulders uncomfortably, I stared at the cards—far more than a standard deck of playing cards. How was I supposed to choose?

"Try closing your eyes," Sabrina advised. "Go by instinct."

I closed my eyes and stretched my hand out. Hovering it over the deck—or where I thought the deck was—I waited for divine inspiration to guide my touch. Ha, yeah right. I was as open to divine guidance as I was to pyramid schemes.

I lowered my hand at random. My fingertips found a card.

"Okay, first one," Sabrina said, her words accompanied by the slithering sound of her extracting the card. "Choose another."

I waved my hand around and dropped it down on another card. We repeated the process four more times, then Sabrina instructed me to open my eyes.

Six face-down cards were now arranged in a circle. She gathered up the remaining deck and set it aside, then studied the six rectangles I'd selected.

Breathing deeply, she composed her expression. "Normally, you would pick the cards while focusing on a problem or question for which you want direction, but the cards' desire to deliver a message is so strong I think they'll tell you what you need to know."

How I would love to snort and roll my eyes at the mystical mumbo jumbo, but this magic was as real as Aaron's fire. I'd seen the evidence already.

"In this spread, we start with the card that represents your current situation." Sabrina turned the top card, revealing a woman wearing a crown and holding a sword and a scale. "Justice. An ominous beginning …"

Why was I not surprised that we were starting with bad news? "What does it mean?"

"You will need to make a decision soon—something that will irreversibly change your future. A choice you can't come back from."

Oh goody. Who *didn't* love those kinds of decisions?

She touched the next card. "This one represents the cause of conflict."

Flipping it, she frowned at the horned creature that dominated the card. A naked man and woman stood on either side of it, loose chains around their necks, the ends held by the beast.

My stomach sank to the floor. Under the illustration was the card's name: *The Devil.*

Sabrina tapped her cheek. "Hmm, not what I expected. Are you having issues with addiction, Tori?"

"Uh, no."

"What about a new obsession? An unusual fixation? Wanton temptation?"

"No, no, and no."

She studied my face, then the card. "Could The Devil represent someone else in your life? Someone trapped by addiction or a compulsion of their own?"

The heavy weight dragging my innards to the earth's core grew colder. I said nothing.

"Let's see what the other cards reveal." Her fingers nimbly turned the next one. The air rushed out of her lungs. "Oh."

Even if her dismayed exhalation hadn't been a dead giveaway, the card's illustration was hardly inspiring: a heart impaled by three swords. How much did I want to bet the heart represented mine?

"The Three of Swords," Sabrina whispered. "Heartbreak. Loss."

I pressed a hand to my hollow gut. "Is someone going to die?"

"Let's keep going." She hastily flipped over the next card, revealing a robed man holding a wand. "The Magician! Yes, this is good. This means the loss you're facing is within your control—you have the power to affect the outcome."

That was encouraging, but also terrifying. "So, you're saying … I can maybe prevent someone from dying, then?"

She nodded and flipped over the second last card. "Oh, hmm. The Seven of Swords."

"I got that card in my first reading. It meant … betrayal? Because someone was deceiving me?"

"The Seven of Swords is the thief." She pointed to the image of a man sneaking off with an armful of stolen weapons. "In this position in the spread, it speaks of you, not others. *You* are the thief."

"I am not a—" I broke off, distracted by the thought of my Queen of Spades artifact. I *had* stolen that … and my fall-spell crystal too.

"The thief keeps secrets and moves with stealth." Sabrina considered the card. "Paired with the Magician, which is the power to enact your goals, this card is telling you *how* to reach the outcome you desire."

"By stealing?"

She gave me a long look. "By embodying the virtues of the thief—caution, cunning, discretion, and deception."

I wasn't great at the first one, or the second, or … well, *any* of those things. Lovely. I pointed at the last card. "That one is the outcome, right?"

"Yes." She glanced at The Fool and Death cards, sitting by themselves like kids in timeout, before touching two fingers to the back of the final card in the spread. Hesitating, she again peeked at the Death card as though making sure it was still there, then turned the last card.

A crumbling tower struck by lightning and lit by flames sparked recognition through me. I recognized it from my first reading.

"The Tower." She sighed unhappily. "A foreboding omen. Chaos and upheaval are coming—soon. Even if you succeed, your life will irrevocably change."

In the card's illustration, a man and a woman had leaped from the burning tower and were plunging toward the dark abyss below. Gooseflesh erupted across my skin and I sucked in an unsteady breath. "Your cards never have anything good to say."

She cleared her throat. "Well, I mean … the Tower is also a card of redemption, so there's that."

"Oh, okay," I replied sarcastically. "That makes it all better."

Her gaze traveled across the spread, and she lightly touched a finger to the Devil card. "Do you know who the Devil represents?"

I studied the cards. The Devil holding a man and a woman in chains. A woman casting judgment. Two victims falling from a broken tower.

A heart pierced by three swords.

The tarot cards or the universe or whatever mystical force powered a diviner's fortune telling was sending damn strong signals my way, and I could almost grasp it. The meaning hovered within reach—but the harder I focused on the elusive message, the higher my anxiety spiked.

I jumped off my stool. "Thanks, Sabrina."

Her forehead wrinkled with concern. "Tori—"

"I need to check on the guys." Squashing my guilt, I rushed to the stairs.

I should've known better. Aaron had once said he'd rather the future surprise him than heed the warnings of a tarot reading. Every time Sabrina's cards got anywhere near me, bad stuff happened. This was the most ominous reading I'd had yet—and that was including the times the Death card had literally stalked me.

On the second level, I crept over to the corner where Aaron and Kai slept. They didn't so much as stir. I lingered for a few minutes, then hurried away, feeling like a voyeur. Creeping down the stairs, I craned my neck to see if Sabrina was still waiting at the bar.

"Who are you hiding from?"

I jolted in surprise and almost fell down the stairs. Sin stood behind me, a tub of potions in her hands and a tattered leather-bound book tucked under one arm. Her blue hair was tied in a messy ponytail, and a colorfully stained apron covered her plain sweater and jeans.

"Sin!" I gasped, clutching my chest. Though her sudden appearance had startled me, I wasn't surprised to see her. She'd arrived a couple of hours ago, escorted by two combat mythics, to relieve Venus as the on-duty alchemist. "Don't sneak up on me."

She arched an eyebrow. "So? Who are you hiding from?"

"Sabrina," I grumbled. "Can you check if she's at the bar?"

Sin descended halfway down the steps. "She's sitting with Felix at the command table."

Good enough. I followed Sin into the pub and we sat at the farthest end of the bar. She set her tub of bottles on the counter and rested the old book on her lap.

"Why does Sabrina have you spooked?" Sin frowned. "Is she supposed to be here?"

"No. She came to do a reading for me."

"What? Why?"

I picked at a chip in the wooden bar top. "Apparently, her cards had an urgent message to deliver."

"What was the message?"

"I have a life-altering decision to make. Also, someone might die."

"*What?*"

I shrugged miserably. "That's the only concrete thing I got out of it." Mostly, I'd gotten a big fat dose of anxiety. Thanks, universe.

She tugged her apron straight. "Tarot reading is imprecise at best. Your future changes with every decision you and other people make. Try not to worry about it."

"Yeah."

"Speaking of worry …" Her eyes narrowed. "I heard all about how you went demon hunting with Aaron, Kai, and Ezra. I have to ask … what the hell were any of you *thinking*?"

"Um, well—"

"You aren't combat trained, and demons are the fiercest, deadliest opponents out there! Why would Darius even approve it? You're all idiots."

I managed a bleak smile. "Thanks, Sin. Appreciate the vote of confidence."

She sniffed angrily. "You know you aren't ready for that, and I'd really prefer my friend not get herself killed."

Couldn't argue with her there. I'd also prefer not to get killed.

Lifting the tattered book off her lap, she smacked it down on the bar. "We need to look at options."

"Uh … options for what?"

"Defensive alchemy." She cast me a flinty stare. "Since you're all for the dangerous jobs now, you need to be armed with more than a couple of artifacts. I heard you used a smoke screen. What else did you take?"

Bemusedly, I watched her flip the book open. "Just flash-bang potions. What is that thing?"

"My grimoire. All Arcana mythics have one—where we record all the spells or transmutations we've learned or invented." She turned several spotted, liquid-stained pages covered in handwriting and diagrams. "I can make smoke bombs and flash-bangs easily enough, but you need something to *stop* an opponent. Personally, I don't like sleep potions. It's easy to get it on your own skin and then you're asleep instead of them."

"Yeah, that'd be bad."

She skimmed a few more pages. "Enhanced strength is useful, but it doesn't last long, and unless you're in excessively good shape, you'll crash hard afterward. Let's see … amnesia, no. Fasting potion, no. Enhanced speed, no."

"What's wrong with speed? I'd like to be faster."

"It's hopelessly impractical. Your body gets faster, but your reflexes don't, so it's difficult to control without training and practice. You'll spend the potion's duration tripping over your own feet and running into things."

"Oh." Too bad. "What's a fasting potion?"

"Drink it and you won't need food, water, or a bathroom for about forty-eight hours. Good for certain situations, but you pay for it afterward." She perused more recipes. "Enhanced perception, air buffer, true sight, anti-emotionalizer, allure-fume—none of these are useful."

"Allure-fume?" I repeated. "What's that?"

She winced. "Uh, it's a ... um ... perfume."

I stared at her pointedly, waiting for an explanation, and her cheeks turned pink.

"A few drops on the skin will make the wearer especially alluring to the opposite sex. Like pheromones."

"Why do you know a potion like that?"

"I tried it out when I was younger, okay?" she muttered defensively. "Lesson learned. You don't have to lecture me."

"What happened?"

"I wore it on a first date with this guy I really liked."

"Did it work?"

"It worked on him, plus every male who got within twenty feet of me. I spent our entire dinner date pushing random men out of our booth. I've never been hit on so many times in one evening. Most of the men were twice my age and married."

Fighting back a snicker, I asked, "Did you go on a second date with your crush?"

"No." She hung her head over the grimoire. "An early sign that my love life was doomed."

I snorted. "You just need to stop acting shy around cute guys you like."

"I can't help it. My brain freezes." She fidgeted with the edge of a page. "Your brother is nice. I should've given him my number."

Another snort escaped me. A couple of months ago, Sin and Justin had met during an eventful night on the town. I'd told Justin to ask for her number but he hadn't, probably because an on-duty cop asking for a girl's number was taboo.

"Do you want me to give it to him?" I asked. It was like junior high all over again.

"N-no. I'm good." She coughed uncomfortably and turned another page. "Immunity booster … freezer potion—it causes any surface it's poured on to freeze," she added at my questioning look. "Oh! How about this one? A babbler potion. It numbs the tongue and vocal cords, inhibiting speech. Great against sorcerers. It only takes a drop or two, but you need to get it in their mouth. That part might be tricky."

"I don't think an enemy sorcerer would drink a potion just because I asked nicely. What if it looked like candy? Think they'd eat candy?"

"I doubt it." She flipped to the next page. "Intelligence elixir. Also no."

"Would it make me smarter? I'll take it."

"It will make you smarter, but it's addictive with terrible withdrawal symptoms. You don't want to go there."

"Damn."

"Maybe some healing spells? I have ones to stop bleeding, replenish lost blood, boost endurance to survive an injury, counter shock, induce a recovery coma, halt burn damage—oh, hey." She stopped on a new page. "A dizziness draft. That could be useful."

"Dizziness?"

"Yeah. I learned it to prank a high school bully, but it would mess up a mythic with a hands-on combat style like a mage. It requires skin contact—a lot, in fact, so you wouldn't need to worry about splashing yourself."

I nodded. "Sure, that could work."

"I'll ask the other alchemists for ideas too." She smiled. "Defensive alchemy isn't my forte, but I like learning new transmutations."

"Battling mythics isn't *my* forte, but I guess I should—"

I caught a glimpse of movement and forgot what I was saying. Still in combat gear, Ezra walked out from the corner where the basement stairs were hidden, his baldric hanging from one hand. My attention narrowed to him alone, everyone else in the pub forgotten.

His mismatched eyes, dull and tired, flicked to mine and he paused.

Our stares connected, and something close to panic buzzed through me. Visions of crimson magic, both his and the demon's, flashed through my mind. His secrets, closer to the surface than ever before, hung in the space between us like an impenetrable wall.

Fear skittered along my nerves—fear of him. Of what he might be.

I gulped, then shoved off my stool. Straightening my spine, I strode toward him.

12

AS I MARCHED TOWARD EZRA, wariness ghosted across his face. His shoulders tensed as though he were bracing himself for whatever I planned to do.

I had no idea what I planned to do. All I knew was I couldn't sit there while fear needled my core. Jaw tightening with determination, I swooped down on him.

Even though I'd had nothing specific in mind to say or do when I got up from my stool, as soon as I got close, instinct took over. Between one step and the next, I reached for him.

He stumbled back a step as I clamped my arms around his neck. Catching his balance, he hesitated, then wrapped me in his arms. I pressed my face to his chest. My spinning anxieties quieted, and the frightening questions faded to the background of my thoughts.

Nothing had changed. He was still the same guy as yesterday. The only difference was that I knew more about what he kept hidden. I'd gone this long without answers, and I didn't need them now. I didn't *want* them. Whatever his crimson magic was, whatever its connection to demons, I'd rather never know.

He crushed me to his chest, then his arms relaxed. I tilted my head back to meet his cautiously questioning stare.

"Are you okay?" I asked softly. "Where have you been?"

"I just needed time."

My hands tightened on his shirt, then I forced myself to release him and step back.

Hands sliding away from my waist, he searched my expression. "Are you ... okay?"

I nodded. We were dancing awkwardly around the truth, around the questions he expected me to ask.

After a final sweeping assessment of my face, he asked, "Where are Aaron and Kai?"

"Still sleeping, last I checked."

He glanced at the stairs. "I'll go see if they're up. Be right back."

As he hastened to the second level, I turned around—and found Sin gawking at me from her spot at the bar. Er, right. We'd had an audience.

"What," Sin whispered emphatically as I returned to my seat beside her, "was *that?*"

"What was what?"

"That *embrace*. You practically jumped him!"

"It was just a hug."

"Sure. Your face is flushed, by the way."

Scowling, I reached over the bar, grabbed a cloth, and started wiping the counter. "It wasn't what it looked like. We hug all the time."

Arching her eyebrows skeptically, she leaned closer. "That looked a lot more heartfelt than just—"

"It was a *hug*, Sin. Would you drop it already?"

Her expression cooled at my acid tone. "Fine."

I scrubbed the bar in angry silence until Ezra reappeared. Setting his baldric and pole-arm on the counter, he slid onto the stool beside Sin.

"They're dead to the world," he informed me, then added, "Hi Sin. How are you?"

"Not bad. How are you after that fight?"

"A bit banged up, but nothing terrible."

"Glad to hear it." She glanced at me as I aimlessly folded and refolded my cloth. "I need to get back to work. See you."

She grabbed her grimoire and tub of potions, then stalked away. I threw the rag onto the back counter, more angry at myself and my temper than her. I should do something productive. My laptop waited at the other end of the bar, the menu proposal open on the screen, but I had no concentration to speak of.

Puffing irritably, I slid off my stool and walked behind the bar, distractedly thinking I should clean something.

"Tori?"

I turned to Ezra, the bar between us. The intensity in his eyes surprised me. "What is it?"

Throat shifting in a swallow, he seemed to hang on something. He opened his mouth—then the bell above the guild door jangled merrily. His gaze darted away, the interruption breaking his fragile resolve. I glanced crossly at the entrance.

Three men walked across the threshold—and cold alarm blazed through me.

Silence rippled across the pub, all eyes turning to the three mythics. Their ugly-ass faces were easy to recognize: Burke, the old contractor; Fenton, the young contractor; and Halil, their hulking champion.

"The Keys of Solomon," I ground out through gritted teeth. "What are *they* doing here?"

Ezra said nothing, his shoulders stiff as he watched the men out of the corner of his eye. The previous times a contractor had appeared in the guild, Ezra had disappeared almost as quickly as Darius could vanish, but this time he didn't move, and I knew why. The moment they'd stepped through the door, the Keys team had fixed their dark, mean eyes on us.

Seemingly enjoying the unwelcome glares coming from all directions, the Keys strolled across the floor, smirking and sneering at the mythics they passed. The three Keys stopped behind Ezra's stool.

"Oh dear," I sighed with snide sarcasm, breaking the soundless power they held over the room before they could do it. "Some trash has blown in off the street."

Burke's deep-set eyes gleamed under his scraggy eyebrows. "Is that how you greet all your customers?"

"This isn't your guild. Get lost."

"This guild is a rest point for everyone participating in the demon hunt. That includes us." Burke slid onto the nearest stool. "I want a drink."

Halil took the stool on Ezra's other side. "Me too."

Fenton stood behind Ezra, grinning nastily. "Count me in."

I met Ezra's terse stare. He was surrounded—and he didn't like it. If he lost his temper in front of the Keys ... if they saw his crimson magic ...

"We're under full prohibition until the alert is over." I pointed at the door. "So too bad, find another bar."

Burke *tsked*. "We just want to wet our whistles alongside our mythic compatriots. What's wrong with that?"

"You can wet your whistles in a puddle outside. Try one near the dumpster."

Smirking, Burke turned on his stool. "Ezra, isn't it? All recovered after your demon encounter yesterday?"

Ezra said nothing, his jaw tight and eyes fixed on me like I was the only safe place to look. I *really* didn't like the way Burke was watching the aeromage—like a crocodile about to ambush a gazelle on the riverbank.

I slapped a hand on the counter to distract the old man. "What part of *vamoose* don't you understand?"

Burke cocked his head in arrogant challenge and lowered his voice. "Make us leave, girl. Go on. Try."

My teeth clenched so hard my jaw creaked. I scanned the Crow and Hammer members scattered around the pub, but not a single experienced combat mythic was present—they were either upstairs sleeping or out hunting the demon. Felix had taken Sabrina upstairs before the Keys came in, and the only person at the healers' station was the apprentice Sanjana. No one stood a chance at intimidating the hardened demon hunter team.

Should I shout for help? What might the Keys do in the minute it took someone to get down here?

While I hesitated, Burke angled toward Ezra again. "You sure you're doing all right, boy? No further injuries? It's quite the miracle you survived the attack, eh?"

Shit. Slipping my hand into my pocket, I felt for my phone, but all I had on me was my Queen of Spades card. My phone was over by my laptop, out of easy reach. I didn't dare walk away and leave Ezra alone with the Keys men.

Halil pressed in close on Ezra's other side. "He didn't just *survive*, Burke."

"No," Burke mused, his feigned thoughtfulness as obvious as his cruel delight. He reached under his coat. "I'd say he did more than that."

With a flourish, he dropped something on the bar top. It hit the polished wood with a hollow *thunk* that echoed through the room. Under the red and orange lights strung behind the bar, the ridged black horn, splattered with long-dried blood, looked even more monstrous than when it had been attached to the demon's head.

"Look what we found in the alley where you fought the demon," Burke crooned. "Hidden in a trash bin. Strange, eh?"

"Very strange," Halil repeated, shifting even closer to Ezra, hemming him in. "So, we asked ourselves, who is this mage who can fight off an unbound demon all alone? He must be someone really special."

Fenton snickered nastily.

Ezra's expression was unnervingly blank—he was fighting not to react. I could feel a faint chill in the air, almost unnoticeable, but that wouldn't last. If I shouted for help now, I was liable to send him over the edge and into violence; I'd done it once before by screaming hysterically during a tense encounter.

"You three must be really *special*," I sneered in a low voice. "I told you to get out of here or—"

"We were curious about you, Ezra," Burke said right over me, "so we looked you up. Fascinating stuff, your history— what exists of it."

My options were running out. Should I slap him? No, that could trigger Ezra too. He *had* to keep his cool. If he lost it now ... I wasn't sure what would happen, but it would be bad.

Burke withdrew a printout from his coat and waved it like a wad of cash.

"Isn't *this* interesting? Your registration paperwork." Angling the top page toward himself, he read, "'Ezra Rowe, registered as an aeromage at eighteen years old.' *Eighteen.* Six years ago! Young mages who fall through the cracks are almost always discovered at puberty when their magic first manifests."

"*Very* interesting," Halil echoed nastily.

Burke shoved the paper in Ezra's face. "Says here: 'six feet tall, one hundred and thirty-five pounds.' *One thirty-five.* You musta been skin and bone at eighteen, but it looks like you've put on weight since then. At least forty pounds of muscle, I'd guess. Am I right?"

He grabbed Ezra's bicep and squeezed. Ezra jerked his arm away. Panic kindled in my chest. I had to stop this, but I had no idea how.

"Were you sick, Ezra? That why you were so skinny back then?" Burke gave a leering smile. "Weird thing, though. We did a bit more poking around and ... you have no medical records older than six years. No immunization records. No school records. *Nothing* until six years ago."

"It's almost like ..." Halil paused dramatically. "Like you didn't exist until six years ago."

"At least, not in any government system."

"Weird."

"Very weird." Burke leaned closer, getting in Ezra's face, and whispered, "What's your real name, Ezra Rowe? Who were you *before* all these forged documents?"

Ezra's lips pulled back, baring his teeth, and I couldn't afford to play it safe anymore. If someone was going to lose their shit, better me than him.

I grabbed the bar top and jumped over it. Having flubbed the move with embarrassing results before, I'd practiced it on quiet nights when no one was around to witness my failures. I had the move down pretty good now—but, as it turned out, not good enough to pull it off while equal parts panicked and furious.

Instead of landing neatly beside Burke, I slammed both feet into his chest.

He pitched backward off his stool and I stuck my landing without even a wobble. As he hit the floor, I pretended that's exactly what I'd intended to do.

Burke launched to his feet, but Ezra was up even faster, kicking his stool out of the way and pivoting so we stood side by side. The air had chilled even more, but no crimson magic yet.

"You three and your fugly asses can get the hell out of my bar," I growled, whipping out my Queen of Spades threateningly, "or you'll regret it."

Lips contorting in a sneer, Burke stepped backward. "You attacked me. I have no choice but to defend myself."

Uh-oh.

A crimson glow lit Burke's infernus pendant, then magic whooshed out of it. The light ballooned in the tiny space between us and solidified into a stocky, scaled demon with glowing eyes in an emotionless face. Stocky but *huge*—over seven feet tall with limbs like tree trunks.

A shiver of silence, then someone screamed.

Terrified cries erupted from the mythics in the room, most of whom had probably never seen a demon. Half of them backpedaled, knocking over chairs, while the rest held their ground, uncertain what to do but ready to help if they could.

Beside me, Ezra was rigid, his face as empty as a mannequin's. I mentally begged him to hold it together. He couldn't let Burke provoke him. The demon hunter wanted to test Ezra—to see what the aeromage could do, to see how he'd survived the first demon attack. What better way to find out than to attack him with another demon?

I couldn't allow Ezra to fight it.

The demon's arm swung up, claws shooting toward us.

"*Ori repercutio!*" I yelled, pointing the Queen of Spades at the creature.

Air rippled and the demon's arm bounced back like it'd punched a wall. Whoa. The demon must be so magical that the artifact could reflect its physical body.

Unfortunately, knocking its arm away did as much to stop it from attacking again as shouting *boo* would have.

It grabbed the front of my shirt, its claws tearing through my brand-new, combat-ready leather jacket. It lifted me off the floor like I weighed nothing.

As fast as the demon, Ezra jammed his fist into the beast's gut. Wind boomed, blowing over all the chairs and tables around us. The demon staggered backward, its grip loosening. Ezra grabbed the back of my jacket and yanked. Leather tore and I dropped onto my feet.

He shoved me behind him as the demon stepped closer. Halil and Fenton hovered on either side of us, blocking any escape, and Burke was grinning like a madman.

His grin suddenly faltered, replaced by shock. Between one instant and the next, a shining blade had appeared, the point pressed neatly against Burke's jugular.

Holding it was Darius. He stood between Burke and Fenton, and the long dagger in his other hand dug into the younger man's throat.

Then Halil hit the floor with yellow magic crackling over him. Girard stood behind the Keys champion, a polished baton in his grasp, the wood carved with runes. His normally sparkling eyes were flat with anger, his expression blacker than a thundercloud.

On the stairs, more movement—Aaron, Kai, and half a dozen combat mythics from the second level were clustered on the steps, alert and waiting. I gripped Ezra's arm, channeling calming vibes into him. His skin was ice cold, all his freezing power contained within.

Holding both contractors at knifepoint, Darius smiled pleasantly. "Gentlemen. It would appear you're breaking protocol."

Standing as stiffly as his demon, Burke swallowed. His throat bobbed and a trickle of blood ran down the side of his neck from the dagger's point.

"Well, if it isn't the Mage Assassin himself," he grunted. "I thought you gave up your blades, Darius."

"Those glory days are long behind me," Darius agreed conversationally. "In my sleepy retirement, I'm but a lowly GM pushing paperwork and destroying anyone who threatens my guild."

Burke paled. "Your bartender attacked me. I was defending myself."

Darius twisted his shiny dagger and more blood ran down Burke's neck. "Call your demon back."

Teeth gritted, Burke turned his gaze to his unmoving demon. Red light lit across its hands and feet, streaking toward his infernus, then the light swept over the demon. It dissolved into an eerie red power that was sucked into the pendant.

"Excellent," Darius said. "Now, listen carefully. If you or any member of the Keys of Solomon set foot in my bar again, you won't leave alive. Understood?"

"You'd kill us for walking into your guild? If the MPD hears—"

"What the MPD hears or doesn't hear won't be your concern, because you'll be dead." Darius flicked his knives up, spinning the hilts in his palms. Burke and Fenton both clapped hands over their necks, stanching the flow of blood from newly opened cuts. "Now, on your way. And take your large limp friend with you."

Furious and silent, Burke and Fenton picked up Halil by the arms and dragged him to the door. While everyone watched their pathetic retreat, I peeked behind me. The broken demon horn sat on the counter, forgotten. I nudged it off the edge and it fell into the garbage bin on the other side, the thump lost in the door bell's jangling. The Keys were gone.

Darius tossed both knives in the air and caught them by the points. "How unpleasant," he remarked to the room.

A nervous titter ran through the mythics, and they uneasily righted the disturbed furniture. As Girard joined them, asking if everyone was all right, the people on the stairs descended to the pub level. Aaron and Kai flanked Ezra, standing close.

Darius's gaze swept over them, his eyes far steelier than his tone. "Aaron, take the other three home."

Aaron stiffened. "Home?"

"You've done all you can in the demon hunt. Now go home to rest. You need peace and quiet."

"But sir—"

I grabbed Aaron's arm, my fingers digging in. He might not want to abandon the demon hunt, but I didn't think the unbound demon had anything to do with Darius's order. Ezra's face was still blank, his jaw was set, and a vein throbbed in his cheek. *He* was the one who needed peace and quiet.

Aaron glanced at me, then followed my gaze to Ezra. He swallowed back his protest. "Yes, sir."

"I'll keep you posted," Darius added.

With a nod, Aaron drew Ezra into motion, leading him behind the bar and into the kitchen. Kai followed on their heels, but as I stepped after him, Darius caught my eye.

"Be careful, Tori," he murmured.

Before I could ask what he meant, he strode off to join Girard. I stared after him. Be careful of … what? What was with mythics and cryptic warnings? Annoyed, I grabbed my laptop, purse, and phone, then stalked after the guys. I had enough to worry about already.

THE MOMENT we piled through the front door of Aaron's house, Ezra made a beeline for the stairs. He cleared two steps before Kai and Aaron hauled him back down and dragged him into the living room.

I followed with my mouth hanging open, no idea what to do or say or … anything.

Aaron pushed his friend onto the sofa. "No, Ezra."

"Don't panic yet," Kai told him.

Ezra glared up at them, then his shoulders hunched in defeat. "But if they know, I have to—"

"One," Aaron interrupted, "they don't *know* anything. They're fishing. They think you're suspicious, but that's all they've got. And two, whether they know or not, you aren't running."

"Don't even try to pack a bag," Kai warned.

Ezra hunched further. "I don't need a bag to leave."

My back snapped straight. *Leave?* That was his plan?

"Good point." Kai dropped onto the sofa beside Ezra. "Now that you've reminded us, we'll make sure to keep you under constant surveillance so you can't sneak off."

Jaw flexing, Ezra growled, "What else am I supposed to do?"

"They don't know anything," Aaron repeated sternly. "They were trying to spook you into revealing something, and if you skip town, you'll just confirm their suspicions. Their whole guild will hunt you."

Ezra braced his elbows on his knees, fingers entwined and pressed against his mouth. "What, then? What do I do? This has never happened before."

Kai and Aaron exchanged a look. I stayed in the doorway, unwilling to enter the conversation.

"We have three options," Kai said. "One, you run for it, which we've already vetoed. Two, we wait them out. When they can't confirm you're anything but an aeromage, they'll go back to hunting the demon. Or three, we kill them."

My stomach dropped through the floor and landed somewhere in the basement.

After a moment's thought, he added, "It's a bit premature for option three."

Aaron sighed. "Kai, this isn't the family business."

Kai leaned back into the sofa. "Killing them would be the safest option for Ezra, and no one will miss them. People have died because those selfish fools are sabotaging everyone's search efforts to get the demon kill for themselves."

"We aren't a mythic mafia," Aaron retorted dryly. "We can't off inconvenient people on a whim."

"We'd need to plan it carefully. Disposing of bodies is a hassle." He shrugged. "But like I said, it's too soon. The Keys are looking for proof. All we need to do is make sure we don't give them any."

Disposing of bodies was a hassle, Kai had said. He'd supposedly broken all ties with his crime-syndicate family seven years ago, so he must've learned that skill before then. Great one to add to his résumé. *Black belt martial artist, master swordsman, and body disposal expert.*

My gaze drifted to Ezra, who was watching the blank TV with a thousand-yard stare. Speaking of young, he hadn't registered as a mythic until he was eighteen. But hadn't he told me he'd always known he was an aeromage? How did *that* work?

Sensing my attention, his gaze turned my way, then dipped down to my chest. He sprang up so fast I started.

Aaron and Kai grabbed for him like he was about to throw himself through the window, action-movie style, but he dodged their hands with unnerving speed. My eyes widened as he strode toward me.

"Tori, you're hurt." Concern softened his voice as he gently took my arm. "I'm sorry. I didn't notice."

I looked down, surprised to see the torn front of my jacket and a bloody splotch above its collar. Oh. Huh. I'd forgotten about that. I pulled the front of my jacket open and was pleasantly surprised that my Kevlar-esque shirt hadn't torn. One demonic claw had nicked my collarbone just above the neckline.

"No biggie, guys."

"We should still clean it," Kai said. "Come with me, Tori."

Leaving the other two in the living room, Kai led me into the kitchen. I leaned against a counter while he retrieved the kit from the bathroom.

As he set it beside me and flipped it open, I lowered my voice and asked, "Kai, how bad is it?"

He tore open an alcohol swab. "The scratch isn't deep."

"Not that. I meant—*oww*." I winced as he swabbed the cut. "I meant with the Keys harassing Ezra."

Kai's dark eyes darted toward the living room. "It's bad. The Keys have no proof, but they don't always care. This wouldn't be the first time they've attacked first and condemned the mythic later."

My jaw tightened, and I scarcely noticed him sorting through bandage options.

"If we keep Ezra out of sight," Kai murmured, "they should give up and refocus on the demon hunt. That's Darius's intent, I think."

I studied him. "And if they don't give up?"

"Then we'll deal with it." He peeled a bandage open. "If you want out, now is the time. I'll take you home as soon as I'm done."

"Funny."

"I'm serious." He pressed the bandage over my cut. "I don't think you're ready to face the reality that comes with staying."

I squinted in confusion. "What reality?"

His eyes met mine, dark as night and deadly serious. "The point of no return is approaching, Tori. If you pass it, you can't go back."

A shiver ran down my spine, his words strangely echoing Sabrina's reading. No going back. An irreversible choice. My life changing forever.

"I'm not going anywhere," I told him.

He gazed at me as though waiting for something, his expression inscrutable. When I said nothing, he eventually nodded. The gesture felt like he was giving me his permission to stay ... a permission he could revoke at any time.

13

"TORI? Tooorriiiii."

Aaron's persistent voice rattled around in my sleep-riddled skull.

"Wake up, Tori."

A hand squeezed my shoulder and gently shook me. Groaning, I lifted my face off the pillow and squinched my eyes open. Pale sunlight leaked through the bedroom curtains.

"Ehhhh?" I slurred.

Aaron's grinning face appeared above mine. "Morning, sleeping beauty. Time to get up!"

I blinked a few times, then laboriously rolled onto my back. A hard, round object pressed against my side, then with a shimmer, Hoshi uncoiled from her small orb form, her long tail spilling across the blankets. She buried her head under the pillow.

Aaron stared at the fae. "Where'd she come from?"

"She likes to sleep beside me." A yawn cracked my jaw and I nestled into the bed. "What are you doing in here? Don't you know how to knock?"

"I did knock. Several times." He waved at me. "Up. Come on. Time to go."

I frowned sleepily, scanning him from head to toe. He wore a loose black and gray tank top and gym shorts, his hair tousled and cheeks flushed. I allowed myself a moment to drool over his amazingly toned arms, which I'd seen far less of since the fall weather had dropped the temperatures, then asked, "Time to go where?"

Aaron crouched at my eye level, a smirk pulling at his mouth. "You know how we keep bringing up that you need training and you keep dodging it?"

Denying that I'd avoided all forms of training for the past six weeks would only make him laugh. I hadn't been particularly subtle about it.

"Yeah, so?"

His smirk sharpened. "You can't dodge it if you're sleeping in our house. Today is day one."

Oh *hell* no. "Pass."

"You don't have a choice."

"Is this really an appropriate time?" I demanded, changing tactics. "With a demon on the loose and the Keys after Ezra—"

"Which means we're stuck at home anyway, so we should make the best of it. Up!"

I yanked the covers over my chin. "You can't make me."

"I'm so glad you said that."

He grabbed the blankets and yanked them right off the mattress. Hoshi shot up above the bed, hissing softly, then faded out of sight. Damn it. She should've stayed to defend me!

Drawing my legs up against the rush of cold air, I curled into a defensive ball—but it was no use. Ignoring the fact I was wearing an oversized t-shirt from Ezra's dresser and no pants, Aaron dragged me to the edge of the bed, got a good hold of my waist, and tossed me over his shoulder.

"Aaron!" I shrieked, flailing. "Put me down!"

"Hold on tight." Laughing, he strode out of the room. I desperately clutched the back of his shirt and cursed him with every bad word I knew. He laughed again as he trotted down the stairs. "Look on the bright side, Tori. We were nice enough to let you sleep in an extra two hours."

"I haven't agreed to this! You can't manhandle me like a child!"

He went down the basement stairs with terrifying speed. "If you'd done any training before this, maybe you'd know how to stop me."

I snarled as he tilted me off his shoulder. My bare feet hit the mats that covered the floor, and I shoved angrily away from him. My borrowed t-shirt was caught around my hips, displaying my purple undies to the whole room, and I jerked the hem down.

Their basement was one big fitness gym, with three treadmills, more cardio machines, and weight equipment on one side. Exercise mats covered the other side. Kai's footsteps thudded against a humming treadmill at a fast jog, his face shining with perspiration. Ezra hung from the pull-up bar, slowly drawing himself up with one arm until his opposite shoulder touched the bar, then lowering himself just as slowly.

My eyes popped at the sight of his bare arms, taut muscles flexing with each one-handed pull-up. He switched hands and pulled himself up with the other arm.

Aaron waved a hand in front of my face, startling me out of my daze. "Get changed. We'll take it easy today, promise."

"Change into *what?*"

He jerked his thumb at the bathroom door.

I folded my arms. "What if I refuse?"

"Do you really want to find out?"

I considered that. Snarling under my breath, I stomped into the bathroom and slammed the door. It featured the most modern décor in the entire house—a granite counter, double sinks, built-in shelves for towels and spare clothes, and a massive shower with more jets than a car wash.

Stacked on the counter were some of my clothes from the assortment I never took home, including a sports bra. When had I left *that* here? My running shoes sat on the floor, and I noted that someone had given them a cursory cleaning for indoor use. I used the toilet first, drank some water from the tap, then got dressed in a summer tank top and yoga shorts.

My hair was sagging out of the ponytail I'd worn to bed, and I reused my hair tie to tame it into a bun. I loitered for another two minutes, then abandoned my refuge. Last thing I needed was Aaron bursting in here too.

When I came out, Ezra was off the pull-up bar and drying his face with a towel. Spotting me, he grinned. "You look like all the puppies in the world just died. It won't be that bad."

"I think it'll be exactly that bad."

Kai, walking on the treadmill now instead of running, switched it off and unclipped the safety line from his shirt. "Over here, Tori. Warm up first."

I groaned and stepped onto the wide belt. As he clipped the safety stop majiggy onto the hem of my tank top, I peeked at the display blinking with stats from his run. Distance: 5.5 km.

He made sure I was ready, then hit a preset button. The track started moving and I broke into a slow amble that accelerated to a fast walk, then a sluggish jog. My calves were burning within a minute.

"How long do I have to do this?" I panted.

"Long enough to warm up." With a brief smile, he joined the other two, who were doing stretches on the mats.

Lungs on fire and legs hurting, I settled into what should've been an easy jog but felt more like death in motion. Luckily, I had plenty to keep me occupied—like the sinfully hot mages going through a routine of stretches and flexibility exercises. All three of them could do the splits. Who knew?

Watching them was fascinating, and I found myself running a detailed mental comparison. Aaron and Ezra were similar in build and almost the same height. Aaron was slightly taller, while Ezra was a shade broader in the shoulders. Kai was a couple of inches shorter and slimmer, but all three packed a comparable amount of muscle. Not body-builder bulges, but lean, hard, athletic figures.

By the time the treadmill slowed back to a walk, I was wheezing and sweating and trying not to throw up. Someone shoot me now, please.

"Good job, Tori!" Aaron called, bent backward in a weird thigh stretch. "You made it!"

"Yeah," I panted. "I'm … in … *great* … shape. Can't you … tell?"

They allowed me three minutes to catch my breath, then Aaron reached into a bin and pulled out padded rectangles. He tossed two to Ezra, who slipped them onto his hands, and carried the other two to the mats' center.

"Shoes off, then over here, Tori." He pointed to the spot in front of him.

Toeing off my runners, I minced onto the squashy mats but was immediately distracted by Kai taking on a fighting stance, facing Ezra. The aeromage held up the two pads, which shielded his hands and forearms.

"Ready."

"Ready." Kai breathed once, then unleashed two rapid punches and a kick into the blockers. The strikes smacked loudly, pushing Ezra's arms back. I could *hear* the power in each blow.

I stopped in front of Aaron. "I can't do that."

Reassuring steadiness had replaced his mischievous smirk. "We'll start from scratch. I know you took a year of taekwondo as a teenager, but I'd rather cover everything."

"All right."

"Let's see your fighting stance."

Feeling self-conscious, I slid my right foot backward and put my hands up by my chin.

"Good." He walked around me, pushing lightly against my shoulder to make sure I was balanced.

At the other end of the mats, Kai was pummeling Ezra's pads at top speed.

"Tuck in your elbows more. There you go." Aaron returned to face me. "Now, fists."

I curled my fingers down, thumbs tucked outside them.

"Excellent." He slid on one blocker pad and held it up. "Okay. Left jab. Give it all you've got."

Bouncing on the balls of my feet, I threw a mean punch into the pad.

"Perfect. Now, right cross."

I flung my right fist across my body and into the pad.

"Not bad, but you aren't moving your hips."

Adopting the same stance, he demonstrated how the cross traveled from his back heel to his hip to his shoulder, adding more power to the strike. We practiced that a few dozen times. Several paces away, Ezra and Kai had switched, with Ezra hammering the pads that Kai held.

"All right," Aaron said. "You'll be smaller and lighter than most of your opponents, so you need to generate as much power as possible. Standing in one spot and punching them isn't ideal. You need to move."

He glanced at the other two as Ezra slammed a roundhouse kick into both pads. Kai slid backward from the force.

"Ezra," Aaron called. "Demonstrate a pounce."

Ezra stepped backward, putting Kai out of his reach. He fell into his fighting stance, then jumped forward and delivered a seamless one-two strike on the pads before bouncing back to his starting spot.

"In and out." Aaron turned back to me. "You stay out of range and only get in close when you're ready to strike."

"Okay," I agreed uncertainly.

Aaron walked me through the steps, making sure I was pushing off my back foot. It took about ten minutes for me to coordinate the various movements into something that resembled what Ezra had done.

"Great!" Aaron complimented. "Now repeat that until you collapse."

My eyes widened.

"Go!"

Gulping, I sprang at him and struck the pads, then sprang back. And again. And again.

Yes, he made me repeat it until my legs were trembling and on the verge of ruin. Finally, he slid the pads off and sent me to the treadmill for a cool-down walk. Breathing heavily, I watched the guys pull more gear from the bins. They donned padded sleeves that covered their arms from knuckles to elbows, leg protectors that covered their feet, shins, and knees, and padded vests.

When they pulled on open-faced headgear like boxers wore, I got nervous.

Aaron and Kai faced off, Ezra refereeing with a stopwatch in hand. He called the start—and the two guys charged each other. They slammed together, grappling, then Kai broke free and jammed three lightning-fast punches into Aaron's padded chest. Aaron blocked the last one, caught Kai's arm, and threw him over his shoulder.

Kai landed on his feet, dropped into a crouch, and swept his leg into Aaron's ankles. Aaron hit the mats and rolled away from Kai's swift kick.

They sparred with sober intensity, landing punches and kicks that sounded horrific despite the padded gear protecting them. Twice they went down grappling but Kai couldn't lock Aaron into a hold.

"Time!" Ezra called.

The two mages broke apart, breathing hard. They took a short break, then Ezra passed the stopwatch to Kai and faced off against Aaron. Kai called the start.

Aaron sprang in, fast and hard. Ezra blocked two strikes then staggered when Aaron landed a kick to his knee.

"Quit it, Ezra!" he barked. "Tori knows you're fast. Don't waste my workout holding back."

Ezra puffed, then leaped at Aaron. The blows flew between them so fast I couldn't follow the action, then Aaron hit the floor on his stomach, Ezra pinning his arm backward. Aaron slapped the mats and Ezra released him.

"Shit," he panted. "Jeez, man."

Not even winded, Ezra rose to his feet and shrugged. "You told me not to hold back."

Aaron growled something and clambered up. "Again."

They launched at each other. Twice more, Ezra pinned Aaron within thirty seconds. Finally, Kai called time.

"All right," the electramage said, tossing the stopwatch aside. "Final round."

Grinning, Aaron faced Ezra again—and Kai took up the spot beside him. Two against one.

Swallowing hard, I stopped the treadmill in case the distraction caused me to wipe out.

The guys got into their stances, and Kai counted down. "Three, two, one, *go*."

Ezra sprang at Kai, but he darted away. He and Aaron split up, flanking Ezra, then attacked simultaneously. Somehow, Ezra evaded their strikes, his movements a blur. He caught Aaron's ankle mid-kick and yanked him off his feet, then went for Kai. The electramage slid aside, but Ezra tackled him from a standstill. They went down in a tangle, each fighting to get on top.

Aaron popped onto his feet, hovered over the grappling pair for a second, then jumped in. Ten seconds later, Ezra was pinned under the other two, slapping at the mats with Kai's legs clamped around his neck and Aaron bending his knee back.

Laughing breathlessly, Aaron flopped on the mats. "Damn. You're always faster than I expect."

I cleared my throat, my heart racing and my brain confused on several levels. The violence was unnerving, but there was something carnally appealing about watching them attack each other. If this was the regularly scheduled programming, I hereby volunteered to work out with them every morning. Yes *please*.

As they stripped off their sparring gear, I finally dared to speak. "Are you done your routine now?"

"Not quite." Aaron tossed his helmet into the bin. "We need to cool down, but first, we'll finish with a round of competitive pushups."

"*Competitive* pushups?"

"Yeah." He didn't sound excited as he got onto his hands and knees in the center of the mats. Kai and Ezra followed suit, taking the spots on either side of him. "We do pushups until one of us can't finish the set. The loser makes breakfast."

As he and Kai steeled themselves for the coming challenge, my eyebrows shot up. Three hours into their workout and they were finishing with a round of pushups? The guys were insane. Or masochists. Or both.

"But Ezra isn't allowed in the kitchen," I pointed out. "He can't make breakfast."

"*Ezra*," Aaron growled as he straightened his body into a tense plank propped up by his extended arms, "has never lost, so it's a moot poi—wait. Oh man. I have a *wonderful* idea."

Equally bemused, Kai, Ezra, and I watched him hop onto his feet. He gestured at me.

"C'mere, Tori."

Eyebrows climbing higher, I kicked my shoes off and walked over. He took my elbow and pulled me to Ezra, who was waiting on his hands and knees, head canted to watch us.

"Get on his back," Aaron said.

My mouth fell open. "What?"

"What?" Ezra demanded.

"Sit on him!" Aaron grinned diabolically. "There's no way he can outlast us with an extra hundred pounds to lift."

I weighed more than a hundred pounds but decided not to point that out.

"That's completely unfair," Ezra protested.

"It's totally fair," Kai interjected. "*You* have the unfair advantage. Do it, Tori."

I looked rapidly between the three guys. "Uh …"

"I want to see him struggle for once." Not waiting for permission, Aaron lifted me off my feet and sat me on Ezra so I was straddling his upper back. "Tuck your feet up. Full weight."

Ezra muttered something unpleasant about Aaron. Eyes wide and voice having vanished the moment my body contacted Ezra's, I didn't know what to do except tuck my feet behind my butt, knees hanging off his sides.

"Perfect." Aaron jumped back to his spot and dropped onto his hands and knees. "Ready?"

"But," I stammered, finding my voice again, "what about breakfast?"

"If it means seeing him drop, I will gladly eat cereal. First set, starting now. Go!"

Ezra pulled his knees off the mats and straightened his body, and I grabbed his shoulders for balance. He inhaled as he lowered his torso, the muscles in his arms and back shifting and tightening. My hands clenched over his shoulders as he pushed up, exhaling sharply.

Oh man. This was a bad, bad, baaaaad idea.

He lowered again, his body flexing under my hands, under my thighs, under my—oh god. Heat radiated off him, soaking into my skin, and perspiration shone on the back of his neck, dampening his curls. He pushed up again, lifting me, and my head spun.

Bad, bad, bad. And *so good.*

My core shivered with building heat as he lifted and lowered beneath me, his breathing labored, faint sounds of effort escaping him. I bit hard on my lip, fighting my rising heart rate. If watching the guys spar had been titillating, that was *nothing* compared to this.

"Set," Aaron announced breathlessly. "I can't believe it. Ezra, you're a machine."

Bracing his elbows on the mats, Ezra grunted wordlessly, chest heaving as he sucked in air. I hadn't been counting. How many pushups had that been? Was I allowed to get off him now? Because if this went on much longer, I would either spontaneously combust or humiliate myself.

"Next set," Kai said. "Three, two, one, go."

He and Aaron pushed up, and Ezra followed a second behind. His muscles bunched and flexed under me, and I bit my lip harder. My hands closed into fists around his shirt. His hot body between my legs. Sweating, panting, flexing. The wild thought that I wanted to be under him, not on top, flew through my feverish head.

His arms trembled with strain as he lowered us. For a moment, he hung there, then he pushed up with a quiet groan that pierced my center. No, Tori. He was groaning from the excruciating effort of lifting my weight. That was it. Focus.

"He's done." Aaron laughed as he dragged himself up again. "You're losing this one, Ezra."

Blowing out air and sucking it in, Ezra lowered again, muscles quivering, veins standing out on his tense biceps. Aaron and Kai stopped at the apex of their pushups and waited with triumphant grins despite their red faces and the sweat beading on their foreheads. I wanted to encourage Ezra, but I didn't dare open my mouth for fear of what sounds might come out.

He pushed up again—and his arms buckled. We dropped and his chest hit the mat with a thud. I tumbled off him.

"Yes!" Aaron crowed. "Let's do this, Kai."

With renewed energy, they completed another six pushups, then flopped onto the mats, Aaron laughing victoriously. He reached over and slapped Ezra on the back as he wheezed.

"You're insane, man. I didn't expect you to finish the first set."

"You ... try it ... next time," Ezra panted.

Aaron snickered. "It's good for you to lose once in a while."

I sat up, hiding my accelerated breathing. That'd be tricky to explain, considering I'd done nothing—nothing except straddle a sexy, ripped mage while he flexed rhythmically under me.

Getting to my feet—shit, my knees were weak—I awkwardly straightened my shirt and glanced across the collapsed mages. "Um, now what?"

"We need to do our cool downs," Aaron answered, eyes closed. "Take a turn in the shower. You've got ten minutes."

Nodding, I hastened off the mats and into the bathroom, and locked the door behind me. Tearing my clothes off, I turned the shower on and jumped into the spray. I gasped as icy water hit me from all sides. Who needed this many shower jets? Talk about overkill.

As my body temperature dropped, I pressed both hands to my face and concentrated on breathing.

My reaction was totally normal, right? Most women would become aroused in that situation, even if the guy was a friend. It didn't mean anything. Just sensory input triggering a hard-coded physiological response. That was it.

I nodded to myself. Yes. That was it.

After washing my hair and scrubbing with a bar of soap, I shut off the water, grabbed a clean towel, and … crap. I stared at the shelves beside the shower, stacked with spare towels and the guys' post-workout change of clothes.

My clean clothes were upstairs. Goddamn it!

As I dried off, I thought frantically. Couldn't put my sweaty workout clothes back on, and I didn't want to wear my PJ shirt again either. No way around it. I twisted my hair into a second towel and piled it on top of my head, then wrapped the big white towel around my torso and tucked in the corner.

Confidence. I strode to the door and flung it open.

Ezra stood on the other side, hand raised to knock.

My stomach dissolved in a surge of molten heat. My mouth went dry, throat closing, toes curling. My gaze raced over his body then up to his face, his hair damp and tousled, cheeks flushed from exertion.

Our eyes met and his widened with surprise—then dropped. Sliding down. Taking me in.

Clutching my towel, I dove past him and sprinted toward my only escape. Aaron burst into laughter at the sight of my towel-clad self bolting up the stairs, but I didn't stop until I was two floors away. I slammed Ezra's bedroom door shut and pressed my back against it.

Way to panic, Tori.

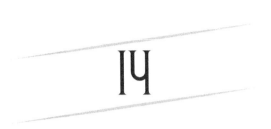

I DIDN'T HAVE TO DWELL on our overly eventful workout for long. When I returned to the main level, something far more pressing claimed my attention:

Fenton, the young Keys contractor, was standing outside on the front sidewalk.

For one horrible, disbelieving moment, I gawked witlessly through the living room window. Then I ran into the basement to inform the guys.

Since the Keys couldn't get at Ezra in or around his guild, they had tracked him to his house—and judging by the black van parked behind Fenton, they planned to hang around for a while. This probably wasn't what Darius had intended when he sent us home.

The three mages and I conferred on strategy. According to Aaron, the Keys wouldn't enter the house because, as per MPD law, violence against mythic trespassers was perfectly acceptable. If they forced their way inside, he and Kai would be free to roast the Keys guys like pigs on a spit.

Short of that, our hands were tied, so we decided to stick with our original plan: wait them out. We'd ignore them and be as boring as possible. We'd stay in. Do nothing. Rot our brains watching TV and eating microwave dinners until the Keys lost interest. We closed all the blinds and did our best to forget they were out there.

Ha, yeah right. None of us could forget even for a minute.

We didn't actually eat microwave dinners. Ezra held true to his pushups loss and toasted a box of frozen waffles for breakfast. After eating, I got to work on my menu proposal. So far, I'd selected which dishes to remove from the existing menu, but I was still struggling with ideas for new meals.

"Guys?" I squinted at my list. "Do fried mac 'n' cheese balls sound good?"

Game controller in hand, Aaron didn't look away from the TV, the split screen displaying two racetracks with careening cars. "Huh?"

"Fried mac 'n' cheese balls. Does that sound appetizing?"

"Fried … mac and cheese … *balls?*"

Ezra dared to look away long enough to smirk at Aaron. "Don't you know everything is better in ball form? Cheese, meat, donuts, snow … pasta."

"Real comprehensive list there, Ezra."

Sighing, I erased that one off the page. While I worked, Aaron and Ezra continued to race the afternoon away. Kai had disappeared upstairs to do who knew what. Maybe he just wanted some quiet; Aaron cursed almost nonstop while gaming.

Ezra played with his usual quiet humor, trouncing Aaron every time—though I now realized his victories had less to do with his skill and more to do with his fast reflexes—but I could see his tension. At every lull in the game, his gaze slid to the curtains covering the front window, his shoulders tensing and brow creasing.

I peeked outside a few times throughout the afternoon. The three Keys members were taking turns standing out front, changing shifts every hour. Their mission wasn't merely surveillance; if it was, they would've stayed in their van. No, they were being deliberately obvious. It was a power play. It was a mind game. They were trying to freak Ezra out.

Unfortunately, it was working.

Their presence wore on him as the day went on. His options were painfully limited. If he fled, they'd chase him. If he confronted them, they'd fight him—which was probably what they wanted. His only option was to stay inside, hiding like a mouse in a burrow, the cat poised over the opening in anticipation.

Apparently, Aaron's neighbors had also noticed our unwelcome company. A cop car showed up midafternoon, but the two officers left after a short talk with Burke. All the Keys had to do to get rid of the police was flash their MID numbers.

We ordered pizza for a late lunch, but Halil intercepted the delivery man, forcing Aaron and Kai to go outside and rescue our meal. The moment Aaron handed over some cash, the delivery man literally sprinted back to his car.

Tense and edgy, we settled in for a Netflix marathon. Thinking a food-related show might help me with menu ideas, the guys picked a cooking competition.

As the show's host dramatically revealed the episode's theme ingredient, I squinted at the spiky dark purple things on the screen. "What are those?"

"Sea urchins," Kai answered.

"Are they poisonous?" Aaron muttered as the camera zoomed in on the round creatures covered in bristling spines. "They look poisonous."

"You need to get out more—to actual restaurants instead of burger bars," Kai said dryly. "Sea urchin is quite good. My favorite is *uni donburi* but it's also delicious in—"

The living room window shattered.

I screamed as glass shards sprayed the floor and something heavy slammed into the hardwood. The guys leaped to their feet and whipped toward the window. Aaron flung the drapes open.

Burke stood on the sidewalk, smirking. As soon as Aaron appeared, he gave a mocking salute, climbed into his van, and slammed the door shut.

"What the hell?" Aaron snarled.

Glass covered the floor, with larger shards heaped beneath the sill. The drapes had caught most of the debris, keeping it from reaching the sofa. I sat frozen in my spot, heart pounding painfully against my ribs.

An object sat halfway under the coffee table. Stretching forward—without stepping onto the sparkling floor in my bare feet—I picked it up. A piece of folded paper, held in place by a rubber band, was wrapped around a heavy red brick.

"Guys," I murmured.

Treading carefully, they returned to the sofa and gathered around me. None of them spoke. Since they seemed to be waiting, I pulled the elastic off, set the brick on the coffee table, and unfolded the paper.

The first thing I saw was Ezra's face. Even in black and white, the bold scar cutting across his pale eye was unmistakable, but he appeared much younger. His cheeks were hollow, his eyes sunken, his hair short and scraggy. He looked like he was ill … or a drug addict.

The photo was a mug shot.

My eyes darted across the page, zipping from one block of info to the next. It was a police report. The date jumped out at me—eight years ago. Then words—*breaking and entering … theft under $5000 … resisting arrest*. The suspect details were blank, with "unknown" written in place of a name and a note that the suspect had refused to provide any identification.

At the top of the report was the title *Portland Bureau of Police*, and someone had circled "Portland" in red—the only color on the black and white photocopy. Written above it in a masculine scrawl were two short lines:

60 miles from Enright, Oregon
4 months after extermination

Aaron yanked the paper from my hands. He scanned it rapidly, Kai squinting over his shoulder.

His hand clenched, crumpling the paper. "This proves nothing."

"It doesn't look good," Kai muttered. "Ezra, you never mentioned …"

They looked at the aeromage. Ezra stood unmoving, his face blank, his jaw locked. His eyes were empty, shuttered, his emotions locked down so tight I wondered if he felt anything at all.

"Never mentioned getting arrested?" he said tonelessly. "It happened a few times."

I could see a sliver of sixteen-year-old Ezra's gaunt face on the paper, his stare in the photo as vacant as it was now.

"This proves *nothing*." Aaron tightened his fist and flames erupted over the page, consuming it in seconds. Gray ash fluttered to the floor. "They can't prove anything."

"They don't need to," Kai said, a sharp, almost fearful edge creeping into his tone. "This is enough for them. If they've linked him to Enright, then they're certain. They won't give up. Waiting them out won't work. They're biding their time until they have a clear shot at him."

Ezra's blank mask cracked, and for a bare instant, despair flooded his eyes. He blinked it away. "Then I have no choice. I need to—"

Aaron and Kai whirled on him and shouted, "*No!*"

He recoiled, his mouth tightening.

"You're not leaving," Aaron snapped. "We're not letting them drive you out."

"We'll handle it, Ezra," Kai promised. "Don't rush to jump ship. We'll come up with something."

With a burning glare, Ezra swept past them and into the front hall. The stairs creaked under his footsteps, then a bedroom door opened and closed. I stared after him. Not once had he looked at me—not once since I'd unfolded the police report.

"We'll have to watch him," Aaron told Kai. "He'll try to sneak out tonight, when it's darkest."

Kai nodded. "The Keys will be waiting for him."

Aaron raked his hand through his hair, mixing ash from the burned paper into his red locks. "This is going to be difficult."

"It might be time for Plan C."

My insides went cold. Plan C? Did Kai mean killing the Keys of Solomon team before they could harm Ezra?

Kai noticed the look on my face. "Ready to go home?"

"No!" I exclaimed. "Of course not."

He and Aaron stood there, waiting, but I had no idea what they expected from me. The seconds stretched into a full minute before Aaron spoke.

"Tori, aren't you going to ask?"

"Ask what?"

He waved a hand. "About any of this!"

My mouth hung open. "I … I mean … I thought I wasn't supposed … to …"

I trailed off as Aaron's expression morphed into disbelief—and Kai's tightened with anger.

"She doesn't want to know," Kai told Aaron cuttingly. "Ignorance is bliss, isn't it, Tori?" Stalking to the stairs, he called back, "Aaron, we have work to do."

Aaron sighed. I swallowed hard, my hands twitching as though I could reach out and scoop the three mages back together—as though I could stop the chain reaction the Keys had set in motion.

My eyes stung. "Aaron …"

He gazed at me for a long moment, and I could feel the weight of his assessment. He was evaluating something … evaluating me.

Sighing more heavily, he turned away. "I'll get some cardboard to cover that window."

As he walked out of the living room, I could still feel the weight of his judgment. I didn't know what he had been evaluating me for—tenacity, commitment, competence, how much of a liability I might be?—but I was certain he'd found me lacking.

15

I STOOD IN THE KITCHEN, alone.

Ezra had barricaded himself in his room, probably planning how to give his friends the slip and flee the city. Kai and Aaron were in the midst of their own planning, the nature of which they'd chosen not to share with me. They were huddled in Kai's room, though Aaron had trekked downstairs several times to dig through boxes.

Everything was falling apart.

The house's front window was covered with cardboard and duct tape. I'd peeked through the door a few minutes ago, expecting to see half the Keys guild out there, but the same black van was still parked on the street. Burke and his team were waiting for us to make a move, then they would attack—and I still didn't know *why*.

Ignorance is bliss, isn't it, Tori?

My eyes started burning again and I blinked rapidly. I was ignorant. Willfully, deliberately ignorant. Since my first chilling experience with Ezra's temper, I'd decided I didn't want the truth. I didn't want to know anything that might change how I felt about him.

And now, because of my determination to keep my happy bubble unblemished, I had no idea how to stop this collapse of everything important to me.

Hands braced on the counter, I closed my eyes. I could see it again: Ezra's crimson power, identical to demonic magic. The scars that raked his torso, identical to wounds inflicted by demonic claws. His face in that mugshot, hollow and sickly and scarred.

I'd seen one other photo of young Ezra. Hidden in the bottom drawer of his dresser was a picture of him and a girl, both around fourteen or fifteen. In it, Ezra was happy, healthy—and unscarred.

A year or so after that photo had been taken, Ezra had suffered irreparable damage to his left eye, lost weight and health, and been arrested for theft in Portland.

His arrest, I suspected, was only significant because of the time and place: sixty miles from "Enright" and four months after an "extermination." That mugshot tied Ezra to the Enright extermination—whatever that was.

And that summed up everything I knew or could guess, because I'd made no attempt to learn a single thing about him.

I opened my eyes and pushed away from the counter. Hiding from this had made me weak and useless. No matter how frightening the truth, I couldn't be ignorant any longer. I needed answers—and then maybe, just maybe, I could help fix this before I lost one, two, or all three of my best friends.

First, I needed to get everyone back together and, if possible, in a better mood. I surveyed the kitchen, then rolled up the sleeves of my sweater.

I'd just put the casserole in the oven and was opening the fridge when a shadow darkened the doorway. Ezra stood a step outside the kitchen, his curls rumpled like he'd been running his hands through them in frustration. Had he been wearing those snug, dark-wash jeans before, or had he changed into "run away from home" clothes?

"Hi," I said softly.

His eyes skimmed over me, somehow wary. The despair I'd glimpsed earlier lurked in them and in the unhappy slump to his shoulders.

"I'm making dinner," I informed him. "About to start the salad. Want to help?"

Something in him relaxed, and a faint smile appeared on his lips. "I'm not allowed in the kitchen."

I arched an eyebrow. "Second rule, my dear mage. Second rule."

He chuckled and stepped onto the forbidden tile floor. "You might regret this."

"Pfff. It's just vegetables. How could that go wrong?"

Grinning, I passed him ingredients—lettuce, cucumber, cherry tomatoes, cheese. Kai must've been planning to cook this week. He was the only one of the three bachelors with an even mildly adventurous palate when it came to home cooking. Aaron would live off baked chicken and boiled broccoli if we let him.

Ezra got out a cutting board while I searched the pantry for croutons. When I emerged, our eyes caught and a dart of anxiety made me falter. I'd sworn to stop avoiding the truth, and here was Ezra—the source of all truth. It was just the two of us. The perfect time to ask. *Ezra, what are you?*

Four little words. I could do it.

My mouth opened obediently, but no words came out. As that subdued wariness returned to his gaze, I hurriedly passed him a colander to wash the lettuce, then moved on to chopping vegetables.

I'd cooked in Aaron's kitchen enough times to know my way around—and to know it was too damn small for anything. It was a tight L shape with a dinky island in the middle, nowhere near enough counter space, and about half the square footage required for two people to coexist.

Our first collision came thirty seconds in. Ezra and I bounced off each other, laughing, and I squeezed past him to rinse off the cucumber. He almost clobbered me while reaching for the paper towel. I got out a big bowl, only for him to bang his head on the cupboard door I'd left open. I babbled an apology, but he was grinning in amusement.

My heart lifted. With a bounce in my step, I threw all the ingredients into the bowl. I asked him to pass me the bottle of dressing; he knocked it over, splattering ranch on the counter. We both reached for the dishcloth and collided again.

Laughing too hard to help, I stepped back to let him wipe up the spill. The timer on the oven beeped. He passed me the oven mitts—no mishaps this time—and I pulled out my cheese-and-noodle concoction, the breadcrumb topping perfectly golden brown.

As I set it on the stovetop to cool, Ezra hovered at my shoulder, peering at the bubbling cheese.

"Don't drool on me," I warned as I ensured the casserole dish was sturdily placed.

"Too late."

Yelping, I twisted to look at my shoulder. He laughed—then grabbed the oven mitt out of my hand before I dunked it in the casserole.

"Kidding. I was kidding!" He set the mitt on the counter. "I have my salivation strictly under control, I swear."

Casting him a suspicious squint, I looked around for the little dish of freshly chopped parsley I'd prepared as a garnish. "You should try to sound like you're joking when you make a joke."

"Where's the fun in that?"

Oh, *there* was the parsley. "Can you grab the plates?"

He opened the cupboard and reached up. Humming tunelessly, I grabbed the small dish, turned toward the casserole—and accidentally jabbed my elbow into his taut stomach. The air *pfffed* out of his lungs and he stepped back sharply.

"Sorry!" I exclaimed, whipping toward him and knocking into his arm.

The four plates tumbled out of his grasp. They hit the floor—

—and the room whooshed as I was whisked away.

Ceramic exploded everywhere with an ungodly crash, but I couldn't see it. Ezra had pulled me clear of the spraying shards, and my face was mashed against his chest, his arms around my waist, my toes brushing the floor. My head spun from the sudden movement, and I tried to remember exactly how I'd ended up face to chest with him.

He loosened his arms and I slid down a few inches, my feet settling on the floor. I gawked at him, my eyes wide. His reflexes were insane. They were *impossible*.

"You okay?" he asked worriedly, craning to look around me at my bare feet. "You didn't step on any shards?"

"I didn't have a chance," I said faintly.

He smiled, then pressed his thumb to a spot beside my mouth and swiped it across my cheek. "You have salad dressing on your face. How did you manage that?"

My shock stuttered into something else—a hyper-awareness of his touch on my skin, his hand on my side, our bodies so close. My fingers gripped his t-shirt, fists pressed to his chest, but I didn't remember moving them.

I wanted to say something witty, but my brain had nothing to offer. "Is it gone?"

He peered at one of my cheeks, then the other. "Yeah, you're good. I'm in trouble, though."

"You are?" Damn, I sounded breathless.

"Four plates at once. Aaron is going to extra-ban me from the kitchen."

By all appearances completely unaware that he'd left me flushed and breathless, he shifted his attention to the mess on the floor and started to step away.

My hands tightened on his shirt and the fabric pulled taut between us. He stopped.

I stared into his mismatched eyes, my pulse racing. Soft, dark brown curls tumbled across his forehead, tousled and begging for fingers to tangle in them. His mouth shifted questioningly.

My fists clenched around the gray fabric. "Ezra …"

His brow creased, and my gaze darted between his eyes, so different from each other. One warm, gentle, sparking with quiet humor. The other pale, cold, unnervingly intense. Two eyes, two sides. Part of him was different. Part of him was dangerous.

The question seared my core, and the words tumbled from my mouth.

"Ezra, are you a demon?"

His eyes popped wide. A storm of emotion rippled over his face, then his expression shuttered into a mask of pain and disbelief.

"No." The word came out hoarse, catching in his throat. "*No*, I'm not—how could you even *think*—"

He pushed my arms away, tearing his shirt out of my grasp. He was backing up, shaking his head, his face closing, his emotions shutting down. His searching stare flicked across me, then he spun around, grabbed the back door, and wrenched it open. As he stuffed his feet in his shoes, his other hand snapped out to grab something sitting on the counter beside the exit.

The door swung shut behind him, and I flinched in anticipation of the bang.

The latch clicked quietly, then silence.

I stood there, arms poised at chest height even though I no longer held his shirt in my fists, my lungs locked and throat burning. What had I done?

16

SOMEONE THUDDED DOWN the stairs from the upper floor, and a moment later, Aaron wheeled into the kitchen.

"I heard a crash." He spotted the mess of broken plates. "Oh shit. What hap—"

The high-pitched snarl of an engine—a familiar sound—interrupted him. I heard that sound every time Kai put his motorcycle through its paces. The engine roared, and the noise rapidly diminished as the bike raced away.

Blank confusion bubbled through me. Kai was upstairs. So how was his bike—

Aaron jerked like he'd been shocked. "Where's Ezra?"

Tearing my eyes off the door, I gaped at Aaron. "He—he just—"

Tires squealed from the front of the house, accompanied by the surge of a larger engine. My head snapped around. Aaron charged into the living room, and I stumbled after him as he ripped the cardboard off the window. The curb in front of the house was empty—the Keys' van was gone.

"Kai!" Aaron bellowed. He rushed onto the front landing and pulled on his shoes. "Ezra is gone and the Keys just took off after him!"

Footsteps thundered down the stairs. Kai skidded to a stop at the bottom and almost collided with Aaron.

"What happened?" he yelled furiously as Aaron shot into the living room. "He wasn't planning to sneak out until later! How did he—"

"He took your bike." Aaron snatched his car keys off the coffee table, and I realized that's what Ezra had taken from the counter—Kai's keys. "We gotta move fast. Those bastards are right on his tail."

Kai seized his shoes from the front landing but didn't stop to put them on as he raced after Aaron. They whipped past me, heading for the back door.

Snapping out of my standstill, I bolted to the front landing, grabbed my shoes and purse, and ran after them. They'd already vanished out the back as I leaped over the broken plates. I rammed through the door, stumbled on the porch, then pelted across the yard. The gate was swinging on its hinges.

Headlights bloomed as Aaron's car started. It backed off the gravel pad, tires spitting rocks into the fence. I sprinted after the car, and as it lurched to a stop so Aaron could shift into drive, I yanked the passenger door open and dove inside.

I landed on Kai's lap. He grunted in pain.

"Close the door!" he ordered.

Aaron was already accelerating as I tugged the door shut. Kai pushed me against it so he could get both hands on his phone, the screen glowing as he pulled up an app.

"Which way?" Aaron growled, slowing as he reached the alley's end.

"North. He's heading toward the guild."

Aaron spun the wheel, the force of the turn throwing me into Kai. "He wants to get a weapon before he books it. That gives us a chance to catch up."

I peeked at Kai's screen. On it was a map with a blinking GPS dot.

"You have a tracker on your motorcycle?" I asked him disbelievingly.

He passed me his phone and reached down to awkwardly pull on his shoes. "Tori, what happened?"

My stomach shriveled to the size of a raisin. "I—I asked him …"

"Tori!" Aaron barked commandingly as he shifted gears. The car tore up the road, streetlamps flashing past, and I flinched as he blew through a yellow light.

"I asked him if he's a demon," I whimpered.

Aaron wrenched his eyes off the road to stare at me. "You *what?*"

"I didn't mean it like that!" I blurted desperately. "It came out wrong. I meant to ask if he was *Demonica*, and it just—I said it all wrong."

"Why would you ask him *that?*"

"Why would I not?" I shot back, my own anger sparking. "Ezra is stronger than a human, he's faster, he can make everything go cold and dark. And he has a secret power that looks *exactly like demon magic.*"

Kai snarled like an angry dog—which was a lot scarier when I was sitting on his lap with no escape. "You've ignored everything about him this whole time, but when you finally decide to ask a question—"

"Where is he now?" Aaron interrupted.

Kai took his phone back. "He ... he's stopped. In Oppenheimer Park."

"What? Why?"

"The Keys must've caught him. Ezra knew better than to bolt right under their noses, but he obviously wasn't thinking about anything except getting away."

My heart clogged my throat, choking me.

Aaron cursed and put his foot down. I clutched the door, petrified that I might go through the windshield, but the streets were deserted even though it was only nine o'clock. Why was it so—oh. I sucked in a breath. We were back in the demon zone, which was still on lockdown. We must've passed a barricade while I was freaking out.

On our left, squat apartment buildings with shops on the ground level were abruptly replaced by dark trees and scattered streetlights. Aaron slammed the brakes, took the corner on two wheels, then jumped the curb in front of a bus stop. The wheels spun on grass as the car shot between two trees.

He wasn't the first vehicle to drive into the small park—a black van was stopped just ahead, its headlights illuminating four figures in the center of the grassy square.

The car slid to a stop a few yards from the Keys' van. Aaron flung his door open as I felt for the handle behind my hip. My grasping fingers yanked the latch and the passenger door popped open, dumping me out of the car. Kai leaped over me and sprinted toward the figures.

I shot up. The car was still running, both doors hanging open.

Thirty feet in front of the vehicles, the three Keys stood shoulder to shoulder, facing Ezra. Kai's bike was lying on its side a yard in front of the van's nose, giving me the horrible impression that the Keys had gone for a round of bumper cars with the bike to unseat Ezra.

The aeromage didn't appear injured. He was pacing back and forth six yards away from the Keys, but not like he was frustrated or nervous. His sharp, aggressive movements reminded me of an attack dog pacing at the end of its chain.

As Aaron and Kai ran toward Ezra, Halil turned. His big, ugly sword was drawn, and he swung it upward. A wall of fire leaped off the blade and roared across Aaron and Kai's path. Oh hell. Halil was a pyromage.

Kai jerked to a halt but Aaron charged right through the flames. He burst out the other side, his clothes charred, and slowed to a cautious walk.

"Ezra?" he called, stopping halfway between his friend and the Keys.

Ezra kept pacing, five steps one way, five steps back, his hands bunched into fists and his teeth bared. With no idea what might happen next, I stuffed my feet in my shoes, then shut the passenger door and circled the car to the driver's side. Should I cut the engine?

Burke laughed, the cruel sound carrying easily through the park. "He's got quite the temper, doesn't he? He's *dying* to attack us."

"Then what are you waiting for?" Kai growled at the contractor. He hadn't tried to get past Halil; without a switch, he was at a huge disadvantage against the pyromage.

"And spoil the fun?" Burke replied gleefully. "You have no idea how long I've waited for this. After Enright, we thought there were none left. If he wants to work himself up first, I'm happy to wait."

"Ezra," Aaron tried again.

The aeromage whirled on Aaron, bared teeth glinting in the headlights' glare. "I'm leaving. This time I'm leaving and you can't stop me."

I couldn't breathe. That furious, snarling rasp sounded nothing like the Ezra I knew.

"You're not going anywhere—" Burke began.

"You should have let me leave the first time!" Ezra shouted at Aaron. He pointed at the Keys. "Now I have to kill them! The one thing—I swore I wouldn't—now I have to because you wouldn't let me go!"

Aaron raised his hands placatingly. "Calm down, Ezra, before you—"

"Why?" he growled. "Why calm down? Why stop? I don't want to kill again. Let *him* do it."

"No, Ezra." Urgency tinged Aaron's protest. "No, you can't. You have to stay in—"

"Go ahead," Burke taunted. "Show us, boy. Give us all you've got."

Paleness gleamed around Ezra's feet—the grass had frozen to sparkling white ice in a two-foot radius around him. He pivoted toward the contractor and hissed, "You want to see?"

"*No*, Ezra. You don't have to do this." Aaron stepped toward him. "Trust me—"

Wind erupted from Ezra. The force threw Aaron backward off his feet.

"Stay away," Ezra snarled.

Burke stepped forward instead. "Show us," the old man commanded haughtily. "Show us what you really are."

Ezra lifted his arm and stretched his hand toward the Keys. "If that's what you want, then so be it. It'll be the last thing you see."

"No!" Aaron roared, shoving to his feet.

Red light lit across Ezra's palm, then raced up his arm in snaking veins. Lungs seizing, I jerked forward against the car's open door, but I was too far to stop this—too far and too late to do anything.

My sudden movement caught Ezra's attention. His gaze shot to me, and for an instant, the rage contorting his features splintered into shame.

But red magic was still surging up his arm. He hunched forward, head bowed. Crimson light burst out of his shoulder and solidified into semi-transparent spines. Veins of power climbed up his neck and the side of his face, and two curving crimson horns formed on the left side of his head.

He lunged for Burke.

He was across the distance in scarcely a blink, but Halil was ready. Sword in one hand, he cut in front of his comrade and swung his fist, brass knuckles gleaming. "*Ori amplifico!*"

Ezra caught the blow in his palm—and a concussion of air detonated around the pair, knocking Burke and Fenton back. Whatever Halil's spell had done, it hadn't slowed Ezra down. He held Halil's fist as crimson power lit his hand. It rippled off his fingers and condensed into shadowy crimson claws that curled over Halil's wrist.

"Finally!" Burke crowed, grabbing his infernus. "Finally, *a demon mage!*"

Red power swept over his pendant as he called on his demon, and Fenton grasped his pendant as well.

One thought jammed itself through my shock: I couldn't let the contractors summon their demons.

I had no magic—no artifacts or weapons that could stop them—so I leaped into the running car, jammed the gearshift into first, and dropped the clutch. The car shot forward, open door flapping, and I cranked the wheel toward the men. In perfect unison, the three Keys mythics and Ezra looked at the oncoming vehicle.

When Ezra looked up, my brain froze.

Luminous power laced the side of his face, and his left eye, normally pale as ice, glowed crimson. The demonic red, deep and cold and gleaming with sinister hatred, was identical to the winged demon's magma eyes.

Shock rippled over his face, then he jumped clear—but the Keys mythics, lacking his inhuman reflexes, weren't as fast.

The car hit Burke like a wrecking ball and threw him backward into Fenton. They tumbled across the grass. Their taller champion crashed onto the hood, slid halfway up the windshield, and fell off the side.

Clutching the steering wheel, I realized my foot was planted on the brake pedal, but I didn't remember moving it. Aghast, I gawked at the car's unmoving nose. Holy. Freaking. Shit. Had I just done that?

Halil's pained groan floated through the open car door. Ezra, glowing crimson eye and all, stared at me through the windshield like I was the one who'd sprouted demonic features. Aaron and Kai stood a ways back on either side of the vehicle, equally stunned.

Fenton, who'd been hit by Burke instead of the car, staggered upright. He didn't seem badly hurt; I'd only had thirty feet of slippery grass on which to accelerate and I wasn't sure when I'd hit the brakes.

Eyes bulging with fury, Fenton grasped his infernus. Aaron and Kai leaped toward the car.

"Pop the trunk!" Kai yelled at me.

I flailed at the dash, found the latch, and pulled it. A clunk from behind told me it had worked. In the side mirror, I saw Aaron throw Kai his katana. Ripping the sheath off Sharpie, Aaron ran back toward the nose of the car.

Out the windshield, Fenton's demon had taken form. Burke was on his feet, and his demon was emerging from its infernus, red magic glowing over its extremities. Both demons faced Ezra, who stood alone, lit by his own demonic power.

Aaron and Kai rushed to help him, but they were behind the demons, their contractors, and Halil. The contractors' champion turned to cut off the mages, fire rippling over his sword and his brass knuckles gleaming. Ezra would have to fight two demons all on his own.

Laughing, Burke pointed imperiously at Ezra. "Now, demon mage, let's see what you can *really* do."

Ezra tensed, his left eye flaring with crimson light. Barehanded, he waited for the attack. The two demons crouched, preparing to leap.

The air thudded with a rhythmic beat scarcely audible over the car's rumbling engine. Ezra's head snapped back, his terrifying stare scouring the dark sky. Burke and Fenton looked up too.

A shape dropped out of the darkness and slammed into the ground beside Ezra. Rising to its full height, two horns missing from its head, the demon spread its curved wings and turned its glowing magma eyes on the Keys contractors.

17

THE WINGED DEMON had returned.

It stood beside Ezra, glaring hatefully at the Keys men and their pet demons. Ezra's eyes, the left one lava red, were wide with shock as he faced the beast beside him.

Aaron and Kai stood frozen, seemingly unable to react. The Keys didn't know what to do either. The demon was standing beside Ezra. Not facing him. Not attacking him. *Beside* him. As though …

As though the demon and Ezra were not enemies, but allies.

But the demon had attacked Ezra twice now. It had wounded him, almost killed him. It wanted to rip him apart.

The demon turned to Ezra. "*Kah kirritavh'athē hh'ainunthēs tempisissā?*"

Its harsh language filled the night, and I remembered: during both their encounters, the demon had spoken to Ezra. But he had attacked the demon without responding.

He lurched backward, his face contorted with disgust as though he couldn't bear to hear the demon's hoarse, growling voice. A malevolent smile twisted the demon's lips, and with its good hand—the other damaged by Ezra in their last confrontation—the demon hooked a clawed finger through the long chain around its neck.

The beast lifted the chain. Hanging from it was a round piece of dark metal—an amulet. The demon held it toward Ezra. An offer.

Ezra looked at the amulet in confusion.

His glowing left eye blazed—and he went rigid. Arching like he'd been skewered on an invisible spear, he gasped. The red veins on his arm writhed and brightened. Then his warm brown eye, wide with panic, flashed to deep, burning red. He lurched back onto his heels, the sudden tension leaving him.

Both eyes glowing like magma, he reached for the offered amulet.

"No!" Aaron shouted.

The instant before Ezra's red-veined fingers touched the dark metal, Aaron tackled him around the middle.

They slammed into the ground. Ezra's crimson claws flashed, barely missing Aaron's throat. Kai burst past the Keys and raced for his friends. With a roar, the winged beast surged toward them too.

Fenton's tall, scaly demon leaped onto the winged demon's back. The winged beast whipped in a violent circle, throwing the Keys demon off, then pounced on its fallen opponent. It ripped its talons across Fenton's demon, slicing easily through its protective scales. The Keys demon made no sound, but its eyes bulged in agony.

A few yards past the battling demons, Aaron broke away from Ezra and rolled clear. Tossing his katana aside, Kai jumped on top of Ezra, slammed his palms down on Ezra's chest—and unleashed a bolt of lightning into his friend.

Ezra convulsed, crackling electricity racing across his body. My heart stopped, and my hands gripped the car's steering wheel so hard it hurt. I couldn't move, couldn't breathe, as Ezra thrashed and jerked under the onslaught. It went on and on, and Ezra was dying, surely he was dying, Kai was killing him—

Kai lifted his hands. Ezra slumped onto the grass, motionless, smoke rising off his clothes. No crimson power glowed over his hands or face.

As I panted for air, I realized Kai's attack had only lasted seconds, though it had felt like so much longer.

A bloodcurdling laugh snatched my attention away from the mages. The winged demon still had Fenton's demon on the ground. In a silent charge, the shorter, heavier Keys demon bowled into the winged beast. The winged demon lurched around and swung the bone-crushing plate on the end of its tail like a mace.

Aaron and Kai grabbed Ezra by the arms and dragged him away from the battle. Getting a better grip, Aaron heaved the limp aeromage over his shoulder and skirted the demons, heading toward the car.

I leaped out of the driver's seat and rushed to the passenger door. I folded the seat down just as Aaron reached me.

Fenton yelled in furious dismay. Aaron, Kai, and I looked over.

Fenton's demon was on the ground in a puddle of gleaming blood, and Burke's demon was locked claw to claw with the winged beast. Clustered dangerously close were the Keys mythics. Halil stood protectively in front of the contractors with his sword in hand.

"Get up!" the younger contractor yelled at his demon. "Get up, *get up!*"

The creature stirred weakly, then slowly pulled its torn limbs under it. Holy shit, it was still alive? *How?*

The other two demons pushed into each other, fighting for dominance—and the stronger adversary was obvious. Burke's demon slid backward, its clawed toes scoring the damp grass.

Aaron shoved Ezra into the backseat, urgency sharpening his movements—and I knew why. The Keys were losing, and once they were defeated, that demon was coming for us.

As Kai raced to his motorcycle, I fumbled to straighten the seat so I could get in. Useless coupe! We needed a van like the Keys had.

Aaron pushed me aside and pulled the lever with steady hands. The seat snapped upright. When had I started shaking so badly?

Leaning into Burke's demon, the winged beast laughed again. A circle of crimson light erupted around its feet. The magic rippled out, and runes appeared among the spreading lines—a sorcery-like spell taking form in seconds. Power rose off the markings, singeing the air.

"Demon magic!" Halil yelled. "Get back!"

The Keys scuttled frantically in retreat. Burke's demon jerked away, but the winged demon held onto its hands, talons piercing flesh as the crimson magic built to a horrific crescendo. I clutched the car door—we were too close, the car was too close, there was no time to get away—

A dart of movement in the night.

Someone flashed between Aaron's car and the Keys' van. Dashing straight for the winged demon and its spell, the stranger spun around in mid-step and landed in a backward skid as he dragged his hand across the crimson spell.

The glowing circle tore, the lines and runes breaking apart. The magic shuddered, then burst like a shattering damn. Red power exploded outward.

The concussion threw me back into Aaron, who hit the car's side panel. Kai ducked behind his bike as dirt showered him, and Burke's demon was hurled to the ground. The winged beast roared furiously, battered by its own failed casting.

The new arrival had sprung nimbly away, dodging to safety as though the detonation had been moving in slow motion. Illuminated by the car's headlights, he paused in a ready crouch, waiting.

It was a demon. A *fourth* demon.

It was the smallest one yet—shorter than Kai and barely taller than *me*. Its build was lean, but defined muscles warned of strength. If not for its reddish toffee skin and long thin tail, I might have mistaken it for a human.

Before I could see more than that, it—he?—leaped into motion again. He shot past the winged demon, and the beast spun clumsily. The new demon ducked, pivoted, and rocketed past the winged demon again—and blood sprayed in his wake. The winged beast shrieked. The new one whirled and sprang. He landed lithely on the winged demon's back, his claws flashing, then he leaped away.

Fast. So fast. The winged demon had seemed impossibly swift and agile, but this opponent was leaving it in the dust.

More blood spilled from gaping wounds torn in the winged demon's back by the new demon's claws. Roaring, the winged beast grabbed for its attacker and completely missed. Thin tail lashing, he darted under the swing, cut behind the larger beast, and grabbed the back of its leg just above the bulging calf muscle. He ripped his claws out again.

A pained screech. More blood. The winged demon dropped to one knee.

The agile demon struck three times so rapidly his movements were a blur—tearing strikes into the winged beast's back. It screamed again, lurched onto its feet, and sprang into the air with its wings beating frantically.

Head tilting back, red eyes glowing, the new demon watched his adversary flee as though considering his options. Then he braced his feet, coiled his body, and leaped.

He might look human-ish, but no human could jump that high.

He slammed into the winged demon in midair and they plunged back to earth—right toward me and Aaron. We scrambled backward as the demons crashed feet from the open car door. Heel catching on a clump of grass, I stumbled and fell on my butt.

That moment of klutziness might have cost me my life, but it didn't matter. The battle was over.

The only movement came from the winged one's head—namely, its head rolling across the grass and coming to a stop at my feet. Its eyes were dark and empty, and gooey icky stuff leaked from the stump of its neck. My stomach attempted to abandon ship.

The new demon crouched over the head he had ripped off—putting him about a foot away from me. His red eyes stared into mine with narrow, vertical pupils. His features were disturbingly human, and terror burst through me, weakening my joints and shaking my hands. I gasped in a shallow breath.

For an instant so brief I might have imagined it, a grin flashed across the demon's face, pointed canines bared in delighted savagery.

Then he rose to his feet, his expression a vacant mask with zero animation. Turning woodenly, the demon walked past the winged corpse. The Keys contractors watched him—no, *it* amble past them, heading toward …

I peered into the darkness.

… toward a short human silhouette standing between two trees at the park's edge. The contractor. Stepping into the glow of the vehicles' headlights, the newcomer waited for his demon.

Er, actually … *her* demon.

If I'd had a chance to think about what sort of badass contractor commanded that demon, I would've pictured someone like Alistair—older and experienced, tough as old leather, all casual confidence and unshakable attitude. Someone who matched the insane lethality of a demon that could tear the winged beast down without getting so much as a scratch.

But this super-killer demon's master was nothing like Alistair. The contractor was a *girl*.

Like … a *girly* girl.

Short, waif-like, her brunette hair cut in a shoulder-length bob, dark-rimmed librarian-esque glasses perched on her nose. Her tough-as-shit contractor outfit consisted of skinny jeans with a pink flower embroidered on one hip, a white tank top, and a purple zip-up sweater, half undone to reveal the infernus pendant resting just below her slim chest.

The demon walked sedately to her and stopped. It was only a couple of inches taller than me, but it towered over her. She barely cleared its shoulder, putting her at, what, five feet? Maybe five foot two?

Not that short people can't be tough. It was just, you know, she looked as threatening as a librarian's assistant. Not even the librarian. An assistant.

She stared first at the Keys, who stood in a cluster with Burke's demon guarding them; Fenton's demon still hadn't gotten up. Then she looked at us—me sitting on the ground, Aaron standing close by, and Kai holding his bike. Ezra, unconscious in the back seat, was hidden from view.

Then she glanced at the lovely demon corpse oozing gore all over the grass in front of my toes.

After a long moment where no one said anything, she twitched her shoulders in a slight, awkward shrug, then slipped her hand into her pocket. She pulled out a phone, and we all watched her dial a number and lift it to her ear.

"Um, hello," she said into the phone, her light alto voice less than confident. "Yes, um … this is Robin Page, from the Grand Grimoire. I'd like to report the unbound demon, please."

I blinked. *Please?*

"Yes … um. It's in Oppenheimer Park. Mm-hmm. Uh … no, the demon is dead." She pushed her glasses up her nose, her demon standing motionless at her side. "Yes, I'm sure. It's definitely dead."

The girl listened for a moment. "Okay, I'll wait here. How long will MagiPol take to arrive?"

At those words, the Keys jolted into motion. Both their demons dissolved into red light, and with their pendants still sucking in the power, they strode for their van. Burke's deep-set eyes dropped to mine and he smirked evilly.

I knew exactly what that smile meant: *This isn't over.*

They piled into their van, the engine started, and the vehicle peeled away, tires skidding on the grass. The van's nose barely missed the back of Kai's bike.

Something cold touched my leg and I started. The pool of thick demon blood under the dismembered head was soaking into my pant leg. I yanked my feet away—and glimpsed a shiny object amidst the bloody grass.

"Aaron," Kai said in a low voice. He swung his leg over his bike. "We need to go. We don't want to be here when the MPD arrives."

As Aaron muttered his agreement, I dipped my fingers into the lukewarm puddle of thickening blood. *Yeeeuch.* Teeth gritted, I pulled the small metal object out and peeked at it. It was the round amulet the demon had offered to Ezra, separated from its host when the demon's head had parted ways with its body.

Aaron stepped in front of me, and I quickly shoved the slimy pendant into my pocket. Taking his offered hand, I let him pull me up, then I jumped into the car. He shut my door and jogged around to the driver's side. Kai's bike started with a snarl.

Through the windshield, I watched the young woman. She made no move to stop us or even call out as Aaron dropped into his seat, slammed the door, and shifted the running car into reverse.

As he backed off the grass toward the street, Kai following on his motorcycle, my gaze shifted to the creature beside her. Its eyes glowed faintly, then the car turned. As the headlights shifted away, darkness swept over the girl and her demon.

18

THE DRIVE BACK was eerily quiet. I sat in the passenger seat, afraid to look anywhere but through the windshield. A few times I peeked at Aaron. His expression was the bleakest I'd ever seen it.

When he drove straight through an intersection instead of turning to go home, I broke the silence. "Where are we going?"

"Your place," he replied roughly. "The Keys might go to my house."

"Oh," I whispered.

We didn't speak again until Aaron had parked at the curb in front of my shabby bungalow. The headlamp of Kai's bike glared through the back window as he parked behind us.

Aaron threw his door open, jumped out, then folded his seat down.

"Hey," he said softly.

I twisted to look behind me, surprised to see Ezra sitting up on the back seat. I hadn't realized he was awake.

Aaron helped him climb out. Ezra moved stiffly, like he was hurting in every muscle and bone—which he probably was, considering what Kai had done to him. Gulping, I slid out of the car and grabbed my purse from under the seat. As Kai joined us, I led the way through the yard.

I unlocked the exterior door, then the door to my apartment. Stepping aside, I let the guys go in first. Not one of them looked at me as they passed.

After locking both doors, I followed them down. Aaron helped Ezra limp into my bedroom, and Kai went in with them. They murmured, their voices too low for me to make out any words. I stared around my apartment like I was seeing it for the first time—my sofa with a new coffee table in front of it, an equally new small flat-screen TV, and two metal stools at the breakfast bar. The crawlspace door, recently replaced, was closed, and I didn't expect Twiggy to make an appearance. He always hid whenever Ezra was nearby.

I'd wondered why, but I'd never asked. I hadn't wanted to know.

Kai and Aaron exited my room and closed the door, leaving Ezra inside. Silently, they walked to the sofa and sank into identical poses—hunched forward, elbows on knees, chins braced on their hands, shoulders slumped. Grim defeat rolled off them as they stared at the floor.

"We should've listened to him," Aaron finally said, his voice hoarse. "He wanted to leave."

Kai exhaled slowly. "I doubt Burke would've given up even if we'd made a run for it on Halloween. You heard him—he's been waiting for this. Searching for one ..."

My throat tightened as Burke's triumphant cry echoed in my head. *Finally, a demon mage!*

I'd heard the term only once before. Alistair, the guild's toughest mage and top combat mythic, had described a demon mage as the "ultimate opponent." None of the Crow and Hammer's other combat mythics had ever faced one.

"What we should have done," Aaron muttered bitterly, "was gotten Ezra out of the city the moment the alert went out."

Kai grunted in agreement.

I slunk to the sofa and stopped beside it, my heart contorting with each beat. "Guys?"

Kai straightened out of his slouch. "Sorry, Tori. We won't stay long."

"Huh?" I mumbled.

"Once Ezra recovers more, we'll get out of here."

"Get out of … where are you going?" When neither mage answered, my chest tightened with the beginnings of panic. "What are you planning?"

"It doesn't matter," Kai said.

"Of course it matters!" My voice went shrill, volume rising. "Tell me what's going on!"

"You don't need to know."

Aaron twitched his head in a faint shake. "A little late for that, don't you think, Kai?"

"No," he replied coolly. "Not yet."

My hands balled into fists. "Don't you *dare* cut me out. I want to know—"

Kai shoved to his feet, his dark eyes blazing. "You *don't* want to know!"

My voice dried up, his sudden anger stealing my protest. Kai almost never shouted—but he was damn close to it now.

"You've *never* wanted to know, Tori. You'd rather pretend everything is fine and normal and *easy*. You're the queen of delusion, an ostrich with your head in the sand, and that's how you like it."

His sharp words hit me like physical blows. Aaron glanced up at us, then looked away, his face pained.

"You had every chance to face this, and you chose not to. So, no," Kai concluded tersely, "we *won't* tell you anything."

Angry denials built on my tongue, but I couldn't speak them. I'd had dozens of opportunities to get answers, but I'd never tried. I could've asked Twiggy why he was terrified of Ezra. I could've asked Zak what he knew. I could've asked Alistair what a demon mage was.

But I hadn't, because I was too scared of the truth. I didn't want to know, because once I knew … everything would change.

"You two have done everything you could to hide the truth about Ezra from me," I said, fighting to keep my voice level. "You didn't want me asking questions."

"I'm not saying it's a bad thing that you didn't," Kai replied. "I'm saying there's no reason to change that now. You don't *want* to know, so you don't *need* to know."

"Tori," Aaron said, getting to his feet too. "We've pulled you into a lot of messes over the past several months, but you always had the option to walk away. Even now, you can transfer to a sleeper guild and go back to living a human life if you want."

"I don't want to—"

"I know, Tori. I know. My point is you have the option, and we're not taking that away from you." He rubbed a hand over his lower face. "You've stuck with us, but you can't anymore. You need to take care of yourself and your future. That means"—pain darkened his eyes—"this is where we go our separate ways."

A bolt of panic ruptured my chest. I gasped in a breath, staring from him to Kai.

They were ditching me. *That's* what he and Kai were saying. I didn't need answers about Ezra because they were leaving me.

Deep-rooted pain, embedded by every excruciating rejection from my past, flared through my core. My eyes burned and I tried to summon anger instead, but it wouldn't come.

My jaw clenched. I glared at them through blurred vision, fighting the tears. "Tell me the truth."

"Tori—"

"*Tell me!*"

Kai was right. I was good at ignoring unpleasant realities. It was a skill I'd learned in my childhood: pretending everything was fine even though my father was an abusive drunk; pretending I was okay after my mother had abandoned me; pretending I could handle it when Justin ran away, leaving me alone with my father for six terrible years.

I was *so* good at pretending that I'd rented an apartment even when, deep down, I'd been expecting to lose my job at the guild any day.

Denial was my coping mechanism, but that wouldn't work anymore. I'd done too much damage by pretending everything was a happy fairytale with no bad monsters ... or demon mages.

Now, I needed to understand. If I didn't understand, then I couldn't stop them from abandoning me.

Aaron and Kai said nothing. Then—

"Tell her."

My head snapped up. Ezra stood in the open bedroom doorway. His arms hung at his sides, his shoulders were bent with pain and exhaustion, and his eyes were dull.

"Tell her," he repeated. "She deserves to know."

He disappeared back into the bedroom. The door closed with a soft thump.

Aaron and Kai hesitated, then Aaron sank onto the sofa. He grasped Kai's wrist and tugged him down too. I perched on the coffee table facing them. The two mages were silent again, but this time, they appeared to be gathering their thoughts.

"In the Demonica class," Aaron began, choosing his words carefully, "summoners and contractors are the two legal orders. But those aren't the *only* orders. Ezra belongs to a third order, an illegal one."

I nervously licked my lips. "He's a ... demon mage?"

He nodded.

"So, Ezra is a di-mythic? Elementaria and Demonica?"

"Not precisely. He wasn't born a demon mage." Aaron drew in a deep breath. "The MPD regulates as much magic as they can, and they have to decide what can be controlled and what has no place in a civilized society. Certain branches of magic are forbidden, and some types of magic-users are forbidden to exist."

Kai pressed his fist into his opposite palm. "Vampires, for example. They don't fit into human society, so we exterminate them whenever we find them."

Words in red pen, scrawled on the police report. *4 months after extermination.*

"Demon mages are the same," Aaron continued. "They're too dangerous to coexist with other mythics, let alone humans. It's an automatic death sentence." His jaw flexed. "Demon mages are so rare and deadly that, to hunters like the Keys, killing one is the ultimate trophy."

I clasped my hands to hide their trembling. "What *is* a demon mage?"

Aaron opened his mouth but couldn't summon the words. His gaze dropped, his expression tight.

"In regular Demonica contracting," Kai explained grimly, "the demon's spirit is housed inside an infernus. With a demon mage, the contractor himself is the infernus."

My entire body tensed. "You mean …"

"Ezra carries a demon inside him."

My limbs shuddered, shaking me from head to toe. A demon … *inside* him. "Is it … permanent?"

"Like all demon contracts, it's irreversible. It'll only end when he dies."

My chest hurt. I rubbed my eyes, denying the stinging tears.

"There are other differences between demon mages and contractors," Kai went on, sounding businesslike except for the slight hoarseness of his voice. "Ezra can't call his demon out. It's bound inside his body."

"And," Aaron added heavily, "Ezra's demon, unlike a contracted demon, isn't powerless. It has its own will—which you saw tonight when it overpowered Ezra to take that amulet."

The vision of Ezra going rigid, of glowing crimson swamping his warm brown eye, flashed through me. The amulet in my pocket pressed against my leg. No one had seen me take it.

I looked at Kai. "So that's why you … you …"

He nodded, and a pained grimace ghosted over his features. "I had to hit him hard. If Ezra had lost consciousness but the demon hadn't …"

Uneasy quiet settled over us.

"The more angry or upset Ezra gets, the more vulnerable he is to the demon's influence." Aaron braced his arms on his knees. "It's one reason demon mages are so dangerous compared to contractors."

I gripped my thighs, fingers digging in. "What are the other reasons?"

"You saw that already. Ezra has full access to his demon's magic. His power is on par with an unbound demon's."

Whereas a contracted demon, devoid of its own willpower, had little to no magic.

"It's why they're called demon *mages*," Kai revealed bleakly. "They wield magic like a mage. Ezra being an aeromage is a lucky coincidence."

"Lucky how?"

"He can blend in with other mythics without raising too much suspicion, since he has magic independent of his demon's."

I nodded, feeling sick. Questions should have been racing through my mind, but only a shocked buzzing filled my head.

Ezra was a demon mage. He had a death sentence on his head. He had a demon *inside him*. All those times his face had gone blank, I'd thought he was restraining his temper … but he'd been resisting *his demon*.

"Does Ezra even *have* a bad temper?" I blurted.

Aaron smiled weakly. "He's the most laid-back guy I know."

It made so much sense. I'd never understood how Ezra could give off such calming vibes while battling an anger management problem.

"Did he ..." I hesitated. "He had to have chosen this, right? Contractors are made, not born, so a demon mage ... Ezra must've chosen it."

Aaron pressed his lips together. "That's something you'll have to ask him."

My eyes darted to my bedroom door and back. With a shuddering breath, I attempted to pull myself together. "All right. Ezra is a—a demon mage. You two have been hiding it, but now the Keys know. What's the plan?"

Aaron and Kai exchanged another long, meaningful look. I watched anxiously, my hands twisting in my lap.

Finally, Kai regarded me. "Burke wants all the glory of killing Ezra for his team, so I doubt he's told anyone else or reported his discovery to the MPD—yet." His expression flattened. "I would prefer to kill the three of them now, before they can—"

"*But*," Aaron cut in sternly, "Ezra won't agree to it. He already told us what he wants to do."

Kai gave a slow nod. "Yes, I know. We planned for this eventuality."

"Is everything ready?"

"It'd be better if we could stop at the house first, but the Keys will be watching it. We'll have to make do with—"

"You're running away," I whispered.

They looked at me, Kai's dark eyes unreadable, Aaron's tight with unhappiness.

"We have no choice, Tori," Aaron murmured. "Once it gets out what Ezra is, me and Kai will be branded as rogues.

Harboring a demon mage is illegal. We'll face the most severe punishments the MPD can give."

My mouth went dry. I tried to swallow but couldn't.

"*You're* fine," he added reassuringly. "You didn't know long enough to get more than a slap on the wrist."

"Like I said, Tori," Kai told me, "we won't be here long. We need to make it out of the city before the Keys can organize a chase."

"But—but—" My gaze darted desperately between them. "There must be another way. There must be … something."

They didn't reply, their silence my answer. There was nothing else they could do. The Keys team knew. If Ezra stayed, they would attack him again, but as soon as he fled, they would reveal him to the mythic world. The entire Keys of Solomon guild would hunt him, as would every other guild equipped to hunt demons.

I thought of the MPD alert about the unbound demon. Would they send an alert about the illegal demon mage in their midst? Would thirty teams of combat mythics set out to hunt Ezra down? Izzah and Mario from Odin's Eye, that Robin girl and her freaky demon from the Grand Grimoire, even Crow and Hammer members?

Panic squeezed my lungs. I pushed off the coffee table with trembling hands.

"Bathroom," I mumbled, hurrying past the guys. I ducked into my small bathroom and locked the door, then grasped the sink's edge and allowed myself to hyperventilate for a solid two minutes.

This was it. This was the end. Aaron and Kai were planning to take Ezra and flee, to drop off the map and disappear forever.

How could I have ignored this for so long? I'd known Ezra's secrets were dangerous, but I'd never imagined something like this. The queen of delusion, Kai had called me.

Gazing at my reflection, I saw shadows of my younger self. She'd learned to fake normalcy to survive. She'd pretended everything was fine until it stymied her ability to act. When you refused to acknowledge that anything was wrong, you couldn't fix it.

I was done being that girl.

Scrubbing my hands over my face, I pushed away from the counter and slipped out of the bathroom. I marched purposefully to my bedroom. Aaron and Kai's low conversation broke off, but neither called out to stop me.

I faced the closed door. Deep breaths. I rapped lightly on the wood, then opened the door without waiting for an answer.

Ezra sat on the floor, his back against my bed and knees drawn up. Surprise flickered over his features at my appearance. As I stepped into the room, I saw both parts of him for the first time.

The Ezra I knew best: soft-spoken, with that straight-faced humor that could catch me off guard, even when I was expecting it. His calm compassion, his unjudging acceptance, his gentle smile that had won me over the moment I met him.

But now I understood his other side. The crushing strength, the enhanced reflexes. The flashes of anger, of power, of violence. The cold and the darkness. The savagery that slept inside him.

It was a demon chained inside his body and bound to his soul.

His gaze dropped away from mine. "I'm sorry."

"Sorry for what?"

"For everything." He didn't look up. "Hiding it from you. Involving you. Putting you in danger. Lying to you."

"You never lied to me."

"When you asked if I was a demon … I denied it."

My hands tightened into fists. Inside him was a beast like the winged demon, its spirit imbued with bloodthirsty brutality. How often did it look out of his eyes? Could it see me right now through his pale, blind iris?

Fear trickled through me, gaining strength and chilling my limbs. I wanted to move, but I didn't know in which direction—toward him or away? I felt chained to the spot, unable to—

Chained. An image of Sabrina's tarot card rose in my mind: the Devil, its illustration showing a man and a woman in the beast's chains. Those two helpless figures … Ezra and me.

Another card flashed in my mind's eye: a regal woman holding scales and a sword. Justice. Judgment. A choice.

Then a final vision: the heart pierced by three swords. Loss and heartbreak. My three mages, leaving me forever.

But I had a choice.

That had been the cards' message. I could change this. I had the power to alter my fate—*our* fate.

"You're not a demon." The words came out flat but ferocious. No doubt or hesitation touched my voice.

Ezra's dull gaze flicked up. "I'm the next closest thing to—"

"*You're not a demon.*"

I closed the short distance between us, and every line of his body tensed in anticipation of my rejection and revulsion. I towered over him for a moment, then sank to my knees. We stared at each other. Confusion and something like dread rose in his eyes.

"Ezra …" My voice went husky with emotion. "Would you like a hug?"

He sat in rigid silence, hesitating, uncertain. The seconds stretched out, an echo of the awkwardness from that first time hanging between us. How many embraces had we shared since then? Some casual, some heartfelt, some more intimate than I'd ever allowed myself to acknowledge.

Tentatively, he lifted a hand toward me.

With no more than that, I was in his arms—squeezing between his knees to press against his chest, burrowing my face into his shoulder, clinging tightly. My arms were clamped around his neck, fists gripping his shirt.

His hands touched my sides, then slid around to my back. He took an unsteady breath, his chest lifting under me, and his fingers closed around my sweater. His arms tightened, crushing but gentle, strength that could break my bones.

I don't know how long we stayed like that before I spoke.

"Let me guess," I said into his shoulder, gently exasperated. "You figured I'd never want to look at you again now that I know."

He made a quiet noise, like he'd started to speak before cutting himself off.

I pushed back to look at him, my hands on his shoulders, his at my waist. He stared up at me like he couldn't believe I hadn't run away screaming.

"Ezra, please." I shook my head. "Do you really think I'd up and abandon you? You already know how stubborn I am."

He blinked, an anxious crease between his brows. "You're stubborn? I hadn't noticed."

On the last word, his mouth pulled into an unintentional smile—the first time his deadpan delivery had failed him. A laugh bubbled in my throat—and a hot flutter ignited in my core. Suddenly, I was acutely aware of how close he was, his face tilted up to mine. My heart gave a weightless lurch.

But his humor was slipping away as despair crept back in. "Tori …"

"Nope," I interrupted. "Don't say it."

"Say what?"

"Whatever heartbreaking farewell you were about to start on there. It isn't necessary."

His eyebrows pinched together, his hands still gripping my shirt tightly. Before he could try again, I tapped a finger against his lips, causing them to part in surprise.

"Not necessary, because I've already made my decision." The Justice card flickered through my mind once more, but I focused on Ezra's mismatched eyes, fully aware that my next words would trigger a fierce battle of wills—a battle I had no intention of losing.

"I know you're leaving, and I'm coming with you."

19

KAI SHOUTED AT ME. Aaron shouted at me. Even Ezra shouted at me—frosting the walls in the process—until Kai banished him into the bedroom to calm down.

They could yell all night about how I was throwing my life away, how I had my whole future ahead of me, how I was perfectly capable of living without them, how I couldn't abandon my brother, how I had no idea what permanent exile entailed, and so on, but it wouldn't change my mind.

They were *not* leaving me behind, and if they tried, I would follow them. *How* I would follow them, I didn't know, but they seemed alarmed at the prospect of what trouble I might get into while trying.

Even then, they were still debating how best to ditch me when Kai had a sudden realization—the Keys knew I was close to them. If they left me behind, the Keys might target me in the hopes I would know where Ezra had fled.

So, with the three mages in varying states of furious disapproval, Aaron, Ezra, and I loaded into the car. Kai would follow us on his motorcycle. I'd packed a single duffle bag of essentials, while the guys would have to rely on the spare clothes and weapons Aaron always carried in his trunk.

As the car pulled away, I watched my dark, sad bungalow disappear behind us. My stomach twisted with nauseating anxiety, but I ignored it. My decision was made. I'd never been the type of person to plan far into the future, and all the potential the guys thought I was losing forever—I had no plans for it. My dream of running my own business was a means to an end, a way to support myself in the least painful way possible. I wasn't particularly passionate about school or entrepreneurship or any of it.

What I was passionate about was my job at the guild—and without the guys, that would be empty too. I'd rather take my chances on the road.

I watched the city lights pass as we drove, Kai's black bike and dark helmet occasionally appearing in the side mirror. Inside the car, Aaron focused on driving while Ezra sat mutely behind me. He was taking my presence the hardest, blaming himself. They were so gloomy that I considered waking Hoshi for company, but she was currently tucked in my purse, fast asleep.

Soon, the city was behind us and we were driving down a treed corridor lit only by the car's high beams. Somewhere on our left was the Burrard Inlet, and in a few more minutes, we would join the Sea to Sky Highway—a beautiful stretch of coastal roadway with breathtaking views of the island-dotted Howe Sound. Not that we'd get to enjoy it in the dark.

"Where are we headed?" I asked conversationally.

"North," Aaron replied in a distinctly unhelpful tone.

"I know that. It's either turn north or drive into the ocean." I cast him a pointed look. "Are you going to sulk all night? That'll make for an awfully long drive."

"It'll be a long drive anyway," he retorted, but his mouth quirked in a half-hearted smile. "We're going *really* north. The Yukon or maybe Alaska."

"I've always wanted to see Alaska."

"This isn't a vacation," Ezra said from his spot behind me, a bitter edge in his smooth voice. "We're fugitives, not tourists. I've done this before, and there's nothing pleasant about it."

"Kai and I have prepared for this," Aaron cut in, glancing in the rearview mirror at Ezra. "We have money set aside in untraceable bank accounts, travel routes and safe houses mapped out, all that kind of stuff. It won't be like last time, when you were on your own with nothing."

His last words chilled me, and I remembered Ezra's sunken cheeks and hollow eyes from his mugshot. No wonder he sounded bitter.

"How much money?" I asked cautiously, thinking of my near-empty account. "Is it enough for me too? Am I screwing up your plans?"

"It's more than enough. It's all from my trust fund." Aaron made an amused sound. "My parents think I invested it, but I'm sure they'd be pleased either way that I'm finally using it."

Aaron had dipped into his trust fund? The only other time he'd touched it that I knew of was to buy his house. I was beginning to grasp how painstakingly he and Kai had planned for this contingency.

"Your parents would be less pleased to realize they won't get to see you for the next few years," Ezra muttered darkly.

"Few years?" I repeated, my brow furrowing. "Aren't we going into hiding permanently?"

Silence. Neither guy answered, and I frowned at Aaron. He kept his eyes on the road.

"We'll have to change vehicles within a couple of days," he said after a minute, giving the dash of his beloved car a glum look. "Kai might want to keep his bike, but it won't be very practical up north. Maybe we'll get an SUV. It'll be better suited for mountain terrain."

Deciding to question Aaron on the "few years" thing later, I suggested, "How about a pickup truck?"

Aaron hummed thoughtfully. "A large pickup truck isn't a bad idea. Kai could strap his motorcycle in the back when he doesn't want to ride it."

We discussed vehicle options for a couple of miles, and Ezra eventually joined in, his tone relaxing into something more natural. Every few minutes, I checked for Kai's headlight behind us. Only a few other vehicles passed in the opposite direction, heading toward the city.

My eyelids grew heavy. As Aaron and Ezra's conversation meandered from vehicles to travel routes, I pillowed my head on my arm and let their voices and the rumble of the car lull me to sleep.

"What the hell?"

Aaron's angry exclamation jolted me awake. I sat up, squinting blearily. The wipers swept across the windshield, erasing a half-hearted sprinkle of raindrops, and everything outside the car was still dark. It didn't feel like I'd been asleep for long.

"What's wrong?" I mumbled.

"The car behind me won't pass." Aaron muttered a curse. "We're the only ones out here, and that asshole can't find another patch of road to drive on. His headlights are driving me crazy."

Unease crawled through my innards and I leaned forward to peek in the side mirror. Kai's headlight flashed, close on Aaron's tail, and behind him was another set of headlights. Too large and high up to belong to a van, they shone brightly in Aaron's mirrors. I relaxed again.

"Some drivers get weird at night," Ezra said, "especially in poor weather. They want to follow someone."

"Asshole," Aaron repeated grumpily. "Whatever. I want to stop in Squamish anyway. Get some fast-food burgers or something."

"Do you think anything will be open?"

"Here's hoping there's an all-night McD's."

A canvas of sparkling lights gleamed up ahead—the town of Squamish, which put us an hour into our drive. I must've slept thirty minutes at most. Aaron slowed, complaining again when the clingy driver failed to pass him. The rain was picking up.

"Is this the turn?" he muttered, flipping on his signal as a darkened shopping center came into view. "I haven't been here in years."

He made a quick left, Kai's bike following. The clingy driver continued down the highway, and I glimpsed the big-ass SUV. Definitely not a van.

"This isn't right," Aaron sighed. "What street are we on?"

The monster shopping center sprawled across endless blocks, the parking lot lights shining on the wet pavement. Aaron turned right, and up ahead, the road diverged in a Yintersection. Muttering some more, he hesitated, then cut left toward a liquor store.

"I think you were supposed to go right," Ezra remarked as we sped past a long-closed grocery mart and straight into a residential block.

Aaron swore. "I'll take the next right and backtrack."

We passed a few dozen houses, then trees closed in. The streetlights ended, plunging the road into darkness, and the rain was gaining force. Aaron sped up the windshield wipers and switched his high beams back on. The slick road stretched onward, but there were no right-hand turns. Instead, train tracks raced alongside the pavement.

Biting back another curse, Aaron let off on the gas. "Should I turn around?"

I pulled my phone out of my jacket pocket—my old jacket, because Burke's demon had shredded my fancy new combat one—but when I pressed the power button, nothing happened. Right. It had died just before we set out.

"Where's your phone?" I asked. "We should pull up a map."

"I think the road is curving right," Ezra said as he passed me Aaron's spare phone over the center console. "It might circle back around."

"But how long will that take?" Aaron shook his head and slowed the car. "We need to go back, especially with this rain. Kai shouldn't be riding on wet—"

He broke off, eyes flicking to his rearview mirror. "Ah, shit, there's another vehicle. Now I can't turn around."

Putting his foot down, he zoomed down the unlit stretch of secondary highway. It was barely wide enough for two cars to pass each other, and turning around would be too dangerous with another vehicle gaining on us.

As I waited for the navigation app to load on the phone, I peered in the side mirror again. Big, bright headlights glared into the car. Kai's bike drifted toward the centerline as though trying to get out of the light.

Aaron checked his rearview mirror, then accelerated more. The black trees flashed by on our left, the train tracks on the right almost invisible. The wipers whipped back and forth, battling the deluge. Kai must be soaked and freezing.

The highway curved left. We were heading farther from the town center. I tapped urgently on the phone's screen but the app was blank, the signal too poor to load anything. "The map isn't coming up."

Growling profanity, Aaron slowed again and scoured the grassy ditches for a side road to turn off. As the highway curved, the train tracks continued straight and disappeared from view.

Now we were driving through pitch darkness. The black trees on the right opened up, and I glimpsed the dark, blocky shapes of an industrial complex. Were we even in Squamish anymore?

"What is that asshole doing?" Aaron demanded.

I twisted to look out the back window, Ezra doing the same. Kai's bike was only a few car lengths behind us—and the other vehicle was right on his tail, looming like a black monster with blazing white eyes.

Aaron hit the gas, speeding up to give Kai room to accelerate away from the tailgating jerk.

I clutched the edge of my seat. "Is that an SUV?"

"I think so," Ezra said. "Why?"

Apprehension clanged through me. "Is it the same SUV that was following us earlier?"

Aaron's startled gaze snapped to me. "How could—"

Light flooded the car's interior—the SUV rapidly closing the gap. Kai's headlight swept past us as he dodged toward the empty opposing lane. The SUV surged forward.

The bike's silhouette lurched—and vanished.

"Kai!" I shrieked, twisting in my seat.

The bike's headlight flashed as the fallen motorcycle slid across the road toward the bank of trees. Aaron slammed the brakes, throwing me against my seatbelt.

The SUV's lights blazed—and it rear-ended the car.

I was flung into my seatbelt a second time. The car swerved, fishtailing violently. Aaron clutched the wheel, fighting for control as the road flew by. The nose steadied.

The SUV rammed us again.

The back end swung out. The car spun, the ditches and the SUV careening past. Hydroplaning on the slick pavement, we reeled wildly, speed barely diminished, and I had one moment to realize what was coming as we spiraled toward the road's edge. Aaron's little sports car hit the ditch.

The car flipped, and my ears filled with deafening bangs, shattering glass, and my own terrified scream.

20

"TORI? Tori, please wake up."

Through a dim haze, I recognized Ezra's voice pleading with me.

I squinted my eyes open, and for a second, I thought I'd gone blind. Then I made out his face hovering in the darkness in front of mine. He had squeezed into the gap between the car's two front seats and cradled my head with gentle hands. My whole body throbbed, limbs tingling with adrenaline.

"Tori!" he gasped in relief.

I drew in a quivering breath. The car had landed upright, but all the windows were broken and the windshield was a pale sheet of cracked safety glass that had somehow stayed in one crumpled piece. The engine was silent, steam rising from the hood, and the only sound came from the rain drumming on the dented roof.

"Are you hurt, Tori? Are you okay?"

"I—I think I'm okay." Nothing seemed broken, at least.

"I'll climb out the back and get you. Just hang on."

He retreated into the back seat, and glass crunched as he crawled through the shattered back window. I blinked slowly in the darkness, and now that Ezra's face wasn't filling my vision, my gaze fell on Aaron.

He was slumped against the steering wheel, the remains of the airbag hanging from it.

"Aaron?" I whispered. "*Aaron?*"

Ezra appeared at my window. He reached through the broken glass to unlock the door.

"Ezra. Aaron i-isn't—" My voice quavered and broke. "Aaron isn't answering."

"He's alive." Ezra almost sounded calm, but panic edged his voice. "I don't want to move him. I don't know how bad …"

He grabbed my door handle and pulled. Metal creaked, but the door didn't move. He wrenched on it. With a loud snap, it gave way and he staggered backward. Catching his balance, he leaned across me and unbuckled my seatbelt.

"What about Kai?" I whimpered, fighting back hysteria. "He fell. I couldn't see where he—where—"

"We'll find him next. He'll be okay. The pavement was wet so he could slide. He knows how to fall safely. He—" Ezra stopped, seeming to realize he was babbling. His hands cupped my face. I could feel them shaking. "We'll all be okay, Tori."

He was as scared as I was. I gulped down my terror and blinked away tears. "Help me out."

Nodding, he slid his hands to my shoulders and gently drew me forward. I grabbed the doorframe to heave myself out.

Light bloomed across us. I squinted, half blinded. Blood streaked down Ezra's face from a cut at his hairline.

He turned toward the light source. Sticking my head out of the car, I spotted a pair of headlights. Someone had seen the accident and come to help us! Wheels grinding over a gravel track, the vehicle lit up the side of a featureless warehouse twenty yards away. Aaron's car had come to a stop at the edge of an industrial lot.

As the vehicle approached, my relief sputtered out. Cold fear sparked in its place.

"Ezra," I gasped. "That's—that's the same SUV! It—"

The vehicle stopped, its high beams pointed at our car like twin spotlights. The doors opened. Three men climbed out.

Ezra didn't move, frozen in place. Then he spun to face me. "Tori, get Aaron and Kai, and get out of here."

"But—"

"I'll lure them away, distract them. They're after me, but they might—I won't let them hurt you. Just get Aaron and Kai away, please."

"Ezra—"

He darted toward the dark warehouse. Laughing, the three familiar silhouettes jogged after him. Burke, Halil, and Fenton were in no hurry to catch Ezra. This was exactly what they'd wanted: a secluded battlefield where they could test themselves against a demon mage's power.

They ran out of the SUV's headlights and vanished in the darkness. I heaved myself out of the car and into the cold rain. Bracing against the crumpled hood for balance, I stumbled to the driver's side, my legs weak and aching. Aaron's window was broken too, and the frame was bent around the door. No matter how hard I heaved, it wouldn't budge, and I wasn't as strong as Ezra. It was jammed shut.

"Aaron?" I crouched to look through the window, panic twisting through me. He hadn't stirred, slouched over the steering wheel with blood running from a contusion on his forehead.

I touched his face and was relieved to find his skin warm. He was unconscious and I shouldn't move him. What if he had a spinal injury? What if—

Pounding footsteps on the gravel reached me through the rain. I jerked upright, terrified one of the Keys had come back. No one appeared in their SUV's lights, but the footsteps were growing louder. I whirled around.

A man's silhouette ran out of the darkness. He was dressed in black and carrying something round in one hand.

"*Kai!*" I wailed, so relieved I almost collapsed.

He dropped his helmet on the gravel and came to a panting stop, his horrified stare locked on the destroyed car. "Tori! You—Aaron? Ezra?"

I snatched his arm and hauled him over to the driver's door. "Ezra led the Keys off that way. Aaron is unconscious and I can't get the door open. We need an ambulance. We need—"

"The Keys? It was *them?*" Kai grabbed the door and yanked, but he couldn't open it either. "Ezra—he can't—he needs—we should—"

He broke off with a heartfelt curse, and my fragile composure threatened to shatter as his shaky voice fell silent. The guys were always so steady, so tough. Nothing was supposed to frazzle them.

With a soft groan, Aaron lifted his head. Kai and I crammed ourselves against the window as he fell back into his seat, one hand pressed to his face.

"What …" he mumbled. "What happened?"

"Aaron, how bad are you hurt?" Kai asked urgently.

"Feel okay, minus my head." He squinted around, horror dawning on his face. "Shit, I remember. We flipped—I felt Ezra buffer us with his magic, but—where is he?"

As I explained where Ezra had gone, he unbuckled his seatbelt and tried the door handle. Kai pulled from the outside while Aaron pushed from the inside, but it was well and truly jammed. Giving up, Aaron crawled across the center console and clambered out the open passenger door. He and Kai rushed to the trunk, and Aaron wrenched it open.

"We have to get to Ezra." He threw Kai his armored vest and katana. "Uninjured and full strength, he might be able to take them, but not—"

He cut himself off as though he didn't want to finish the thought. He lifted out Sharpie. With his other hand, he passed me my new combat belt. Three alchemy bombs had miraculously survived, but I didn't have a chance to check for the missing one before Aaron thrust Ezra's pole-arm at me. I caught the heavy weapon and commanded my trembling limbs to steady. Rain ran down our faces.

"Which way, Tori?" Kai demanded as he slid his vest on.

I pointed at the warehouse, and they started running while still buckling on their weapons. I took a few steps after them, then pulled up short, clutching Ezra's weapon. Darting back to the open passenger door, I reached inside. My searching fingers found my purse jammed under the dash.

My hand met a round sphere, and I pulled it out. "Hoshi?"

The silvery-blue orb shuddered but didn't uncoil. Praying the sylph wasn't hurt, I stuffed her into the back pouch of my belt and sprinted after the guys as they vanished around the corner of the warehouse. My limbs throbbed painfully.

Around the corner, minimal light from the SUV penetrated the darkness, but a faint glow flickered out of a steel door hanging open with the handle broken off. I ran inside. Two dozen yards ahead, firelight cast a sharp silhouette over Aaron, the flames dancing above his palm as he and Kai jogged across the room.

Metal pillars, concrete walls, railings, and overhead beams broke up the massive space. It wasn't a warehouse but a factory—though judging by the garbage strewn across the floor, the rust, and the water leaking through the roof, it had been abandoned for years. Aaron and Kai passed a disused forklift, then skirted around something on the floor.

Light very different from Aaron's fire flashed.

The magical glow swept across the floor and both guys fell as though their feet had been yanked out from under them. They hit the concrete and skidded across it, dragged by an invisible force. Scrabbling in vain for purchase, they slid to a dark patch on the floor and fell into blackness.

"Guys!" My cry echoed off the bare walls.

A stomach-turning crunch answered me, and I sprinted to where they'd disappeared. The magical glow faded and darkness plunged over the space.

Firelight erupted again, emanating from a ten-foot-wide hole where the floor had collapsed. Glinting near its edge was a silver pyramid—the artifact that had dragged its victims into the hole.

Aaron and Kai were twelve feet down, hemmed in by old machinery and a concrete wall. A rusted steel beam lay amidst the debris—it must have fallen and punched a hole through the floor, years ago by the looks of it. Holding a palmful of fire, Aaron was crouched beside Kai, who was lying on his back.

"Aaron! Kai!" I dropped onto my hands and knees and set Ezra's pole-arm aside. "Are you okay?"

"I landed on him," Aaron said tersely. "Shit, I'm sorry, Kai. Are you hurt?"

"I'll live," Kai panted. "You—"

A boom shook the floor. Equipment rattled and dust drifted from the ceiling.

Aaron's pale face looked up at me, his eyes wide and jaw clenched. "That's Ezra."

I glanced deeper into the building, seeing no sign of the battle that had triggered the explosion, then looked back at Aaron and the twelve-foot wall of the pit. "Can you get up that?"

In answer, he backed up as far as he could, then ran at the wall. Leaping, he scrambled up the vertical surface. I lunged forward and caught his wrist. His shoes scuffed the wall, but he slipped and fell backward. His weight wrenched my arms, then he dropped back into the pit.

I grabbed the edge, stopping myself an instant before I fell in after him. Another distant explosion shook the floor.

"Try again!" I cried desperately.

Aaron backed up, then sprinted a second time. He sprang at the wall, scrambled up it, and I grabbed his wrist again—but my grip instantly started to slip. I wasn't strong enough. He didn't have enough room to get a running head start, there was nothing to grab on to, and I couldn't—

Hoshi burst out of my belt pouch in a whirl of silver and blue. She dove over my head and grabbed the back of Aaron's shirt.

Half his weight disappeared. I heaved, my muscles screaming. Tail lashing, Hoshi pulled. Aaron grabbed the edge with his free hand. He hauled himself out and we sprawled across the dirty ground.

Aaron sat up, and we both turned back to the pit. Panting, Kai grabbed a piece of machinery and pulled himself to his feet—without putting any weight on his left leg.

"I'm stuck," he said shortly. "Go help Ezra."

"But—"

"*Go!*" he shouted.

Aaron gave a sharp nod and pushed to his feet. My lungs squeezing at the thought of leaving Kai trapped in that hole with an injured leg, I sprang up after Aaron.

Whirling around, he grabbed me and crushed me to his chest.

Fire exploded—but not from Aaron. Scorching flames tore over us in a red and gold maelstrom, their roar deafening. Heat pounded against me, sucking the air from my lungs. Aaron's arms and magic were all that was keeping me alive.

He thrust his hand out. The flames scattered, releasing us from their suffocating embrace. Pushing me away, he whipped around.

Halil walked toward us, fire coating his massive sword. He was so tall, so strong, that the heavy length of steel seemed weightless in his grasp. The brass knuckles on his other hand glinted in the firelight as he rubbed his jaw.

"Thought I heard something," he remarked. "Looks like my little spell caught one of you."

I was tempted to glance at the pyramid artifact, but I kept my glare locked on him. "Where's Ezra?"

"Burke and Fenton are having fun with the demon mage." Halil smirked. "It's a shame, actually. The boy got too banged up in that rollover, we think. Not moving as fast this time. Burke is disappointed."

"You almost killed us all," I hissed.

"Oh, but don't you realize?" His sunken eyes glinted. "We're going to kill you all anyway. You're defending a demon mage. Your fate is the same as his."

He swung his huge sword and a wall of flame surged at us. I ducked behind Aaron and the fire broke over him like a wave over stone, charring his clothes but not harming him. As the fire died, Hoshi poked her nose out from the pit where she was hiding.

"You're good, Sinclair." Halil smiled hungrily. "It's been a long time since I fought a pyromage I couldn't burn."

Aaron drew Sharpie. "Then why don't we see if I can burn *you?*"

He planted one hand against the flat of the blade, then whipped his weapon through the air. An inferno roared out of the steel and the white-hot fire crashed over Halil. The man reappeared, his clothes smoking and a smirk on his thin lips.

"In that case," Aaron snarled, "I'll just have to run you through instead."

He set his feet, then he and Halil charged each other.

I retreated as they collided in an earsplitting clang of steel. More fire burst over them as they sought to overpower the other with either magic or brute strength. Aaron slid backward, outweighed and probably out-muscled by the larger man.

They slammed their swords together again, fire bursting everywhere. The flames formed flickering patterns as though the mages were trying to summon more complex attacks, but they were too evenly matched and disrupted the other's attempts over and over.

Breaking apart for an instant, they clashed again, steel ringing. Swinging their weapons, they parried violently and Aaron gave way. Halil drove him backward and Aaron stumbled on the uneven floor.

In that instant of distraction, Halil took one hand off his sword hilt, fingers balled into a tight fist. His brass knuckles gleamed.

"*Ori amplifico!*"

He punched Aaron in the side—and Aaron flew backward like he'd been hit by a speeding car. He crashed to the floor, and his sword slid away with a clatter.

My whole body froze in panic. Halil had used that same artifact on Ezra with no effect aside from a boom of air—but Ezra must have countered it with his own magic. Aaron didn't have that ability, and Halil's hit had thrown him ten feet. He was clutching his side, unable to rise.

Grinning, Halil strode toward Aaron, flames rippling over his broadsword.

I launched forward, my hand scrabbling at my belt. My fingers closed around a smooth glass sphere and I locked my focus on Halil. The mage looked up, smirking in cruel amusement at the thought of me trying to fight him.

Six feet away, and just before I entered the reach of his sword, I whipped the sphere at his face.

He whacked it out of the air, but it shattered against his hand. I squeezed my eyes shut against the blinding flash as an earsplitting bang pierced my eardrums. Eyes flying open, I lunged at him, my fall crystal in my other hand. All I had to do was touch it to his skin and he would go down.

I reached for him—and his fist swung out. I whipped my arm up and his knuckles struck my forearm, throwing me backward. The fall spell flew out of my hand as agony flared through my wrist, but adrenaline numbed the pain. I staggered for balance, relieved the punch had lacked the power of his brass knuckles' spell.

I coiled to leap at him again, but he pointed his hand at me. Fire flared over his palm and launched for me in a boiling wave.

Hoshi dove in front of me. Wind swirled in a mini tornado around us, and the fire was swept into the spiral. Everything turned red. The heat blasted my skin, but the flames didn't touch me.

Halil burst through the fiery whirlwind, blade swinging. The flat side caught Hoshi in the chest, hurling her out of the air. Then his other hand flashed out and grabbed me by the throat. His skin, hot as a stovetop, burned my neck and I screamed. I scrabbled at his scorching fist and brass knuckles.

He drew his sword back to strike. Snatching wildly at my belt, I grabbed my second-last glass orb and smashed it against his face.

With a shout of pain, he let me go. I fell, my nails dragging over his hand and catching on his brass knuckles. They came off in my grasp as I crumpled to the floor amidst a rapidly expanding cloud of smoke that hid everything more than three feet away.

Fire ignited above me—Halil, readying a new attack. Gasping, I rolled away from him as a second inferno erupted.

Aaron appeared out of the fog, a fiery wraith with a sword—his torso wreathed in white flames and rippling heat. He slammed his blade into Halil's and a cannon blast of white-blue fire leaped from him, hitting the Keys man in the chest.

Halil howled in agony. The flaming assault died, but the remains of Halil's shirt were still burning. His skin was black and blistering, his face streaked with blood and peppered with shards of glass.

He stumbled back a step, then bared his bloody teeth. "You think this will stop me?" he snarled, raising his sword again. "You think after the demons I've fought *you* could ever—"

He jolted forward, then twisted to look over his shoulder. A small silver knife stuck out of his lower back.

Leaping out of the pit directly behind him, a bolt of lightning struck the knife. Crackling white power engulfed Halil's body. Convulsing, he collapsed backward, hit the edge of the pit, and tumbled into it.

The lightning dispersed as Halil hit the ground with a crunch.

Trying not to whimper, I crawled to the edge and looked down, but I couldn't see anything in the darkness. Faint silvery light bloomed. Hoshi undulated over to me and her softly glowing body illuminated the interior of the hole.

Drawn sword in hand, Kai leaned against a bank of machinery, sneering at the pyromage crumpled on the ground a few feet from him. I didn't know if Halil was unconscious or dead, and I didn't care.

Panting harshly, Aaron hobbled to the edge too. "You okay, Kai?"

"Fine." He still wasn't putting any weight on his leg. "Hurry!"

Aaron straightened with a pronounced wince, his hand pressed tightly to his ribs.

"Hoshi, stay with Kai," I said breathlessly, reinforcing the words with a mental image of what I wanted.

As she drifted down into the pit and Aaron sheathed Sharpie over his shoulder, I stumbled to my feet and raced to retrieve

Ezra's pole-arm. When I grabbed it, agony speared my palm and it fell from my grasp.

Shards of glass were sticking out of my bloody hand. Teeth gritted, I pulled out the big pieces, then grabbed the pole-arm again, ignoring the pain. A deep, worrying throb filled the wrist I'd used to block Halil's punch, but I ignored that too.

Red glinted on the dirty floor. I grabbed my fall spell and stuffed it back in my belt, along with Halil's brass knuckles.

Aaron conjured a small flame to light our way. As he limped behind me, holding his chest, I hurried deeper into the abandoned factory. Half my attention was on spotting more booby traps, while panicked questions consumed the other half. How long had that battle taken? Was Ezra still alive? Was he still fighting? Was he—

A deep boom rattled the walls, and directly ahead, a brief crimson glow illuminated the pillars and equipment blocking our path. I ran forward, then stopped to scan the machinery for a way past.

"There," Aaron panted, pointing with his palmful of fire. Off to the side, a metal ladder connected the ground level to the steel mezzanine twenty feet above.

I darted to the ladder, stuck Ezra's pole-arm through the back of my belt to free my hands, and started to climb. The rusted rungs bit into my palms and scraped the bloody cuts.

A loud clang below me. I stopped short and looked down.

Aaron wasn't on the ladder. He stood on the ground, clutching his side and wheezing. Gulping for air, he grabbed a rung with one hand, the other braced against his ribs. He stepped onto the ladder, only to drop back to the floor with a stagger.

"Tori," he panted. "I can't ... Go. Don't wait for me."

My throat closed. Go? Alone?

"I'll follow," he added, unnaturally winded. "I'll be right behind you."

I stared down at his white face and knew he couldn't follow. He couldn't climb the ladder, and even if he'd been able to, he was hurt too badly to fight demons.

Unable to find my voice, I nodded. My heart shuddered beneath my ribs and panic coursed through me like acid, but I started to climb again—leaving first Kai and now Aaron behind.

21

I CLAMBERED onto the mezzanine, a platform of heavy steel beams with metal grating as a floor. Flickering light from Aaron's fire lit my way as I jogged across the platform, my steps clanging. The farther I went, the darker it grew, until the rotting pallets and half-manufactured machinery stacked along the wall were no more than black shadows.

Aaron's warm light glowed behind me, calling me back. Ahead was nothing but darkness. Slipping Ezra's pole-arm out of my belt, I pushed onward. Ezra was somewhere ahead. He must have lured the Keys as deep as possible to buy his friends time to escape.

I slowed to a trot, one hand stretched out blindly. Crimson light flared in a thin, rectangular shape—the outline of a closed door set in a blank wall that cut across the mezzanine. Breaking into a run, I reached it just before the guiding light vanished. I shoved the rusted metal door open.

A stack of pallets blocked my way forward, but more white light glowed dimly beyond it. I scooted around the stack and burst out on the other side.

The mezzanine stretched another twenty yards, then ended without so much as a safety railing. Two figures stood at the edge, lit by a blocky artifact on the grating between them that glowed like a dim lantern. They were looking down into the space below—where red light blazed and something banged against a metal surface.

The silhouettes belonged to Burke and Fenton—and below them, on the ground level, their demons must be battling Ezra. No wonder Halil had felt safe leaving the contractors unprotected. How was Ezra supposed to reach them from twenty feet down?

Swallowing my terror, I grasped Ezra's pole-arm like a baseball bat and charged.

My clanging footsteps announced my arrival, but Burke scarcely glanced at me before refocusing below. Fenton, however, turned sharply and scrabbled for something in his pocket. He whipped out a wooden ball carved with runes.

"*Ori impediar—*"

I swung the pole-arm at his head. He ducked, and I brought it down on his arm with a sickening crack. The artifact popped out of his hand and bounced over the floor's edge.

In the open space beyond the mezzanine, yellow crane machines with heavy chains were affixed to huge steel tracks that crisscrossed the high ceiling. Along the walls were stacks of unfinished machinery, each piece as large as a car, and massive pillars thicker than oak trees supported the building's roof. Thirty-foot-tall overhead doors lined the farthest wall.

Suffocating darkness engulfed the loading bay. Icy mist rose from the floor, frost sparkling across every surface. And in the open space where workers had once loaded trailers with machinery for shipment, Ezra battled the two demons.

Crimson magic veined his arms and semi-transparent spines jutted from his shoulders. Two small red horns had reformed above his glowing left eye, and his fingers were tipped with claws that looked lethally solid instead of eerily translucent.

Fenton's tall, scale-plated demon stood statue-still in the middle of the bay, its body crisscrossed with ugly wounds from the winged demon's earlier attack.

Burke's short, squat demon, its back bristling with spikes, swung at Ezra's face. He caught the demon's arm, but it wrenched free and slammed Ezra with its other fist. Ezra staggered back, blood splattering the floor.

Too much blood already marked the dark concrete. Ragged tears in Ezra's clothes revealed where the demons' claws had found his flesh. He was moving slow and favoring one leg, his left arm tucked against his side. From my single training session with Aaron, I knew his stance was all wrong. He was hurt and trying to protect his injuries.

At the sound of the pole-arm hitting Fenton and his pained howl, Ezra's head snapped up. His mismatched eyes—one crimson, one brown—found me on the ledge.

"Ezra!" As I screamed his name, I hurled his pole-arm off the mezzanine.

I knew it wouldn't reach him—I was a terrible throw—but he snapped a hand into the air. Red runes spiraled over his fingers and a streak of crimson light shot for the pole-arm. The magical wire whipped around it in midair, then retracted like a fishing line. His weapon smacked into his palm.

At the same time, Fenton's hand closed around my arm and he yanked me toward the platform's edge.

Shrieking, I snatched for any part of him I could reach—which ended up being his head. He bowed forward, flailing for balance, then wrenched back. The motion pulled me away from the edge, and I broke free from him.

Below, Ezra had split his pole-arm into two short swords, and crimson magic flowed down the steel. Burke's gaze was fixed on the scene below, his face tight with concentration as his demon circled Ezra, searching for an opening. Fenton's demon still hadn't moved.

Snarling, Fenton tackled me. I hit the grating, his weight landing on top of me. He jammed his forearm into my neck. I cried out and scratched frantically at his wrist, but he was bigger and far stronger than me. He pressed harder into my throat and cut off my air. Black spots popped in front of my eyes. I scrabbled at my belt and pulled out my fall crystal, but I needed air to speak the incantation.

Fenton spotted the artifact and jerked back like it was a live bomb, freeing my throat. Saved by his idiocy, I gasped in a breath. "*Ori—*"

He grabbed my wrist—and bones ground under his fingers. My vision went white with agony. He tore the leather tie out of my hand and threw it. The small crystal fell through the grating.

"Finish her!" Burke barked. "The boy is armed and I need your—"

Crimson power exploded, shaking the mezzanine. Fenton twisted to look behind him. Gasping for air, I grasped my last alchemy bomb and threw it at the back of Burke's head.

I scrunched my eyes closed as the glass sphere burst with a blinding flare and a crack that jolted through my chest. As I opened them, Burke pitched to one side and almost fell off the mezzanine.

Ezra unleashed another earth-shaking blast, and beyond the mezzanine's edge, I glimpsed Burke's demon hurtle through the air and slam into an industrial tank.

"No!" Burke yelled furiously.

Fenton grasped the front of my shirt and heaved me off the floor. I slapped hopelessly at my belt. My remaining artifacts— the Queen of Spades reflector spell and the green-crystal interrogation spell—would be useless against him.

My fingers collided with something hard in a pouch. I yanked out Halil's brass knuckles. With no time to put them on, I clutched them in my fist and swung at Fenton's chest.

"*Ori amplifico!*" I shouted.

The air boomed and Fenton was thrown backward. He stumbled, arms windmilling, and stepped off the mezzanine's edge. As he fell, he snatched my outstretched wrist.

He wrenched me off the mezzanine with him. A scream tore from my throat as the concrete floor rushed toward my face—then wind gusted under me. My fall slowed at the last moment, and I thudded against the floor.

Across the bay, Ezra's hand was stretched toward me, red magic crawling over his arm.

Burke's demon slammed into Ezra, throwing him into an overhead door. Metal screeched as it bent, then crimson light exploded out of Ezra, throwing the demon off. I lifted my head, struggling to move through the throbbing pain. Arctic cold burned my skin, and my quick, desperate breaths puffed white.

I had to get up. I had to ... do something. What was I supposed to do now?

A few feet away, where he'd landed, Fenton was groaning. He sat up and fumbled for his pockets. He pulled out a tiny vial, tore the cork out, and downed it. Sucking in a deep breath, he pushed gingerly to his feet, pain clearing from his expression. His attention snapped to the demon and mage in battle.

For the first time since I had distracted Fenton, his demon moved. Fenton locked his eyes on Ezra, and his demon broke into a silent, slinking run. Its horrible wounds, inflicted by the winged demon, weren't slowing it down.

Burke's demon, already back up on its feet, stood with one of Ezra's short swords embedded in its gut. It pulled the blade out, gripped the handle, and snapped the weapon in half. It too slunk forward, the demons closing in on Ezra from either side. His head swung back and forth as he gauged their approaches.

I pushed myself up. I had to distract Fenton. His demon could only fight when he was commanding it. If I could keep one demon out of the battle, Ezra might have a chance.

Both demons charged Ezra, and he whipped his remaining sword in front of him. Runes raced down the blade, and a flash of crimson blinded me. The accompanying boom thundered through my chest.

Burke's demon landed on its back halfway across the room, spines scraping the concrete, but Fenton's demon had dodged the blast. It swung its scale-plated fist at Ezra, who blocked with his forearms and retreated with limping steps.

Panting, I spun toward Fenton. I had to stop him, but how? I had no alchemy bombs left, my crystal artifact had fallen under the mezzanine, and I'd dropped Halil's brass knuckles somewhere. With nothing else left, I pulled out my Queen of Spades and ran toward Fenton.

A huge shape cut across my path.

Burke's demon, its magma eyes glowing, snatched at me with massive claws. I dove out of the way and its talons raked across my upper arm. Hot blood soaked my jacket sleeve. Gasping, I rolled over—and rolled again, barely escaping the demon's foot as it tried to stomp on my head.

Up on the mezzanine, Burke was laughing.

Crimson magic blazed—Ezra battling Fenton's demon. He had to be exhausted. He couldn't keep fighting much longer. Burke knew it, so instead of using his demon to attack Ezra, he would kill me first.

I scrambled backward on my butt, panic blanking my thoughts. The towering demon, spines jutting from its back, its blank stare fixed on me and fanged mouth slack, reached for my face.

"*Ori repercutio!*" I cried, thrusting my card at it.

The air rippled and the demon's arm bounced backward.

But with nothing else to reflect, that's all the card did—it knocked its arm back. And like the last time, the demon barely faltered. It reached for me again.

"*Ori repercutio! Ori reper—*"

It grabbed the front of my jacket and lifted me into the air—again, just like the last time I'd faced this demon. Through the hysteria screeching in my head, I could almost hear Burke's cruel, laughing voice—*time to finish what you started, foolish girl.*

I wrenched at the demon's thick fingers, my useless Queen of Spades fluttering from my hand, its spell wasted. The demon lifted me higher, my feet dangling above the ground, and its other hand rose, fingers curled to strike.

I fumbled desperately at my waist, at my belt and pockets, searching for a weapon, even though I knew I had none left. As my hand ran roughly over my hip, something jingled, the sound almost lost in the clamor of battle between Ezra and Fenton's demon.

The belt's pouches were empty, but there was something in my pocket?

My fingers dove into my jeans and met fine links, the metal warmed by my body heat. I whipped it out: a dark metal chain with a round disc. The amulet I'd taken from the winged demon's corpse.

A wail of despair rose in my throat that it wasn't a weapon, but I lifted it anyway, the amulet swinging wildly.

Claws flashed for my neck.

The swinging amulet landed on the demon's hand that gripped my jacket—and the creature froze. Its claws hovered inches from my jugular.

Magma eyes blazed. The vacant mindlessness in the demon's expression vanished, and its reddish skin contorted—its brows drawing down, lips pulling back, nose wrinkling in a snarl.

An expression of absolute bestial fury.

From above, a shocked gasp escaped Burke. The demon's claws were dangerously close to my throat, but it still didn't move. Staring into its eyes, I knew that a living, thinking being stared back. Seeing me. Judging me with sinister intelligence.

Terror liquefied my innards and my hands jerked convulsively. The amulet slipped off the demon's wrist and swung on the end of its chain like a pendulum.

The moment the amulet broke contact with the demon, the rage on its face melted back into blank nothingness. The intelligence in its eyes died. Burke shouted something, and the demon drew back its arm a second time, ready to repeat the strike it had failed to perform.

I slapped the amulet against the demon's wrist again.

Life flared in its eyes, and that rage reappeared. Its claws curled, and muscles bunched.

"Don't move!" I gasped. "Or I'll take the amulet away again!"

The demon bared its sharp fangs—but otherwise, it didn't move.

"Put me down—slowly."

It lowered me until my feet touched the floor, but it didn't release my jacket. Probably a good thing, because I wasn't sure my trembling legs could hold me up.

We stared at each other, the scant seconds stretching out as I thought frantically. The demon was assessing me with equal intensity, those intelligent eyes gleaming. Its claws were still poised to strike.

Somehow, the amulet's power had severed Burke's control over the demon's will. Holding the front of my shirt was a demon in full command of itself.

A very, very angry demon.

It could kill me in an instant, but if the amulet broke contact with its skin, it would fall back under Burke's power. It didn't seem eager to take that risk.

"Listen," I said, my voice shaking. "Let's make a deal. I'll give you the amulet if you get rid of the other demon—and d-don't kill me."

The demon stared at me, then its mouth curved into a vicious grin. Did that mean it agreed?

A blast of red light from Ezra blinded me, and I didn't have time to find out. I yanked the amulet off the demon's wrist and shoved it against its other palm.

The demon's fingers snapped over the amulet, claws scoring the back of my hand. It released my jacket and I crumpled at its feet, my legs turned to jelly. The demon glared down at me—then turned away.

My jaw hung open. It—it hadn't killed me? It was honoring our deal?

Amulet clutched in one hand, the demon sprang forward. But it didn't go for Fenton's demon, which had just slammed Ezra into the floor. Instead, Burke's freed demon took aim at the other human.

In three loping steps, it grabbed Fenton in its huge, powerful hand—and ripped out his heart.

The unsuspecting contractor didn't have a chance to scream. Bones crunched, blood gushed, and his body collapsed to the floor.

A screeching laugh erupted. Fenton's demon had stepped back from Ezra, its mouth gaping as it cackled, its delighted stare fixed on its slain master. Red light gushed from its hands and whooshed over its body. Its form dissolved into a blur of crimson power that shot for Fenton.

The light rushed into his body, making it glow like a scarlet light bulb, then it faded. The crimson radiance blinked out, leaving an empty, lifeless corpse splayed on the blood-drenched concrete. The scaled demon was gone.

I was too shocked to move. Had that final moment of possession been the demon stealing Fenton's soul and using it to escape this world?

Gasping harshly, Ezra braced one hand against a broad pillar. His left eye still glowed, but most of the red magic had faded from his arms. He stared at Burke's demon—and fear edged his expression.

"What are you doing?" Burke roared from the mezzanine. "Obey me! You have to obey me!"

The demon looked up at its shouting contractor. Lips pulling back in another hideous grin, it lifted its free hand toward Burke. Crimson runes sparked over its fingers and spiraled up its wrist. A glowing red wire shot out of its hand— identical to the spell Ezra had used to catch his pole-arm.

The coil of power snapped around Burke and yanked him off the edge. He plunged twenty feet and landed with a horrifying thwack. Laughing in a deep, hoarse voice, the demon ambled over to its former master. Leaning down, it sank claws into Burke's shoulder and lifted him. Burke grabbed at its wrist, his face white with terror.

"N-no!" he stammered. "You must obey me! You accepted the contract!"

Another bone-rumbling laugh. With a casual flick, the demon raked its claws across Burke's face. Blood splattered and Burke screamed. The demon dropped him.

Burke hit the ground, still screaming, and pressed his hands over his eyes as blood ran down his cheeks like macabre tears. Chuckling, the demon turned away from its master. Its magma eyes slid to me, and it offered a mocking nod of acknowledgment. It had agreed not to kill me. It was holding to our bargain.

Then it continued its turn—and faced Ezra.

My body went ice cold. I'd told the demon not to hurt *me*, but I hadn't mentioned Ezra. How could I have forgotten?

Ezra shoved away from the pillar, holding his remaining short sword, but he could barely stand. His breath came in ragged pants, one arm hanging uselessly at his side. The magic blazing over his body had mostly faded, and the only bright spot left was his glowing left eye.

With bloodthirsty delight etched on its face, the demon I had freed launched its attack.

22

WINTRY COLD swept over the room. Darkness sucked at the artifact Burke and Fenton had left glowing on the mezzanine. Frost reformed over every surface.

And the demon slammed into Ezra.

It drove him into a stack of pallets with crushing force. Wood splintered and crunched. Ezra slashed with his sword, but the demon didn't flinch when the blade parted its flesh. It had many injuries, none of which bothered it. Hadn't Ezra told me himself? Demons could take a lot of damage.

Crimson light spiraled around the demon—magic no longer chained by the demon's contract. Instead of fighting a slow, witless, magic-less demon controlled by a distractible human, Ezra now battled a fully powered, fully autonomous demon that could wield more magic than the demon mage.

All because of me.

I spun in a wild circle. A dozen feet away, Burke was crawling blindly, searching for an escape. My gorge rose at the sight of his face. The demon could have immobilized him with magic, but instead, it had blinded him—a far more vicious way of keeping its former master from escaping.

With an explosive roar, power erupted. Thrown backward, Ezra slammed into the central pillar supporting the mezzanine. Metal groaned under the impact, and he slumped, legs sprawled, his torso held up by the pillar. Without it, he would've been flat on the ground.

His short sword spun across the concrete and slid to a stop at my feet.

The demon stalked toward Ezra, its claws uncurling. He lifted his head, his left eye gleaming with faint red light. Blood ran from his mouth and dripped off his chin. He didn't make any move to stand as the demon approached.

I looked down at the sword.

The demon stopped in front of Ezra, smiling malevolently. Four yards away, on my other side, Burke was inching along the concrete with soft grunts of pain and panic.

I had to stop the demon. I had to save Ezra.

The demon lifted its arm, thick claws glinting in the faint light as it took aim at the exhausted, injured, defenseless mage. Seconds. In seconds, Ezra would die. I couldn't let that happen. I had to stop this, no matter what it took. I had to act.

Seconds. No time. Go! *Go now!*

I snatched the sword off the ground and sprinted. A scream burst from my throat—a tearing outcry of panic, of denial, of desperation. I raised the blade over my head, the deadly point gleaming.

And I slammed it down into Burke's back.

The foot-long steel drove between his ribs. The edges scraped against bone. The hilt hit his body and he collapsed without a sound, his weight pulling the sword out of my hands.

My breath came in fast, urgent pants. I stared at him, at what I had done, then I raised my head. Crouched over Ezra, the demon gazed at me, its cold, harsh features unreadable.

Then it tore its claws out of Ezra's chest.

The force pulled him upward before the claws came free from his body. He fell back into the pillar, limp, slumped, head lolling, blood running down his chest. My throat spasmed, another scream fighting to escape, but I'd forgotten how to make a sound.

Cackling softly, the demon opened its other hand. The amulet fell to the ground with a clink, then light swept over the beast's body. Dissolving into a luminous blur, the crimson spirit hurtled toward me.

I stumbled back as the demonic spirit plunged into Burke, claimed his dying soul, then faded out of this world.

A sob crawled up my throat and made my lungs heave. I burst into an unsteady run, racing to Ezra's side. Hands outstretched, I dropped to my knees beside him.

This close, he looked even worse—clothes torn, cuts and lacerations leaking blood, blue-black bruises darkening his skin. But it was the three piercing wounds in the right side of his chest that had me shaking so hard I couldn't breathe. The demon had driven its claws in deep, and blood flowed steadily from the punctures.

Wet, ragged breaths trembled through his lungs. His head twitched, then his eyes cracked open.

"Tori," he rasped. His left eye shone with a hint of red.

"Ezra!" I reached for his arm but hesitated, terrified that even the gentlest touch would hurt him more. "Ezra, I—"

His hand fumbled for my wrist, and his fingers closed in a surprisingly powerful grip. "Tori, *get away*."

"What?"

"Get away. Run away."

"The demons are gone, Ezra."

He sucked in a horrible, gurgling breath. "Get away."

His eyes rolled back, and his fingers slipped off my wrist. His hand thudded lifelessly on the floor.

"Ezra!"

He was still breathing—barely. More blood than air filled his lungs. He drew in another tremoring gasp. His eyelids flickered, showing nothing but the blank whites of his eyes.

For a long moment, he didn't move. Didn't even breathe. Then his eyes snapped open—and both irises were consumed by glowing crimson that deepened to near black in their centers. Two circles of hellish, inhuman magma.

The temperature plunged. Ice coated everything nearby. The heat left my body in a trembling wave and I fell backward out of my crouch, my butt landing on a lumpy fragment of debris. My whole body quaked with violent shivers. The light vanished, and only Ezra's demonic eyes, glowing with power, existed in the consuming darkness.

More crimson light sparked—runes appearing on his chest. Lines spread from them, coiling over his torso and sinking into his body. A luminescent circle flashed to life under him, filled with runes. I shoved myself backward, away from the glow.

Scarlet light brightened and deepened, burning black at its core. His red eyes were wide and staring, but concentration tightened his face.

Then he spoke—and his voice was a guttural growl, deep and rough. The words rose and fell in an unbroken stream, and I recognized the cadence of an incantation. The magic he had conjured blazed brighter, then drew inward like water flowing down a drain—except the magic was draining into the punctures in his chest.

Ezra arched off the pillar, hands clenched and teeth bared in agony. He shuddered violently as the final wisps of power melted into his flesh. With a gasp, he slumped again, head falling forward, limbs sagging to his sides. The frigid cold lessened and the blanket of unnatural darkness lifted, allowing the faint light from the artifact on the mezzanine to illuminate the loading bay again.

"Ezra?" I whispered.

The mysterious spell was gone—as were the punctures in his chest. The three marks from the demon's claws no longer wept blood. They no longer looked like gory holes.

"Ezra?" I tried again.

He didn't react, his chest rising and falling with slow, smooth breaths. Barely daring to hope, I inched closer. Beneath smears of blood, the deep punctures had transformed into three jagged-edged scars.

Shivering from lost body heat, I hesitantly peeled apart the blood-soaked tears in his shirt. Not only was his chest whole again, but the other slices and claw marks had healed, leaving fainter scars, and the bruising had faded to reveal unmarked bronze skin.

In awe, I lightly touched a new scar. The speed of the healing eclipsed anything I'd seen the Crow and Hammer healers accomplish. My stare dipped to the old scars that raked up his side and stomach, then I sat back.

That hard fragment poked my backside again. I slid my hand under my butt, searching for the debris to toss it away.

Ezra's chest rose in a deep inhalation. His shoulders went back, his spine straightening, and he raised his head. His eyes opened—and his irises glowed like crimson fire.

My empty lungs froze. His gaze slid over the bay, touching first on Fenton's body, then Burke's, then lingering on the demon amulet lying on the ground a yard away. Finally, his stare turned to me. My hand closed around the small object I'd sat on.

The demon inside Ezra smiled. Crimson power flared over his hands and raced up his arms in snaking veins.

He lunged for me.

I flung my hand out and mashed the ruby artifact into his face. "*Ori decidas!*"

The screamed incantation left my lips as his claws grazed my throat. He crumpled under the spell, his muscles slack. I kept the crystal pressed to his face as he hit the ground, limbs splayed and body immobilized.

I panted, terror weakening my muscles. With my free hand, I gingerly touched my neck. Stinging cuts marred my throat and trickled blood, but since the wounds weren't spurting, my jugular must be intact. What was it with everyone going for my throat tonight?

Under my hand, the ruby artifact glinted against his cheek. Once, an irritatingly wise druid had told me that the world was rife with mysterious magical forces that may or may not be sentient. If those forces could indeed influence a human's puny life, then I owed them a big favor. Either that, or I was one hell of a lucky girl to have found my fall spell—dropped while grappling with Fenton on the mezzanine—right when I needed it most.

Keeping the precious artifact in place, I met Ezra's gaze.

His demon looked back at me. Even without the crimson eyes, I would've known this was not Ezra. Never could he have looked at me with such primal loathing. Never had bloodlust and viciousness contorted his face like that. There was nothing of Ezra in this cruel monster that had taken over his body.

Kai's passing comment, his unintentional warning, repeated in my head. *I had to hit him hard. If Ezra had lost consciousness but the demon hadn't …*

Ezra had tried to warn me. *Get away*—not from our defeated foes, but from *him*.

The demon twisted Ezra's lips into a cold mockery of a smile. "Such disgust on your face, *payilas*."

I shuddered. Ezra didn't sound like that—his voice was too deep, too growly, the words sharpened by an alien accent.

"Shut up," I told the demon, proud that my voice was steady. "You aren't supposed to talk, especially not with Ezra's mouth."

A soft, hissing laugh. "This body is mine. He will give it to me … soon."

I tried to ignore the demon, but seeing the beast behind Ezra's familiar face twisted something inside me in the most painful way.

"They did not tell you."

"Didn't tell me what?" I asked before I could stop myself.

"His fate," the demon taunted. The glowing power in his eyes didn't seem as bright as before. "He is mine. His body and his soul."

My throat tightened. I pressed the crystal harder into his cheek.

"But you can save him." Magma eyes blazed again. "Give me Vh'alyir's *imailatē vīsh* and he will be free."

My gaze darted to the dark amulet lying a mere three feet away on the ground.

"Do you not wish to save him, *payilas talūk?*" Another laugh hissed from Ezra's throat. The gleam in his eyes was fading rapidly. His face was slackening. "Either way ... he will be mine."

With those final whispered words, the red glow disappeared, revealing Ezra's human eyes—one pale and the other warm brown. His eyelids drooped over his glazed, empty stare. I waited, scarcely breathing, as seconds stretched into minutes, but he was well and truly unconscious—the human *and* the demon.

Above me on the mezzanine, the soft light from the Keys' glowing artifact flickered. It dimmed. Then it went out, plunging the room into darkness.

Rain pattered on the roof and leaked through cracks, dripping onto the floor. In the cessation of the life-and-death battle, the drumming filled my ears. I stared at the invisible mezzanine, my breath coming faster and faster. Why couldn't the spell have lasted just a few minutes more?

Fingers trembling, I carefully settled the spell crystal in the hollow of Ezra's throat where it couldn't slip off. Then I sat back, my butt thumping on the ground, and buried my face in my bloody hands. As my adrenaline faded, pain grew—my palm full of glass, my burned and scraped neck, my broken wrist, my sliced upper arm, my strained and bruised muscles, and more aches than I could identify. I sat unmoving, fighting the pressure building in my chest.

A whimper slipped from my throat—and the dam broke. Sobs shook my body. I couldn't stop myself. I wept from the terror, from the horror, from the dread and panic and pain.

I cried because it was so much, too much, but it wasn't over. Somehow, I had to find the strength to stand. I had to find a way out of this building in the pitch darkness. I had to make my way back to Aaron, and I had to figure out how to get Kai out of the pit. I had to somehow move Ezra, even though I was weak and hurt, because Aaron and Kai had sustained far worse injuries.

I couldn't do it. It was too much.

A scrape of metal against metal snapped me back to the present. I lifted my tear-streaked face and squinted through the darkness. I couldn't see anything, and suddenly, I was terrifyingly aware of the two dead bodies so close and now unseen.

The darkness lifted.

I stared in confusion. The room had brightened, but it wasn't light as I'd ever seen light before. There was no spell, no lamp, no flare or glow or beam. The darkness simply … lightened. The source-less luminescence came from everywhere and nowhere, as omnipresent as the darkness had been before.

A man stood just inside a gap in one of the overhead doors, his hand raised, palm upturned as though he had physically lifted the darkness and cast it away. I couldn't believe my eyes. Surely I was hallucinating.

"Darius?" I whispered.

He strode forward. The ground crunched reassuringly under his feet, the splashing puddles proving he wasn't a figment of my imagination. Sweeping to my side, he knelt and leaned over Ezra, two fingers finding the pulse in his neck. Then Darius's solemn gray eyes turned to me and his warm, solid hand settled on my shoulder.

A dozen questions spun through my head, but I couldn't speak. My voice had disappeared along with the darkness—darkness the guild master, the rare luminamage, had banished.

But I didn't need to speak. My questions didn't matter. We were safe now.

23

I SAT IN THE PASSENGER SEAT of Darius's SUV and listened to the rain.

Behind me, the guild master was arranging a blanket across Kai. The electramage was slumped in the seat, already buckled in, his broken leg splinted and wrapped in tensor bandages. Darius had fed him a healing draft, and he'd dozed off within seconds of finishing it.

In the middle was Aaron. Darius and Alistair had given the pyromage the initial round of first aid, and he was also comatose from a powerful healing potion. Ezra was tucked in the third seat, still deeply unconscious. He wouldn't be waking, either, because Darius had dosed him with that same yellow sleeping potion mythics kept shooting at me in paintballs. I couldn't fault Darius's logic; it wouldn't be good for Ezra to wake up trapped in the back seat of a vehicle with no idea where he was.

I looked down at my wrist, splinted and tied against my chest in a makeshift sling. My hand and arm were tightly wrapped in gauze and tape, bandages pulled on the skin of my neck, and a cooling salve was slathered over my burns. It was nice that I wasn't bleeding anymore, but the first aid treatment had done nothing to dull my pain.

Crunching gravel mixed with the sound of the downpour. Darius tucked in the last corner of the blanket, ensuring all three mages were covered, then straightened.

"I found it." Alistair's deep, gravelly voice carried through the open door of the vehicle. "Scratched up but seems to be working just fine."

I craned to look through the open door. The sturdy volcanomage, his leather jacket zipped tight and the collar turned up against the cold, wet breeze, stood beside Kai's recovered motorcycle.

"Can you ride it?" Darius asked.

Alistair grunted, but it sounded more amused than grumpy. "I'd prefer my Harley, but I can make do with this little crotch rocket."

"Good. Let's get moving, then."

Closing Kai's door, Darius got into the driver's seat. The engine was already running, and heat pumped from the vents. He unbuckled the weapons belt around his waist and tucked the sheathed daggers under his seat, then turned on the window wipers and shifted into drive.

Kai's bike snarled to life, its headlight flaring, and Alistair pulled out first. The SUV rolled out of the lot after it, gravel grinding noisily under the tires. As we pulled onto the secondary highway, I closed my eyes. I didn't want to see the road again, not when my last view of it had ended in such disaster.

If Darius and Alistair hadn't shown up, I didn't know what I would've done. Kai, it turned out, had called for help after the Keys had driven him off the road. Darius and Alistair had come to our rescue, but it had taken them almost an hour to reach us. Still, I wasn't complaining.

"How are you doing, Tori?" Darius asked softly.

I reluctantly opened my eyes. We were approaching an intersection, and Alistair had just turned Kai's bike onto a new road—the area where Aaron had taken a wrong turn. If we hadn't gotten lost in the town, would any of this have happened?

"I'm okay," I whispered.

"Tell me about it," Darius said. The words weren't a command, but a gentle suggestion.

We turned onto the Sea to Sky Highway, the high beams sweeping across glistening pavement, and our speed picked up significantly. What did the darkness look like to Darius's eyes? As a luminamage, was anything ever too dark to see? I swallowed against the dry soreness in my throat and adjusted the nearest vents to blow hot air into my face. Hoshi, back in orb form, was nestled in my lap.

"Do you know?" I asked abruptly.

"About Ezra?" Darius didn't look away from the road. "Yes."

"For how long?"

"Since the very beginning. He told during our interview for his membership."

My eyes widened. From everything I'd seen, Ezra guarded his secrets more carefully than his life. But he'd straight up told

Darius? And Darius, knowing the truth, had allowed Ezra into the guild?

"But …" I protested in disbelief. "But Ezra is …"

"An illegal demon mage? A danger to everyone around him? A walking, talking crime so severe that the MPD would imprison me, Aaron, and Kai simply for knowing him?" He nodded. "Yes, he is all those things, but during our interview six years ago, he was also a scared, scarred eighteen-year-old who'd never known a normal life."

Scarred. Somehow, I knew Darius wasn't talking about Ezra's physical scars.

"I've watched Ezra very closely," Darius added. "As have Aaron and Kai. If Ezra had ever seemed like a danger to anyone in the guild, we would have taken the necessary steps."

I opened my mouth but didn't speak. I didn't want to know what the necessary steps were.

My jaw clenched as I caught myself in the thought. No, I couldn't do that anymore. I needed to face and understand the ugly truths. "What would you have done?"

"Exactly this," Darius replied. "I helped Kai and Aaron with their escape plan years ago. If Ezra needed it, they were ready to run with him at any time."

I eyed the guild master. That wasn't all. There was another "step" he wasn't sharing.

"So, you now know what he's been hiding," Darius continued before I could ask. "What do you think?"

"Huh?"

"Are you afraid of Ezra?"

Startled by the question, I considered it for a long moment. "I'm afraid of his demon."

"Good. You should be."

"I—" I inhaled shakily. "I talked to his demon."

Darius's head snapped toward me. He quickly looked back to the road. "Did you?"

With another unsteady breath, I told Darius first about the winged demon and the amulet it had tried to give Ezra, then how I'd used the amulet to free Burke's demon, and finally the request Ezra's demon had made.

"His demon wanted the amulet," Darius murmured, more to himself than to me. "Tori, I would hazard to guess that anything the demon wants is unlikely to be good for Ezra."

"That's what I thought too."

"The amulet is an immensely dangerous artifact. Under no circumstances should Ezra ever touch it. He could lose all control over his demon, and an out-of-control demon mage is even more volatile than an unbound demon."

I frowned. "Why's that?"

The glow from the console cast eerie shadows over Darius's face. "An unbound demon kills in a desperate attempt to find a way home. The demon trapped inside a demon mage, however, can never go home. It's bound to the mortal flesh. When Ezra dies, the demon will die with him. It's the reason his demon is so motivated to keep Ezra alive and has gone to the effort of healing his injuries."

Oh. I hadn't thought about *why* the demon would heal Ezra, only how shocking its magic had been while doing it.

"The demon within a demon mage is highly invested in the survival of its host. It wants the body for itself, perhaps so it can live the longest life possible, perhaps to seek revenge on the humans it blames for its fate, perhaps to search for a way home." Darius smiled grimly. "It's difficult to unravel the thought processes of a demon, but regardless, it makes the demon extremely dangerous."

I still wasn't sure I understood what made a demon mage's survival-minded demon deadlier than an unbound one on a killing spree, but I didn't argue. Hidden in my pocket, the dark amulet weighed against my hip. I'd collected it, along with all my other artifacts and Halil's brass knuckles, before leaving the building.

The winding road flew beneath the SUV's headlights, Alistair speeding ahead of us. I watched the wipers slashing back and forth, resisting the urge to look at Ezra.

"Why did he do it?" I whispered. "Why did he choose to become a demon mage?"

Darius slid his hands over the steering wheel. For a long moment, he was silent as he concentrated on the drive.

"Ezra," he finally said, his voice a low murmur, "didn't understand that he had a choice."

My breath caught. "What do you mean?"

"He'll tell you when he's ready, but don't blame him for it, Tori."

How could a person fail to grasp that they could choose *not* to summon a bloodthirsty monster out of a hellish realm and permanently embed it inside their body? I didn't understand, but for now, I would take Darius's word on it.

"What's special about Enright, Oregon?" I asked.

"Enright is an abandoned railroad town deep in the Oregon Coast Range." Darius rubbed his salt and pepper beard as though to relax the sudden tension in his jaw. "It's significant to the mythic community, and demon hunters in particular, because eight years ago, on private property near the town, a well-hidden group of demon mages was discovered and eradicated. It was the largest congregation seen in about a century."

Ezra's mug shot. He'd been arrested in Portland, Oregon, four months after the demon-mage purge, looking sick and homeless. Combined with his lack of history prior to joining the Crow and Hammer, I could understand why the Keys considered that police report to be definitive proof of Ezra's origins.

I wanted to know more—if Ezra had been part of that group, how he'd ended up there, how he'd escaped the extermination—but I figured the demon mage himself should be the one to answer those questions. I fidgeted with the splint on my arm. "What now? Is it safe to take Ezra back to the city?"

"I don't believe Burke told anyone outside his team about Ezra. If he had, more teams would have been on your tails tonight."

I watched Darius's profile closely. "Then Ezra's secret is safe?"

"For now."

For now. Well, that was something, at least. "What about … Burke and Fenton … and Halil? Their bodies …"

"I've already called some trusted mythics to clean up the location, and we should pass them heading north soon. You can guess why I don't want to involve the MPD." He glanced at me, an eyebrow arched. "Alistair and I would've taken care of the cleanup ourselves if not for two reasons. First, I thought it best to get all three boys to our healers as soon as possible."

I finally allowed myself to look into the backseat. Aaron, Kai, and Ezra almost appeared to be sleeping peacefully—except for their torn, dirty, bloody clothes and various bandages and splints.

"The second reason?" I prompted as I settled back into my seat and adjusted Hoshi in my lap.

"I need to return immediately. Alistair, Girard, and I are in the middle of something."

Seriously? I shook my head. "Do you ever rest? The unbound demon was *just* slain earlier tonight, and I figured everyone would be heading straight to bed for a nice, long sleep."

Darius smiled faintly, but something dark and mean hardened his features. "Our task is tangentially related to the unbound demon … and the ones who set it loose."

My mouth popped open in a silent "oh." The Crow and Hammer's deadliest team was no longer hunting the slain demon—they were hunting the ones responsible for it.

"Well," I said airily. "We definitely don't want to keep you from that."

"Most appreciated, Tori."

We drove in silence for a long time. At one point, a single pair of headlights appeared on the road, driving in the opposite direction, and Darius flashed his hazards in greeting. I stirred out of my doze, exhausted but kept awake by my throbbing injuries. Darius didn't reveal who the cleanup crew consisted of.

Finally, hazy lights appeared in the rain—the northwestern tip of the city, bright and cheerful and undimmed by the trauma of the night. I sank into my seat, relief rolling through me.

"Tori," Darius murmured, his voice startling me after so long in silence. "You made a choice tonight that few would make. And you repeated that rare choice over and over throughout the night."

I stared blankly, too tired to puzzle out his meaning. "Huh?"

"You chose to stand by your friends despite the terrible danger."

"Oh … right."

An amused smile twitched his short beard. "Should I praise your bravery or your stubbornness?"

I scowled.

"Either way," he continued, his amusement fading, "it's past time for you to take your own safety seriously. I've warned you repeatedly that your wellbeing is as crucial as anyone else's, and my tolerance for your poor attitude toward self-preservation has reached its limits."

My displeasure melted into a guilty cringe.

"Since you clearly have no intention of sitting on the sidelines, that means you must learn how to defend yourself. Properly," he added when I opened my mouth.

How had he known I was about to protest? I mean, yeah, I'd taken a beating, but I'd gotten through it all alive. Then again, if I hadn't avoided Aaron's every mention of training over the last two months, maybe I could've done better. Maybe I could've spared Ezra from a life-threatening injury.

"I will be speaking to Felix about a training regime." Darius glanced at me, and there was no hint of compromise in his tone. "He'll coordinate with Aaron and Kai, and I'll expect regular reports on your progress."

I gulped, understanding the unspoken warning that consequences would follow if I failed to meet his expectations. "Yes, sir."

"Good. And my final instruction …"

I straightened attentively. "Yes?"

"Ask Ezra to teach you everything he knows about demon mages—everything he knows about how his power works." Darius's mouth thinned. "I think it's knowledge you'll need … sooner or later."

A chill crept through me, and my eyes were drawn to the back of the vehicle where Ezra leaned lifelessly against the window, his pale face streaked with dried blood and his cheek marked by an unknown demon's claw.

24

"**ARE YOU READY YET?**" Aaron shouted from the second floor.

I shot a glower toward the stairs as I hastened into the living room with my arms full.

"Almost," I shouted back. "Quit nagging!"

"We're going to be late."

"I know!" I snarled as I rushed across the kitchen, only to find the main bathroom's door closed. Kai must be in there, finishing his own preparations.

Growling, I whipped around the corner and loped down the stairs. The basement was dark and cold, the sparring mats empty, and the bathroom door hung open. I hurried inside, used my hip to swing the door most of the way shut, and dumped my armload on the counter.

My reflection frowned back at me, and I paused to tilt my head. Faint pink lines marked my neck—the remnants of Ezra's demon claws, which had come so close to opening my jugular.

I'd almost rather face his demon again than what I had coming tonight. My gaze inadvertently dropped to my outfit.

Correction: my *costume*. Ugh.

Nose wrinkling, I gave my hair a final check, ensuring my curls were the right mix of tidy and sexily mussed. But not frizzy. Frizzy was not sexy. And my hair was about the only sexy thing I had going for me with this getup.

I glared mutinously at the last pieces of my costume, then picked up a crinkly package containing a black wide-brimmed hat with a feather plume. I ripped the clear plastic open with more violence than necessary, then lifted the whole package and upturned it over my head, intending to drop the hat right onto my crown.

The hat fell out, bounced off my head, and landed in the sink. What *did* land on my head was a grenade's worth of colorful confetti.

"*Argh!*" I yelped in furious dismay.

The plastic packaging crinkled merrily, and I belatedly noticed the bold yellow text in the corner—*Free pirate confetti with every hat!* Snarling my favorite bad words, I carefully shook my hair. Dislodged confetti showered the counter and floor, but even more shiny bits sank into my curls.

"Goddamn it!"

"Tori?"

With a light rap, the bathroom door opened. Ezra stood in the threshold, scanning me with concern.

My frustration evaporated. In the week since our battle with the Keys, I'd scarcely seen him. I was pretty sure he would've skipped all socialization tonight too, but Aaron and Kai had bullied him into it.

He'd bounced back from his demonic healing faster than Aaron or Kai had recovered from their injuries, but a hollowness lingered in his face. A tiny new scar marked the edge of his jaw just below his right ear.

His worried gaze flicked over me, searching for the cause of my yelping and swearing. I knew the moment he spotted the confetti—he blinked, then smiled, then quashed the smile.

I huffed and turned back to the mirror—but that didn't help, as I could now see his reflection. And that was a problem because he was in costume too, and sexiness was not an issue for him. Heat slid through my core, my hormones completely ignoring my stern admonishments.

"How did you—" he began as another wave of confetti spilled out of my hair.

"Don't ask," I grumped as I started picking the shiny stuff out. Curly hair forbade the use of hairbrushes, and if I shook it around too much, all my hard work containing the frizz would be ruined.

Ezra watched me pluck confetti out piece by piece, then stepped into the bathroom. Moving behind me, he reached up. The first slight tug on my hair as he removed a piece of confetti sent tingles rushing down my spine.

I cleared my throat. "So, you guys never said whose idea this was."

When I gestured at our reflections, Ezra's crooked smile reappeared. "I'll give you one guess."

"Aaron's," I concluded grouchily. "The Three Musketeers are so lame."

"Four Musketeers," he corrected.

My scowl deepened. Indeed, four. I'd already put on my tight breeches, white shirt with billowy, tight-cuffed sleeves, and a draping blue tabard with a shiny *fleur-de-lis* on the chest. The hat and leather gloves were the last part of my getup, and I wasn't pleased about any of it. I looked ridiculous.

Ezra, on the other hand …

He would be wearing the exact same outfit, but he hadn't donned his tabard yet. The breeches hugged his strong legs, and the way the white shirt hung off his broad shoulders looked downright dashing. On my smaller frame, the shirt looked more like a pillowcase with sleeves.

Our shirts dipped into a sharp V-neck, but he'd left the ties on his undone, allowing a tantalizing hint of his bronze chest to peek out. I yanked my gaze away and focused on picking crap from my hair. He was standing so close that his intoxicating scent filled my nose.

That night a week ago felt like a terrible dream. Ezra's flight from the house, his confrontation with the Keys, my finding out he was a demon mage. Abandoning the city, racing north, the car accident … and everything that had followed. The blur of darkness, rain, battle, blood, and crimson magic. It all had the hazy obscurity of a half-forgotten nightmare, but when I lay in bed at night, waiting for sleep, it all came back with crisp, terrifying clarity.

Ezra carefully lifted my hair away from my neck and brushed confetti off my shirt collar. My gaze lifted to the mirror. We hadn't had a proper conversation since that night. Every time I entered a room, he'd disappear shortly afterward. He was more elusive than an antisocial housecat.

I spun around. He blinked, his hands hovering in the air, ready to resume searching for confetti. He started to step back, but I grabbed his wrists, halting him.

"You've been avoiding me," I accused bluntly.

DEMON MAGIC AND A MARTINI

He opened his mouth but seemed to realize denying it would be stupid.

"Why?" I demanded.

He gave his wrists a tug. I didn't release him.

"Tori …" he muttered. He pulled away again, more strongly, but instead of letting go, I stepped with him, keeping close and pressing my advantage. His back bumped the wall. The bathroom wasn't cramped, but it didn't leave much room to maneuver either.

I glared at him. His gaze darted away, seeking a safe place to look besides my face. He settled for gazing pointlessly at a spot above my head.

"Spill it, Ezra."

"Spill what?"

"The reason you've been avoiding me all week and won't look me in the eye."

His mouth thinned. "Isn't it obvious?"

"No."

Surprise brought his gaze down to mine. He searched my eyes—probing for signs of deceit. I held his wrists between us.

"No," I repeated sternly, staring him down. Or staring him *up*, since he was taller than me. "I *don't* know why you're avoiding me and I'm getting seriously annoyed about it."

"Annoyed?" Uncertainty flickered over his features. "I thought you'd prefer …"

"Prefer *what*?"

"To … see less of me?"

I squinted angrily. "Because you're a demon mage?"

He flinched.

"Well." Still gripping his wrists, I leaned closer. He tried to lean back and banged his head against the wall. "In case you hadn't noticed, I don't care. If I cared, I wouldn't have gone with you guys that night, would I?"

His expression shuttered, emotions hidden. "How can you not care?"

"Oh, I see. You think I'm a coward."

"What? No, I don't—"

"Then you think I'm selfish."

"No, you're—"

"Then what? Why do you think I would turn my back on you just because your inner demon is more literal than usual?"

A small, amused snort escaped him.

"Ezra, nothing has changed except I understand now." Actually, that wasn't true. Damn near *everything* had changed— but one thing hadn't. "*You* haven't changed. You're the same person you were before that night, so why would my feelings for you change?"

He went very still. "Your feelings?"

"Uh." Something near to panic jumped through me. "I—I mean, you still want to be my friend, don't you?"

His gaze skimmed my face, then settled on my eyes like he was trying to peer inside my head.

"Of course I do," he said softly.

I'd expected one of his deadpan jokes. Or at least a smile. But he was staring at me with a strange intensity, his steady gaze still seeking something. I suddenly became aware that I hadn't released him, holding his wrists hostage between our bodies.

He seemed to realize it too, because his arms moved—but not away from me. His hands drew closer to my face. Hesitantly, as though expecting me to cringe in disgust, he touched his fingertips to my cheeks.

Not daring to breathe, I stared up at him. My brain had gone blank, buzzing and useless.

His fingers brushed lightly across my cheeks, his eyes fixed on mine as they searched my soul. "Tori … can I have a hug?"

My heart jumped into my throat, choking off my voice. I started to lift my arms.

He pulled me into him before I could complete the motion, and I yipped in surprise as he crushed me against his chest. His warm breath stirred the curls above my ear, his face pressed into my hair.

"You must be crazy," he muttered. "It's the only explanation."

"Are you complaining?" I asked, managing to inject a tart note despite my breathlessness.

"No. No, I'm not."

My chest tightened at his quiet response, and I wiggled my arms free so I could slide them around his shoulders. Our hugs had always been friendly—familial, even—with only the occasional rogue thoughts on my part about hard muscles and mouthwatering scents, but that had changed too. Pressed against him like this, my awareness was consumed by every inch of his warm, sculpted body against mine, his strength easy and overwhelming.

As heat flushed through my center, his fingers brushed the back of my neck, tangling in my hair. I couldn't help it—I shivered as a fresh wave of hot tingles whispered down my spine.

His head turned just slightly. Had he noticed me shiver? Embarrassed, I tried to pull back, but he tightened his arms.

"Oy!" Aaron's shout cut through the quiet basement. "Tori, are you ready yet or—oh."

A body filled the doorway. I looked around in time to see Aaron stop dead in his tracks, staring at Ezra and me entwined in a tight embrace. His eyes widened.

"Oh," he said again. "Does this mean Ezra has stopped hiding from you?"

A soft footstep, then Kai appeared beside Aaron. "I'm guessing Tori ambushed him."

"Uh." I tried to step back, but Ezra hadn't released me. Heat rose in my cheeks.

"Well, good." Aaron waved. "Let's go already. Darius is making a big announcement tonight and I don't want to miss it."

"Wait, we should check first." Kai fixed his dark eyes on Ezra. "Are you finished sulking and avoiding us now?"

Ezra gave his friends a long, hard stare, his expression inscrutable. "You know, the fact that *I'm* the sanest one in this house is extremely alarming."

Aaron, Kai, and I exchanged looks. Since we were perfectly happy to be friends with a demon mage, we couldn't really argue, could we?

Silence hung for a moment more, than a grin flashed across Ezra's face. I groaned that he'd gotten us again, and Aaron laughed. Chuckling, Ezra finally released me. He picked up my plumed hat, shook the confetti off it, and set it on my head.

"Looking good, D'Artagnan."

I snorted *and* rolled my eyes, making sure he had no misconceptions about my feelings regarding the costume.

We rushed back into our preparations, and five minutes later, we were clustered by the back door in our identical Musketeer costumes—the guys nothing less than alluring in their blue tabards and snug breeches, their wide-brimmed hats placed at jaunty angles. Actual steel rapiers were sheathed at their hips, and they looked ready to whip the swords out with a haughty, "*En garde!*"

I had a rapier too, but I didn't feel particularly charming, bold, or medieval. I just felt silly. Costumes were the worst.

We piled into the silver Mustang parked out back—Aaron's rental. He had yet to shop for a new vehicle. His poor baby had been totaled, and I suspected he had a grieving process to complete before he could replace it.

He drove to the Crow and Hammer at a higher speed than strictly legal, but we were running late. This was our second visit to the guild today—the first had been at ten this morning so Aaron, Kai, and I could set things up for Halloween Party 2.0.

Yes, we were over a week into November. It had snowed last night—though the light dusting had already melted. Halloween was well over.

But our original party had been canceled under the worst circumstances. When I'd returned to work after having my broken wrist healed, Clara and I had put our heads together. Everyone was tired and stressed. They all needed a pick-me-up. And what better way to do it than revive the party they'd been looking forward to?

After parking in the back, I followed the guys around the building to the front door, nervously adjusting my tabard and rapier. Flashing a grin over his shoulder, Aaron pushed the door open.

A wave of noise rolled out. Yeah, we were definitely late.

The pub was crammed with mythics, music was thumping, and conversation rang through the room. Everyone in sight was in costume, wild colors mixing in a collage of fantasy, horror, pop culture, and randomness. The people nearest to the entrance cheered and waved at us to come in.

Holding the door with one hand, Aaron extended the other to me. Laughing, I grabbed Ezra and Kai, and together, we swept inside.

HUMMING QUIETLY, I mopped a puddle of pink punch off the bar top. The party had wound down an hour ago. Colorfully costumed mythics had made their way out the door in twos and threes, and only twenty or so people were left.

I sighed, tired but content. I'd never seen the pub so packed. Not only our members, but spouses, plus-ones, and even a few mythics from other guilds had packed the building. The noise level had been deafening, filled with chatter and laughter. The lingering notes of stress and worry from the demon alert had vanished in the revelry.

Yep. It had been worth all the work—and the musketeer costume.

Giving the counter a final wipe, I headed along the bar to the end, where a tiered tray marred by smeared icing and crumbs held the last cupcake. I considered it carefully, glanced around to ensure no one was watching, then picked it up and bit into the icing-coated top.

"Isn't that your fourth cupcake?"

I jumped guiltily. Ezra had just walked out from the short hall behind the stairs. His mismatched eyes sparked with amusement.

"So what if it is?" I asked mutinously.

"I only had one."

"Oh." I looked down at the cupcake, my taste buds crying for more cream cheese icing, then held it out. "You can have it. I only had one bite."

He chuckled. "It's fine. Go ahead."

"You sure?" When he nodded, I took another bite. Oh my god, so good. These were too delicious to be legal. "I'm so glad we got more. Losing the first batch was a crime against desserts everywhere."

"Maybe I should've kept them for self-defense." He studied me somberly. "Demons can't resist cupcakes."

I arched my eyebrows. "Demons can't? Or *you* can't?"

His poker face was infallible. "I'm admitting nothing."

Snickering, I took one more bite of the cupcake, then held it out again. He gazed at it longingly, then caved and took the half-eaten dessert. He bit the icing-covered top off and his eyes rolled back in bliss.

"That's not how you're supposed to eat cupcakes," I chastised.

"Don't tell me how to achieve nirvana." He slid onto the nearest stool and rubbed a hand through his messy curls. His wide-brimmed musketeer hat had vanished a while ago. "Kai and Aaron should be tired by now, shouldn't they?"

Amused, I looked past him. Across the room, Aaron and Cameron were having a mock sword battle—rapier versus lightsaber—and a cluster of guys egged them on. While Aaron ducked a swing from the plastic weapon, I scanned the scattered tables. Sabrina, Sin, Kaveri, and Kier were sitting together, listening raptly to a story Kier was telling. Darius, Alistair, Girard, and Clara had claimed another table and were deep in a serious discussion.

In the farthest, quietest corner of the room, two people were sitting together in the shadows, empty drinks on the table in front of them. I smirked.

An hour or two into the party, a group of Odin's Eye mythics had joined us. And with them? Izzah, looking utterly ravishing in a Greek Goddess costume that featured a draping white dress, gold belt, and a golden laurel wreath on her head, nestled in her raven hair. Every single guy in the pub—and a few non-single guys—had stopped to stare.

Kai had made a beeline straight for her, and they'd been glued to each other's sides since. Tucked in a corner by themselves, they'd been lost in conversation for hours.

"We need to do something about that," I murmured thoughtfully, watching them.

"About what?" Ezra asked, casually licking the icing off the cupcake wrapper.

Ignoring his poor manners—if it were my wrapper, I'd be doing exactly the same thing—I gestured at the electramage. "We need to do something about Kai and his family not letting him be with anyone."

Ezra peered into the corner. "What can we do, though?"

I tapped my lips. "I'll think about it."

He made a quiet sound of agreement, and my mind drifted to other impossible dilemmas … like the demon amulet hidden in my apartment. Ezra didn't know I had it. Neither did Aaron or Kai. I'd told them what it did and that I'd given it to Burke's demon, but I hadn't mentioned how the demon had dropped it before escaping this world.

The words Ezra's demon had whispered were carved into my brain. *He is mine. His body and his soul.*

Darius had told me that when Ezra died, so would his demon—but if the demon thought it would get Ezra's soul, it clearly had a different opinion on the matter. I agreed that handing Ezra the amulet was all kinds of bad idea, but I had no intentions of ignoring his looming fate. I'd never thought much about souls, but if Ezra's was in danger, then we needed to save him.

Kai's family. Ezra's demon. Both things I planned to think about.

"Tori?"

Jarred out of my thoughts, I realized I was staring intently into Ezra's face.

He canted his head. "What's wrong?"

"Nothing," I blurted, but he didn't look convinced. Luckily, Kaveri and Kier called goodbye from the door, and I waved energetically. As they left, Sin and Sabrina wandered over.

I almost hadn't recognized Sin at first. Her teal hair was now midnight black, and her eyes were done up in smoky makeup. Fitted black clothes covered her from head to toe, and an oversized postage stamp was pinned to her left shoulder.

Her costume had stumped me, Aaron, and Ezra, but Kai had guessed it immediately: blackmail.

"I'm exhausted," Sabrina declared, sliding onto the stool beside Ezra. She'd gone for a classic gypsy fortuneteller costume and had spent half her night carrying around a crystal ball and pretending to see terrible portents of doom in its misty depths. "Tori, could I get a water?"

"Sure thing." I hurried to my station, poured one, and returned as she was setting her crystal ball on the bar top.

"Bringing this was probably a mistake." She rubbed her wrists. "My arms are aching."

"Nah, it was perfect," Ezra said, grinning. "Really made the whole costume. I loved your vision of 'death by fire-breathing dragon' for Aaron."

She giggled. "I told Darius to beware of narrow bridges and whips."

We laughed. Maybe hearing his name, Darius glanced at us from his table. A pointed gray hat was perched on his head, with matching wizard robes draped around him. Gandalf's wooden staff was propped against the table, and whenever the mood had struck him, the luminamage had made the crystal on top glow dramatically.

I wondered what announcement Darius had been planning to make. Aaron had mentioned it several times, but the GM had made no attempts to speak at large to the partygoers.

Sin propped her chin on her hand, ignoring renewed shouts from the nearby battle reenactment. Aaron was now dueling Luke Skywalker and two Power Rangers, while complaining loudly that he needed musketeer backup. Neither Ezra nor I moved to aid him.

"Tori, when can we see the new menu?" Sin asked, squinting at the wall above my head where the chalkboard menu had been wiped clean and replaced with my terribly drawn pumpkins and bats.

"First of December," I answered promptly. "Darius approved my proposal yesterday. He was busy before that. Though we'll be lucky to have everything ready to go in three weeks."

Darius had been in and out nonstop since rescuing me and the guys a week ago. I hadn't had a chance to ask him how his hunt for the demon summoners had gone.

"I can't wait," Sabrina said brightly, absently tapping her crystal ball. "I hope there'll be some less greasy options for—"

"Uh, Sabrina?" Sin interrupted. "Is it supposed to be doing that?"

The diviner looked at her crystal ball—and gasped. The white mist inside it was streaked with red. Eyes wide, she placed her hands on either side of the orb.

"That's a *real* crystal ball?" I muttered nervously, watching as the scarlet streaks ebbed and flowed like ink in water.

"Mm," Sabrina mumbled. "Why would I buy a fake one just for my costume?"

Fair point.

"There's something ..." She lowered her face and peered into the mist. "A vision ..."

We all leaned in as the red streaks thickened, the color deepening. Just as I wondered if she was pranking us, the sphere darkened to pitch black—and a pair of glowing crimson eyes flashed within it.

Sabrina let out a tiny shriek, Sin jerked back so fast she fell off her stool, and I jumped about a foot but managed not to scream. Ezra alone didn't react. As the crystal ball returned to swirling white, his grim expression smoothed back into his usual good humor.

"What's wrong?" Aaron, breathless and clutching his rapier, hurried over. "What happened?"

"Just—just the crystal ball surprised us," Sabrina stammered.

Aaron helped Sin to her feet. "That's all? You sure?"

"We're good," I said, giving him a meaningful look. He took the hint and stopped asking. We all stood silently for a moment.

"Tori, I've been meaning to ask." Sabrina shifted forward on her seat. "Did you make your decision?"

"Decision?"

"From your tarot reading," she prompted.

"Right!" Sin exclaimed. "Sabrina predicted that someone would die and you had to make a big life-altering decision to save their life." She playfully arched an eyebrow. "How did that work out?"

I didn't answer, and it took her a moment to realize she was the only one who seemed entertained. Her amusement quickly faded.

"Sabrina," Aaron said quietly, "did you really predict that?"

She nodded, watching me closely. "It wasn't just *anyone* who was in danger, though. Someone Tori cared for was going to die ..."

Against my will, my eyes slid to Ezra. He stared back at me, but I couldn't tell what he was thinking.

"Oh!" Sabrina gasped.

I jerked my attention away from Ezra. "Huh? What?"

"Nothing!" With scarcely concealed glee, she grabbed her crystal ball and dumped it unceremoniously into the largest pocket of her gypsy dress. "Nothing at all. Well, we should go! Sin, want to split a cab? I already called one."

"Sure," Sin muttered, looking as confused as I felt. "See you later, Tori. Great party!"

She was still calling her farewell when Sabrina dragged her off. Halfway across the pub, the diviner started whispering feverishly in Sin's ear. Both girls stopped and looked back at me, Sabrina with a knowing expression and Sin with disbelief.

"Uh," I said blankly, watching them hurry to the door. "What was that all about?"

DEMON MAGIC AND A MARTINI ♠ 277

"I was going to ask you the same thing," Aaron muttered.

As the two girls pushed through the door, Kai stepped inside. I blinked in surprise. When had he left?

He strode to us, frowning over his shoulder. "What were those two giggling about?"

"No idea," I answered. "Where were you?"

"I just saw Izzah off."

I braced my elbows on the bar top and grinned. "Did you have a nice visit with her?"

"No, it was extremely unpleasant. Are we ready to go?"

"Almost. I've got a few more things to clean up first. I just need to fortify myself. One more drink?"

Aaron grinned. "Okay, one more. But Ezra will have to drive us home."

"You sure you want to trust me with that?" Ezra asked, amused.

"It's cool. The car's a rental."

I zipped to my station, considered my options, then started mixing drinks. Five minutes later, I set four martinis on the bar top and plopped an olive in each one.

"Finishing the night in style," I said brightly.

"Perfect! But first, we need …" Aaron looked to the end of the bar. "Hey! Where's the last cupcake?"

I flinched but recovered quickly. "It got eaten."

"But that was Kai's birthday cupcake. I even got a candle." He pulled a small pink candle from his breeches' pocket. "Who ate it?"

"You—you never said it was for Kai!"

Aaron's expression shifted to incredulity. "*You* ate it? I saw you eat at least two cupcakes already."

"Why is everyone counting how many cupcakes I eat?" I demanded furiously. "And Ezra ate some of it too!"

"Hey!" Ezra protested. "I only finished it because you—"

"It's fine," Kai interrupted with an exasperated roll of his eyes. "I don't need a cupcake."

"But it's your birthday," I said guiltily. "I didn't even know."

"That's because it *isn't* my birthday. It was a week ago, and we spent the entire day with the healers." He picked up his martini. "This is fine. Better than a cupcake."

"You didn't try one, did you?" Ezra asked. "Nothing is better than those cupcakes."

"Not helping, Ezra," I muttered out of the corner of my mouth. "Let's do a toast to Kai, then. How old are you?"

"Twenty-five."

"Wow. Old."

"Thanks, Tori."

"I turn twenty-two in a few weeks," I told him smugly.

Giving me another eye roll, he swirled his drink. "Let's toast to the four of us, not just me."

I grinned at their matching *fleur-de-lis* tabards. Throughout the night, we'd all misplaced—or in my case, deliberately discarded—our plumed hats, but the overall effect of our costumes was still strong.

Holding out my glass, I began dramatically, "All for one?"

They stared at me, then identical grins split their faces. They raised their drinks and our glasses clinked loudly. "*And one for all!*"

We took long gulps of our martinis, kept our composures for two more seconds, then burst into laughter. I gasped in mirth, patting my chest before I choked. Maybe it wasn't that funny, but I couldn't help seeing the parallels between our costumes and real life. If all four of us hadn't been together that night, none of us would've made it out of the factory alive.

Before the thought could sober my mood, Darius and Clara rose from their table and headed our way. Girard and Alistair were still deep in discussion, their heads bent together.

"Tori!" Clara gushed as she joined us. "What a success! You have a real talent for event planning."

"Do I?" I didn't feel talented. I'd felt in over my head and wildly unprepared.

"An excellent job," Darius complimented, smiling through his Gandalf beard. It looked convincingly real, and I wondered if he'd gotten some alchemic help to grow it twelve inches long in a matter of days. "You're welcome to head out. Clara and I will finish up here."

"Are you sure? I don't mind—"

"You've done enough, Tori!" Clara interrupted sternly.

"And we need to stay longer either way." Darius glanced at the door. "Unless they changed their minds? I expected them hours ago."

Clara glanced at the clock on the wall. "It's after midnight. They must not be coming after all."

"Who—" I began curiously.

My unfinished question was answered by a cautious rap on the guild's front door. Alistair and Girard fell silent, as did the other mythics scattered around.

"Ah," Darius said. "That must be them."

He pulled his wizard hat off and left it on the bar before striding across the pub. Clara followed, and as they passed, Alistair and Girard rose to join them. Darius reached the door and pulled it open.

With four people in the way, I couldn't see who was outside, but they must've come in because the door swung shut again. Darius spoke in a quiet murmur, and a moment later, Clara offered a warm welcome to the guild's visitors.

I looked at Aaron, Kai, and Ezra. They stared back blankly, equally nonplussed. Other members wandered closer to see who had come in, so I planted my hands on the bar top and sprang over it—hell yeah, I was getting good at that—and together with the guys, we headed over.

"… glad you made it safely," Darius was saying. "Though it's a shame you couldn't arrive sooner. I would've liked to introduce you while everyone was present."

A feminine voice mumbled an answer I couldn't make out.

Glancing up, Darius took note of his audience. He turned with a broad smile and gestured grandly at the unfamiliar girl beside him. She was around my age with long, dirty blond hair in a style that fell somewhere between "sexy tousle" and "just got out of bed." Smoky makeup darkened her cautious eyes.

"Ladies and gentlemen," Darius proclaimed. "I'd planned this announcement for the whole guild, but as a reward for your impressive late-night endurance, you'll hear it first. May I present the Crow and Hammer's newest members!"

A mix of emotions jumped through me. A new member? Since my first day in the guild, I'd been the new girl. I wasn't sure how I felt about passing that title off to someone else.

The blond girl grimaced awkwardly.

Darius placed a hand on her shoulder. "Please welcome Amalia Harper, a sorceress in her third apprenticeship year. And …"

And? Wait, he'd said new *members*, plural. But I could only see the young blond sorceress. Who else was joining?

Darius reached around Amalia and scooped a second person from behind him and Clara. She was so petite she'd been completely hidden from view. Apparently, no one else had noticed her either, because a murmur of surprise ran through the gathered mythics.

The girl was also in her very early twenties, with shoulder-length brunette hair and dark-rimmed glasses slipping down her small nose.

"And this," Darius continued, his voice carrying through the hush, "is Robin Page—"

My lungs spasmed, adrenaline spiking in my veins.

"—our very first demon contractor."

Robin's large blue eyes, framed by thick lashes behind her glasses, turned to me. As I gawked, her gaze drifted to Aaron, Kai, and Ezra. Silence pressed on the room, every member equally shocked by Darius's casual revelation. For the first time, the Crow and Hammer included a demon contractor.

But not just any demon contractor.

Robin Page, the waif of a girl who commanded the lithe and lethal demon that had slaughtered the unbound winged demon without breaking a sweat. The girl who'd saved me, Aaron, Kai, Ezra, and the Keys team from near-certain death at the winged beast's hands.

Our first demon contractor. But unbeknownst to the rest of the guild, not our first Demonica mythic.

And I could only guess what Robin Page's appearance in the guild would mean for our dangerous, secret, and highly illegal demon mage.

TORI'S ADVENTURES CONTINUE IN

THE ALCHEMIST AND AN AMARETTO

THE GUILD CODEX: SPELLBOUND / FIVE

As a guild bartender, I can handle pretty much anything—mages, sorcerers, witches, the occasional demon. But show me anything family-related and I'd rather run for the hills. It doesn't even have to be *my* family.

So I have no idea why I thought spending the holidays with Aaron's mom and pop was a good idea.

Meeting his famous parents is already terrifying enough, but I've got a bigger problem. Students of his family's renowned mage academy are being attacked on the grounds—and somehow no one has seen a single assailant? Unexplained tracks litter the nearby woods, rumors of forbidden alchemy are circulating the campus … and Ezra has been acting strangely since we arrived.

Something deadly is brewing in the shadow of Sinclair Academy, and the longer we take to uncover it, the more dangerous it becomes. But no matter the risk, we'll protect the students.

And Aaron's parents too, I suppose. If we have to.

www.guildcodex.ca

TAMING DEMONS FOR BEGINNERS

THE GUILD CODEX: DEMONIZED / ONE

Meet the Crow and Hammer's most recent recruit in this
exciting new series set in the world of mythics.

Rule one: Don't look at the demon.

When I arrived at my uncle's house, I expected my relatives to be like me—outcast sorcerers who don't practice magic. I was right about the sorcery, but wrong about everything else.

Rule two: Don't listen to the demon.

My uncle chose a far deadlier power. He calls creatures of darkness into our world, binds them into service contracts, and sells them to the highest bidder. And I'm supposed to act like I don't know how illegal and dangerous it is.

Rule three: Don't talk to the demon.

All I had to do was keep my nose out of it. Pretend I didn't find the summoning circle in the basement. Pretend I didn't notice the shadowy being trapped inside it. Pretend I didn't break the rules.

But I did, and now it's too late.

ABOUT THE AUTHOR

Annette Marie is the author of YA urban fantasy series *Steel & Stone*, its prequel trilogy *Spell Weaver*, and romantic fantasy trilogy *Red Winter*.

Her first love is fantasy, but fast-paced adventures, bold heroines, and tantalizing forbidden romances are her guilty pleasures. She proudly admits she has a thing for dragons, and her editor has politely inquired as to whether she intends to include them in every book.

Annette lives in the frozen winter wasteland of Alberta, Canada (okay, it's not quite that bad) and shares her life with her husband and their furry minion of darkness—sorry, cat—Caesar. When not writing, she can be found elbow-deep in one art project or another while blissfully ignoring all adult responsibilities.

www.annettemarie.ca

SPECIAL THANKS

My thanks to Erich Merkel for sharing your exceptional expertise in Latin. Any errors are mine.

My heartfelt thanks as well to Umayal for your time, enthusiasm, and endless patience. Izzah wouldn't be the amazing character she is without your help.

THE
GUILD CODEX
SPELLBOUND

Tori has finally uncovered Ezra's secrets and experienced the danger he faces ... and the danger he represents. Keeping her friends safe won't be getting any easier, and she's ready to learn just what it means to be a combat mythic.

Welcome to the Crow and Hammer.

DISCOVER MORE BOOKS AT
www.guildcodex.ca

THE
GUILD CODEX
DEMONIZED

Robin Page: outcast sorceress, mythic history buff, unapologetic bookworm, and the last person you'd expect to command the rarest demon in the long history of summoning. Though she holds his leash, this demon can't be controlled … but can he be tamed?

Demonica. Enter at your own risk.

STEEL &STONE

When everyone wants you dead, good help is hard to find.

The first rule for an apprentice Consul is *don't trust daemons*. But when Piper is framed for the theft of the deadly Sahar Stone, she ends up with two troublesome daemons as her only allies: Lyre, a hotter-than-hell incubus who isn't as harmless as he seems, and Ash, a draconian mercenary with a seriously bad reputation. Trusting them might be her biggest mistake yet.

*The only thing more dangerous than the denizens of the
Underworld ... is stealing from them.*

As a daemon living in exile among humans, Clio has picked up some
unique skills. But pilfering magic from the Underworld's deadliest
spell weavers? Not so much. Unfortunately, that's exactly what she has
to do to earn a ticket home.

A destiny written by the gods. A fate forged by lies.

If Emi is sure of anything, it's that *kami*—the gods—are good, and *yokai*—the earth spirits—are evil. But when she saves the life of a fox shapeshifter, the truths of her world start to crumble. And the treachery of the gods runs deep.

This stunning trilogy features 30 full-page illustrations.

GET THE COMPLETE TRILOGY
www.annettemarie.ca/redwinter